GUNFIGHTER JAKE

The Most Unusual Gunfighter the West Has Ever Seen

GUNFIGHTER JAKE

The Most Unusual Gunfighter the West Has Ever Seen

WILLIAM HAGENBURG

ARPress
45 Dan Road Suite 5
Canton MA 02021
Hotline: 1(888) 821-0229
Fax: 1(508) 545-7580

Ordering Information:
Quantity sales. Special discounts are available on quantity purchases by corporations, associations, and others. For details, contact the publisher at the address above.

Printed in the United States of America.

ISBN-13:   Softcover   979-8-89389-655-8
           eBook   979-8-89389-656-5

Library of Congress Control Number: 2024921589

Contents

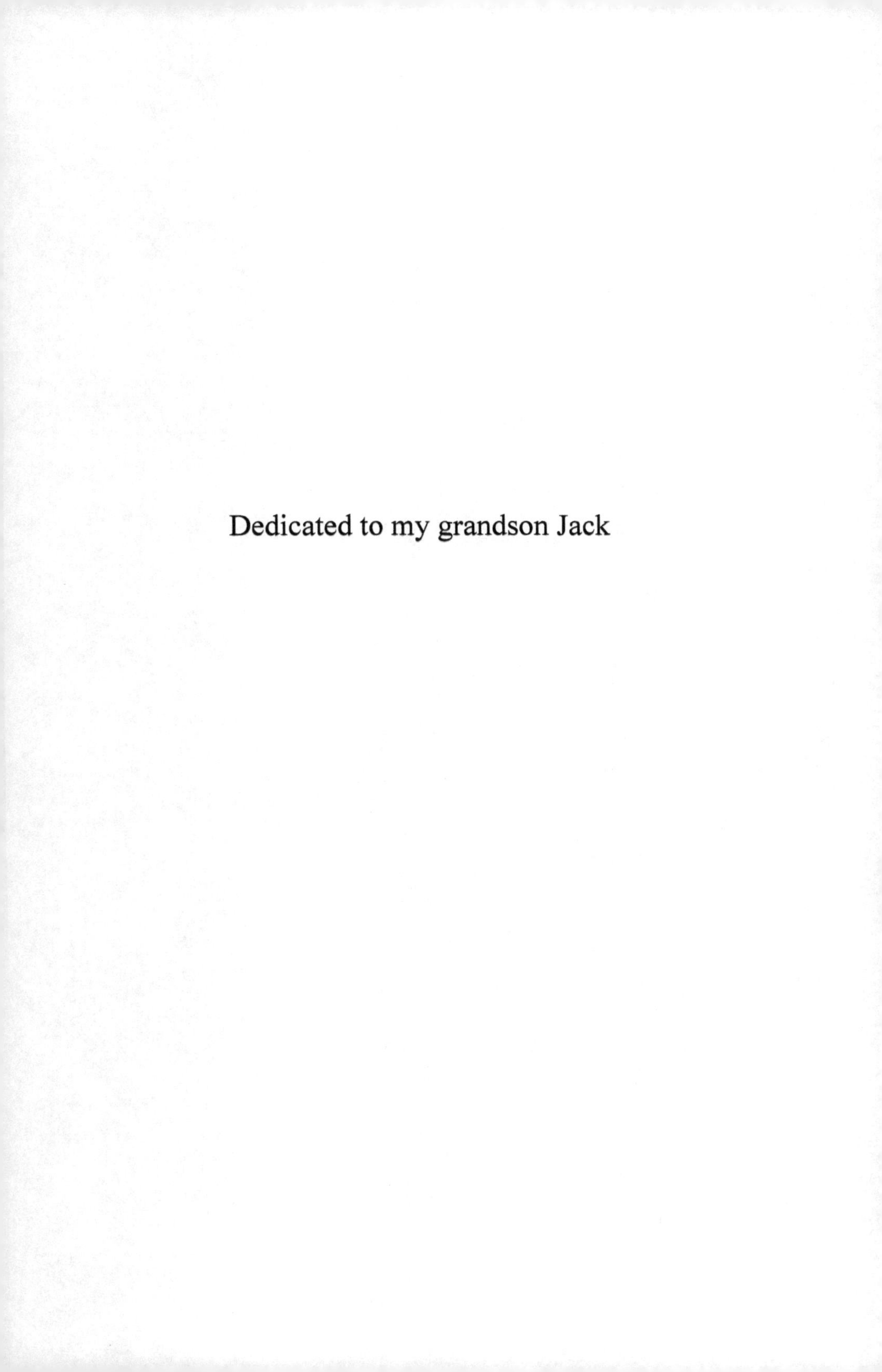

Dedicated to my grandson Jack

GUNFIGHTER JAKE
THE MOST UNUSUAL GUNFIGHTER
THE WEST HAS EVER SEEN

"Sam, this here saloon's crowded tonight."

"It sure is, Pete. Those cow punchers must've got paid."

"Yup. There's a few gunfighters in here right along with those cowhands. Hope there ain't no shootin'."

"Want another beer, Pete?"

"Nope. I'm a-headed home, Sam. See ya at Sara's store for coffee in the mornin'."

"Got a new yarn to spin, Sam?"

"Yup. I'm a-gonna tell ya boys about the most unusual gunfighter the West has ever known."

"Be lookin' forward ta hearin' it."

In the morning, the sun was just rising over the mountains when four old cowboys walked into Sara's store.

"Good mornin', Sara. Coffee on?"

"Now ya boys know I always put the coffee on first thing."

"Yeah, we know, Sara."

"Seen Sam yet this mornin'?"

"Nope. It's a little early for Sam. He has to get the boys at the ranch a-workin' before he gets here."

"Say, Sara, the coffee's extra good. Just what do ya do to this here coffee ta make it so good?"

"Boys, that's my secret."

"Say, Sara, where did Sam get that ranch from anyway? He never talks about it."

"Well, boys, someday he'll tell ya the story."

"Hey, boys! Sam's a-comin' down the street."

"What's the matter, Sam? Couldn't ya roll outta bed this mornin'?" "Never you mind—pour me a cup a that there coffee."

"Sam, I been a-tellin' the boys ya was gonna spin a yarn about a gunfighter."

"Yup. His name was Jake—the fastest gun that ever lived."

"Sam, did he kill a lotta men?" "Enough, Pete."

"How many?"

"Nobody knows. He would never talk about it."

"Well, Sam, we wanna hear about Jake."

"Cut me a piece of that chew and pour me another cup a that there coffee, and I'll tell ya the yarn about the life of Jake—the most unusual gunfighter the West has ever known."

"It begins back at the turn of the century. The West was wild in those days.

A family livin' on a small ranch, located on some prime land, worked tryin' to make a livin'. A man, his wife, and ten-year-old son worked from sunup to sundown, seven days a week. There was a nearby rancher that wanted the land. He was ruthless and sent his men to raid the ranch. One night, they rode in a-shootin'. The rancher grabbed his rifle and began shootin' back at the raiders. He got a couple of 'em.

One of the raiders shot the rancher through the window and killed him dead. His wife picked up the rifle and began firin' out the window. One of the raiders burst in through the door and shot her. He didn't see the boy a-hidin'.

The gunmen left, the woman a-dyin' on the floor. The boy ran to his mother. She told him to get the metal box on the shelf and run and hide. "Son, always keep the box with you. Open it when you get older." She pulled her son close and kissed him, then her eyes closed for the last time.

The boy ran out the back door and hid in the rocks. He was cold, scared, and cried all night long.

In the mornin', an Indian brave rode to the top of a hill. He stopped and looked down at the ranch. He took a deep breath and shook his head, seein' the livestock layin' dead on the ground. He noticed the boy in the rocks. He rode down to where the boy was hidin', stopped his horse, and got down. He walked toward the boy. The boy, afraid, crawled deeper into the rocks.

"Boy, come. Me friend, not hurt you. Come out of rocks. I help you. Wait here, look in house."

The Indian walked into the house. He could see bullet holes in the side of the cabin. Then he saw the bodies layin' on the floor. Knowin' the white man's ways, he buried the two bodies and marked the graves. While he was doin' this, the boy came out of the rocks and stood by the graves.

"Boy, come. Take to village."

The boy mounted the horse behind the Indian, and they rode to the Indian village. An old Indian woman took the boy into her teepee, cleaned him up, fed him, and put him to sleep.

In the mornin', the old Indian woman told the brave that the boy should be with his own people. The Indian brave told her he would take the boy to Hank Black. He rode out with the boy to Hank's ranch.

Hank saw the Indian ridin' through the gate of his ranch.

"Two Arrows, how are you? Who's that you have with you?"

"Boy, Hank."

He told Hank the story of how he found the boy.

"Well, boy, get down off that horse, and I'll fix you some vittles."

The boy got down off the Indian's horse. He didn't speak.

"Boy, what's your name?"

The boy answered, "They call me Jake."

"Jake, what's your last name?"

"Just Jake."

"Well, Jake, I need a strong hand like you to help me run this ranch. How would you like to live with me?"

Jake shrugged his shoulders. He was still in shock from the events of the past few days.

"Two Arrows, how have you been? Haven't seen you in a while."

"Me good, Hank. You okay?"

"I've been good. How's your wife?"

"Squaw good. I go now, Hank. Be back, see boy."

"Stop by anytime, Two Arrows."

"Hank, Two Arrows is a funny name."

"Well, you see, that Indian can fire two arrows as fast as other braves can fire one, so they call him Two Arrows."

They stood and watched Two Arrows ride out of sight. Then Hank said, "Let's go in the house. You must be hungry."

A few months pass and Jake is more like himself. He comes out one morning and notices that Hank's ranch is the nicest ranch he ever saw. He walks over to the corral, climbs on the fence, and sits on the top rail, patting an old horse. Hank comes walking out of the house and walks over to Jake.

"Like that old horse, Jake?"

"Yes, he seems to like me too."

"Jake, would you like to have that horse?"

"Oh yes, for my very own?"

"Yes, Jake, for your very own."

"Thanks, Hank, I'll take good care of him."

"I know you will."

"Jake, I have something else for you."

"What is it, Hank?"

Hank has a small gun belt and revolver. He unwraps it and shows Jake.

"Is that for me?"

"Yes, Jake, it's yours. Tomorrow morning I'll begin to teach you how to use it."

"Oh boy, can I shoot it today?"

"No, Jake, it will be sometime before you shoot it. First, you must learn to handle it safely."

Jake, all excited, is up before the sun waiting for Hank. Hank gets up and fixes breakfast. Jake eats fast — he wants to begin learning how to use his gun.

"Jake, hold your horses. We have to attend to the stock before we do anything else. Remember, the stock always comes first."

After they fed and watered the horses and cattle, Jake asks, "Hank, can we shoot my gun now?"

"Jake, I told you that you have to learn how to handle a gun before you shoot it."

"Ah, Hank, I want to shoot it."

"You will in due time."

"Jake, this is tough country. A man needs to know how to handle a gun." Hank knew the horse and gun would help take Jake's mind off the loss of his parents, so he began to teach Jake how to handle his gun.

"Jake, a gun is a tool, not a toy. It is dangerous and you must learn to respect it. I was a sheriff for thirty years. I never drew my gun unless I planned to use it. I never drew first. I was lucky — I was always a little faster. I had to use my gun to protect the citizens of the town. There was always someone that wanted to take something belonging to the townspeople."

"Men like those that took my father's ranch?"

Hank, in a soft voice, says, "Yes, son, just like those men."

"Now, the first thing you must learn is that no matter how fast you become drawing your gun, never use your gun for pay. Use it only to protect yourself and others from serious harm."

Hank would tell Jake this over and over: never use your gun to make money. Hank would let Jake wear his empty gun for days until he learned to handle it safely.

"Jake, leave that gun alone in the holster. When you're ready to learn to draw, I will teach you. Otherwise, you will develop bad habits."

One day Hank said to Jake, "Come here, boy, it's time you learned to draw." Hank waited until the novelty wore off and Jake was used to wearing his gun without touching it.

Hank began to show Jake how to draw the right way. Jake practiced every day when his work was done. Hank would watch Jake from a distance. One day he called Jake.

"Jake, remember how to safely handle that gun?"

"Yes, Hank."

"Let me see it."

Hank loads the gun and tells Jake to draw and fire, put it back into the holster, and do it again, and again.

"Jake, how many bullets did you shoot?"

"I was so excited I don't know."

"Jake, part of using a gun is to know how many bullets you shoot and how many you have left. Never empty your gun — always reload before you fire the last bullet. Never be caught with an empty gun." "Here's a box of bullets. Go practice your draw. Pick a target to shoot at." "Jake, what's the first thing you look at before you draw and shoot?"

"What's behind the target I'm shooting at and where the bullet would go if I miss my target."

"Okay, son, go practice your draw."

Weeks go by, Jake practices every day. Soon, years begin to roll by. Hank is always watching from a distance. He walks over to Jake and says, "You're almost as fast as I am. You're a natural, and you've become a dead shot. I'm gonna tell you somethin' that was taught to me when I was very young. You probably won't understand right away, but in time you will."

"What's that, Hank?"

"You're drawin' physically. You gotta learn to draw and fire with your mind. Don't make it happen—let it happen."

"You're right, Hank, I don't understand."

"In time you will, boy. Just keep practicin'."

One day, when Jake was about twenty, he excitedly calls Hank. "Hank! I got it! I know what you meant when you said draw with my mind—watch." Jake draws and fires.

"That's it, boy! You're the fastest gunman I ever seen. Remember, son—never put your gun out for hire."

"I won't, Hank."

Hank is at the corral unsaddlin' his horse. Jake is in the barn brushin' down his old horse when three men ride in, up to the corral.

"Hey there, boys, what can I do for ya?"

"Is your name Hank Black—Sheriff Hank Black?"

"Yes, boys, I was Sheriff Hank Black. Just Hank Black now."

"Do you remember us?"

"Don't say that I do."

Hank's instincts, gained from bein' a sheriff, told him somethin' was wrong. He puts his saddle down and moves away from his horse.

"Sheriff, you put us away ten years ago. We just got outta prison."

"Glad to see you boys are out."

"I waited ten years for this."

As he says that, the three men draw their guns. Three shots ring out—two men fall dead. Hank falls against the corral fence, blood comin' outta his chest. One of the gunmen was too fast for Hank to get off a third shot. The gunman laughs, holsters his gun, turns, and begins to walk away.

Jake comes runnin' outta the barn. He sees Hank holdin' his chest, bleedin'. Jake yells. The gunman turns and draws his gun—one shot is heard. It was Jake's. The gunman lays dead on the ground with his two friends.

Jake takes Hank into the house and lays him on the couch.

"I don't know what to do."

"There's nothin' you can do, boy. Jake, you passed a serious test today. You can shoot a man while lookin' him in the eyes. That may not be a good thing. Don't get used to killin'. Don't begin to like it. Remember what I told you—never put your gun out for hire. Never use your gun to make money killin' with it. Put your ability to good use and never draw first."

With those last words, Hank's head slumps. He becomes silent.

Jake buries Hank on a hilltop overlookin' the ranch and the river— his favorite spot.

Jake turns the livestock loose, goes into the house, and opens the metal box his mama gave him. In the box, he finds the deed to his father's ranch. He closes up the house, mounts his old horse, and rides out without lookin' back.

Ridin' out through the gates of Hank's ranch, he wonders what his father's ranch looks like after all these years. He decides to go have a look at the ranch where he lived as a small boy with his mama and daddy.

On the way, he stops at the Indian village to tell Two Arrows about the passin' of Hank. They mourn Hank, Indian-style.

"Jake, your clothes torn, your horse old. You grow to my size—I have new buckskins, give you. Go put on."

Jake knows it would be an insult to an Indian to refuse a gift. He goes into a teepee and puts on the buckskins. When he comes out, a group of Indian braves is waitin' to see him.

"Jake, you tall, black gun belt—you look okay. Real Indian." They all laugh.

Just then, a young Indian boy comes around the teepee leadin' a big black stallion.

"Jake, you horse old—put in field. Take Big Black. He broke to ride, not with saddle. You train."

All the Indians let out an Indian yell of joy.

Jake trains the big black horse to take the saddle and rides into the Indian village. Two Arrows says, "You go now. Soon I be with ancestors."

Jake knew it was time to leave when Two Arrows told him to. He mounts Big Black and rides out of the Indian village. He rides a short distance, stops, and turns his horse around. Sittin' there on his horse, he knows it's the last time he'll see Two Arrows. He turns his horse and slowly rides away—then kicks him up and rides for town.

When Jake reaches town, he rides up to the sheriff's Office and dismounts. He walks in and shows the sheriff the deed to his father's ranch and tells him where he's been for the past ten years.

"I don't know what to tell you, son. I gotta think about it for a while. Mr. Randal runs that ranch now."

"Why don't you leave that deed with me and I'll check into it for you?"

"No sheriff, I think I'll hold onto it and look into it myself."

Rememberin' what Hank told him about crooked sheriffs, he walks across the street into the saloon. He sits by a window, watchin' the sheriff's Office. The sheriff comes out, gets on his horse, and heads in the direction of Jake's father's ranch.

The sheriff rides directly to the ranch and tells Randal about the deed.

"What does this saddle tramp look like?"

"He's tall, wearin' buckskins, rides a big black horse, and looks like he knows how to use a gun."

"How do you know that?"

"The way he wears it—low and tied down."

"Go back to town and stay in your Office. I'm sendin' a couple boys to get that deed."

Later that afternoon, two gunmen ride into town and walk into the saloon. Jake is sittin' in the corner, watchin' them. They each get a beer and then turn around and look at Jake. As they walk toward him, they set their mugs on a table.

Jake stands and says, "Don't come any closer."

"Hey, buckskin—what's your name?"

"They call me Jake."

"Looks like you think you're fast with that gun."

"No, I don't think I'm fast—I know I am."

When Jake says that, he draws and breaks the two beer mugs sittin' on the table. He's so fast they didn't even see him draw. They run outta the saloon, get on their horses, and gallop outta town.

"Randal, I tell you—he's the fastest gun we ever saw."

"Ride over to Johnson City, find Ross and Slim, tell 'em I got a job for 'em."

When Ross and Slim hear this, they ride right to Randal's ranch.

"This saddle tramp has a paper I want. I don't care how you get it. Matter of fact, I don't care if you kill him."

"Okay, Randal—let's ride to town."

"I'm not goin' with you."

"If you want this job done—you're goin'."

"I don't know why, but I'll ride with you."

Jake decides he'll ride out and have a look at the ranch. On the way, he sees three riders comin' down the trail toward him. He stops his horse and waits for 'em. Ridin' up to Jake, the three stop their horses.

"You must be Jake."

"You must be Randal. Who are these cowboys you got with you?"

"These boys are gonna convince you to give me the deed to the ranch."

"Well, boys—I need your names, if you want 'em on your graves."

They both draw. Two shots ring throughout the desert. Two men sittin' on their horses—each side of Randal—are dead before they hit the ground.

"Don't shoot! Don't shoot!" Randal quickly says.

"Get outta here."

Randal turns his horse and races away. Jake puts the two dead gunslingers on their horses and leads them back to town. He rides up to the sheriff's Office and calls the sheriff out. He tells him what happened back on the trail.

A member of the town looks at the bodies and says, "Do you know who these men are?"

Jake answers, "Nope. Can't say that I do."

"They're the Cain brothers—hired killers. There's a bounty on'em."

"Is that right, Sheriff?"

"Yes—two thousand dollars."

"Give it to the poor family that lives on the edge of town."

"You don't want it?"

"I don't make money with my gun killin' people."

A few days later, Randal rides into town and goes into the sheriff's Office.

"Sheriff, I want you to arrest Jake for murder." "Suppose he doesn't want to be arrested. Just do what I pay you for, or I'll get another sheriff."

The sheriff walks into the saloon, very nervously. He tells Jake he has a warrant for his arrest. Jake tells one of the men at the bar to hold his shot glass out in front of him. Knowing the sheriff won't draw his gun, Jake tells the sheriff, "When you drop the shot glass, draw."

"No, no, I'm not drawing down on you."

"Take that badge off. You just quit bein' Sheriff. Now get outta town and never come back."

The Sheriff runs out of the saloon, gets on his horse, and races outta town as fast as his horse will run.

"Hey, Jake, will you take the job as Sheriff?"

"No, this gun's not for hire."

A few days later, a prospector comes walking into town leading a burro. He walks into the saloon and orders a beer. Every day, he goes into the saloon, orders a beer, and stands around, never saying a word. The swinging doors to the saloon open, and a tall man dressed in a black suit walks in and up to the bar. Jake notices he wears his gun low and tied down— he's a gunman. Jake, expecting trouble, loosens his gun in his holster. The man in black turns around, and Jake sees a silver star pinned to his coat. He walks over to Jake and says, "You must be Jake."

"Yup, that's me."

"Well, Jake, I've been sent here to find out what's been goin' on."

"What are you talkin' about, Marshal?"

"Jake, are you used to runnin' Sheriffs outta town?"

"No, Marshal, not at all."

Jake tells the Marshal the story.

"This Randall is livin' on the ranch you hold the deed to. May I see the deed?"

The Marshal looks over the deed. "What about the two men you shot on the trail?"

"Marshal, they drew first."

The prospector is quietly standing by the bar drinking a beer. He speaks up.

"Marshal, his story is true. I was just comin' outta the mountains and saw those two boys draw first. This here fellow shot 'em both outta their saddles. The third man turned his horse and galloped away."

The Marshal says, "Let's get a posse together and ride out to see this Randall fellow."

The prospector asks Jake, "If I can round up a horse, could I go with you?"

"Sure, come on along. What's your name?"

"Curly."

"I can see why they call you Curly."

One of the men in the saloon lets Curly borrow his horse. Jake watches Curly walk over to his burro and take a gun and holster out of the pack on his burro. The way he straps on the gun and wears it, Jake says, "Looks like you know how to use that gun."

"A little."

They ride to the Randall ranch. When Randall sees Jake leading the group of men, he runs into the house and grabs his rifle. When he comes out, he sees the Marshal's badge on the man ridin' beside Jake.

"What can I do for you, Marshal?"

"Your name Randall?"

"Yes, that's me. What of it?"

"Randall, this young fellow holds the deed to this ranch."

"How is it that you claim to own this ranch?"

"I bought it some years back. Here's my bill of sale."

"You purchased this ranch without a deed?"

"I was told the deed was destroyed in a fire."

"Randall, I have enough on you to put you away for a long time, now this..."

"Maybe I could pay Jake for the ranch."

"Jake, would five thousand be enough?"

"Yes, Marshal, that would do just fine."

"Randall, what do you think?"

"That's a lotta money."

"Randall, you could just leave this ranch and come in with me. Jake will take over this property right now."

"I'll pay Jake the money, I have it inside."

"I'll go get it, Marshal."

"Here's your money, Jake. Now hand over the deed."

Riding back to town, Jake asks the Marshal, "What do you have on Randall?"

"Nothing. It was a bluff. I'm sure Randall's guilty of enough illegal activity. He didn't know what I knew, but was sure worried."

"Jake, what are you gonna do with the five thousand?"

"Sheriff Hank Black left me his ranch. Think I'll go back and stock it up with the money."

They laugh, kick up their horses, and head for town.

When they get back to town, the Marshal says, "Let's go in the saloon and have a beer."

"I'm buyin', Marshal."

"Guess you are, Jake."

When they walk up to the bar, the bartender tells Jake that there was a young kid in town lookin' for him.

"He thinks he's a gunfighter. He said he's faster than you, and he wants to prove it."

"Well, Marshal, I guess it's time for me to leave town and let this kid live another day. I sure do thank you, Marshal. I'm headed for my ranch that old Hank left me."

"Thanks for tellin' me, barkeep. When you see him, tell him I'm headed for Silver City."

Jake looks at the Marshal and says, "I'm headed in the opposite direction."

"Hey, Curly, come here a minute."

"What do you want, Jake?"

"The man that raised me left me his ranch. I'm headed there to start it up again. How would you like to ride with me and run the ranch for me?"

"Why, Jake, I would like that just fine."

"Come on, I'll get you a good ranch horse before we leave town."

"Curly, this here is a fine-lookin' horse. He just was fed, his shoes are okay. Let's water the horses before we leave."

Jake checks the shoes on his horse and mounts Big Black. "Curly, here's some money. Go over to the general store and pick up some supplies. Put 'em on your burro."

"Curly, you better get that gun and belt outta your pack and strap it on. We'll be ridin' through some tough country."

They ride to the hills around the rim of a canyon stopping for the night they make camp.

"Curly, in a couple of days, we'll reach Pine River City. The ranch is a few miles outta town."

Riding into Pine River, they see three men wearing masks coming out of the bank shooting, they mount their horses. From the other end of the street, they see the town's sheriff come out of his Office. He shoots one of the bank robbers, then the sheriff gets wounded. The two riders race up the street towards Jake and Curly. Jake draws and shoots both men off their horses. Jake rides to the Sheriff's aid—he's wounded in the shoulder. The townspeople take the sheriff into the doctor's Office.

Jake and Curly walk into the saloon.

"Some shootin', boy."

"Thanks, old man."

"Jake, is that you? Look at you, all grown up and wearin' buckskins. That was some shootin' out there in the street."

"Why, Bob, how are you?"

"Just fine, Jake."

"Curly, Bob and I grew up together."

"Say, Jake, are you the fast gun we've heard about?"

"Could be, Bob."

"Bob, meet Curly."

"Good meetin' ya Bob."

"Jake, what brings you back to these parts?"

"Hank Black left me his ranch. We're on the way to run it."

"Jake, that is a fine ranch, one of the best in the county."

"Say, Jake, could you use a ranch hand?"

"Why, sure, Bob. Can't pay you much at first."

"That's okay, Jake. As long as I have a roof over my head and some food to eat, I'll be fine."

A man comes running into the saloon yelling, "Hey Jake, the sheriff wants to see you. He's still over at Doc's place."

"I'll be right back, Curly. Here, Bob, buy yourselves a beer." Jake walks over to the doctor's Office.

"Hello Sheriff, how ya doin'?"

"Just fine, boy. That was some good shootin' out there today — you saved the bank's money. Well, son, you made yourself a thousand dollars today. There was a bounty of five hundred dollars on each of those two boys."

"Well, Sheriff, I don't make money with my gun. Give the reward money to the poor families in town."

"That's quite generous of you, son. May I ask why?"

"Yup. Hank taught me to use this gun and had me promise I'd never take money for usin' it."

"Hank? You mean Sheriff Hank Black? Are you Hank's boy?"

"Guess you could say I was."

"Jake, would you let me deputize you till I get back on my feet?"

"No, sorry Sheriff, I'll be leavin' in the mornin'."

The next morning, Curly, Bob, and Jake head out of town. They reach Jake's ranch in a few hours.

"This sure is a good-lookin' ranch, Jake."

"Curly, as soon as we get it back in shape, it will be. It's been vacant for a few years."

"It don't look too bad."

"Bob, after we clean up and make some repairs, it'll be the finest ranch in the county."

"Let's ride up to the house and see what that looks like inside."

"It's kinda dusty — we'll clean up in the mornin'."

"Let's get some rest. Each of you take one of the bedrooms on the left. This here's my old room."

In the morning, Jake is up early makin' breakfast. The aroma of fresh coffee brewin' wakes Curly and Bob. After breakfast, they go outside and look around the ranch.

"The front porch, corral, and barn are gonna need some minor repairs. Let's ride out and see if there's any stock runnin' around — I let 'em all loose when I left."

"Hey look, Jake — over there — some young horses and cattle!"

"Yeah, Bob, they've been breedin' in the wild. After we make repairs, we'll round 'em up. There's some good-lookin' young horses there."

"Curly, the sun's gettin' high — let's head back to the ranch. C'mon, Bob."

They work a few days makin' repairs to the buildings and the corral. Then they begin roundin' up the livestock runnin' loose on the ranch.

"Curly, I'm headin' out to buy some cattle across the valley."

"Do you need any help, Jake?"

"No, you boys keep cleanin' up. Make sure the corral's good and strong. I'll be back in a few days." Jake rides out on Big Black.

"Hey there, cowboy, what can I do for ya?"

"Jim, you don't recognize me?"

"Nope, don't reckon I do."

"I'm Jake — Hank Black's kid."

"Jake! I'll be darned. How are you, boy?"

"I'm good, Jim. It's been a long time."

"Yeah, you rode out right after Hank got shot. Where ya been all this time?"

"Just wanderin' around."

"Say, Jim, I'm gonna work old Hank's ranch — he left it to me, ya know. I was thinkin' maybe I could buy some stock from you."

"Sure thing, Jake. What did you have in mind?"

"I wanna start a herd of cattle and a string of horses."

"That's a fine-lookin' stallion you got there. I've got just the mare for you to breed him with. They'd start a fine string."

"How many cows did you want?"

"A couple dozen would give me a good start."

"Well, you're gonna need a bull. I've got the perfect young bull for you too."

"That'd be great, Jim."

"How's the old ranch look after all these years?"

"I brought a couple of boys with me to work the ranch. We fixed it up — looks like the old place again."

"Jake, that's the finest ranch in the entire county. Prime land too, especially with the river runnin' right through the middle of her."

"Jim, this is more stock than I figured on. You think one of your hands could help me drive 'em back?"

"Sure. When do you wanna leave?"

"First thing in the mornin', if that's alright with you."

In the morning, Jake and one of Jim's ranch hands leave for Jake's ranch. Jake is ridin' his new mare, and Big Black is followin' behind. They drive the herd for a few hours until they reach water. They water the stock, rest a while, then set out for the ranch. The sun is risin' high in the sky — it's hot and dry. Curly looks up and sees a cloud of dust comin' toward the ranch.

"Hey Bob, look — it must be Jake drivin' a herd of cattle. Open the gates and get mounted — we'll go help him bring 'em in." They ride out to meet Jake.

"Bring 'em in, boys. Smokey and I are gonna ride in, get this dust off us, and grab a beer."

"Okay, Jake."

"Yah! Let's go, you mavericks!"

They drive the stock through the gates of the ranch and into the corral.

"Curly, would you cool off and brush down Big Black?"

"Sure thing, Jake."

A few months pass. Big Black has bred the mare, and the ranch is in great shape. Jake, Curly, and Bob sit down for dinner at the end of the day.

"Boys, you've done a fine job with the ranch. Think I'll hit the trail in the mornin'. I trust you boys to take care of things."

"Jake, where you goin'?"

"No place special. I wandered around for so many years, I just need to travel."

"When will you be back, Jake?"

"Oh, in a few months or so. I'll stay in contact by mail with you."

"Think I'll turn in now. I wanna start early before the sun gets too high."

"Good night, boys."

"Good night, Jake."

Jake is up before sunup, has his breakfast, and feeds Big Black. He saddles his horse, fills his canteen, then wakes Bob and Curly.

"Well boys, I'm headin' out. See you in a few months."

"Take care, Jake." He rides out and down the trail, headed for town.

Reaching town, Jake is tired and hungry from his long ride. He stops in front of a coffee shop. He sees a young boy in the street and asks him his name.

"My name is Rob."

"Well, Rob, can you take my horse down to the stable and have him fed and watered?"

"Yes, sir."

Jake gives him a silver dollar, and the boy leads Big Black away. Jake brushes the dust off himself and walks into the coffee shop.

"Hey, cowboy, what can I get for you?"

"A cup of coffee and something to eat."

The girl working in the coffee shop pours him a coffee and makes him a sandwich. Jake looks out the window and sees a man coming out of the saloon. He wears his gun low and looks like a gunfighter. Jake asks the girl if she knows who the man coming out of the saloon and headed this way is.

She says, "He calls himself Nevada, thinks he's a fast gun. Says he's been looking for someone called Jake."

"Oh no."

"Sorry, what did you say?"

"Nothing. I was just thinking out loud."

Nevada crosses the street and walks into the coffee shop. He sits down next to Jake.

He says to Jake, "Looks like you been ridin' awhile. You're kinda dusty."

"Yup, just rode into town."

"I saw you from the saloon. You were ridin' a big black horse."

"Yup, that I was."

"I been lookin' for a man that rides a horse like that. Haven't seen him, have you?"

"What's he look like?"

"He's a big man, about your size. He wears buckskins."

"I've heard of a man like that. Haven't seen him. They say he's fast with a gun."

"Yeah, that's what they say. But I'm gonna prove he's not so fast."

Nevada doesn't recognize Jake. He's not wearin' his buckskins—he still has on his ranch clothes. Jake says, "Good luck, son, if you find him. Say, how old are you?"

"I'm eighteen. Old enough to gun this Jake. I know I'm faster."

"What do you call yourself?"

"Nevada."

"Well, maybe I'll be seein' you over at the saloon."

Jake leaves and walks over to the hotel, gets a room, and goes right to sleep.

The sun shinin' through the window wakes Jake. He gets up, has a bath and a shave, then puts on his buckskins. He puts on his black boots and gun belt, then walks to the saloon.

When he walks into the saloon, he sees Nevada standin' at the bar with his back to the door. Jake walks up behind him.

"Hey boy, heard you were lookin' for me."

Nevada turns around. "You're Jake?"

"That's me, boy."

Nevada thinks, He's a lot taller than I thought, as he looks at Jake. Jake stands straight and tall. His buckskins are a light tan, his boots, gun belt, and hat are black.

"Why you been lookin' for me, Nevada?"

"To prove you're not so fast, and I'm faster than you."

"You know, in order to prove it, one of us must die."

Nevada doesn't say a word.

"Kid, have you ever killed a man lookin' him straight in the eye? You look a little nervous. Not a good way to enter a gunfight. If you draw on me, I'll put a bullet straight through your heart."

"I think I have a better way to prove who's the fastest. A way that you'll be able to say you drew against me and lived. Nobody'll die today."

Jake tells one of the men standin' at the bar to get two beer mugs and a shot glass from the bar and come outside. Everyone follows Jake and Nevada outside and over to the corral. Jake tells the man to put the mugs on the fence rail and stand aside.

"Nevada, stand next to me. When he drops the shot glass, draw and break the mug in front of you."

"Drop that shot glass whenever you're ready."

He drops the shot glass. Jake fires, breakin' the beer mug before the shot glass hits the ground. Nevada hasn't cleared his gun from his holster when Jake's gun is already back in his. Thinkin' what would've happened if he'd drawn on Jake in the saloon, Nevada grows weak and pale.

"Come on, kid, I'll buy you a drink. Looks like you need one."

They walk into the saloon and order a beer.

"Jake, how did you know I was so slow?"

"You stand all wrong. You wear your gun too low, and your arm's too far forward."

"Hey Buckskins, beer mugs don't shoot back."

Jake looks into the mirror and sees a man standin' behind him. He can tell this cowboy knows how to use a gun.

"Nevada, move away."

"Hey Buckskins, I'm talkin' to you. You think you're a gunfighter?"

Jake turns around and says, "I don't think I'm a gunfighter. I know I am."

"What's your name, Buckskins?"

"Jake."

"Jake what?"

"Just Jake."

"Never heard of ya."

Jake says, "Do you plan to draw? If you do, tell us what name to put on your grave marker."

When Jake says that, the man draws. Two shots ring out through the saloon. Jake's bullet goes straight through the man's heart. The second shot goes straight into the floor from the man's gun. He's dead before he hits the floor.

Jake looks at Nevada. "That could be you layin' on the floor. I think your gun-slingin' days should end right here."

"I think you're right, Jake."

"The second thing you better do is quit callin' yourself Nevada. Use your real name."

Nevada is shaken up after seein' Jake outdraw the man and kill him.

"Kid, come over here and sit down. How would you like to learn how to be a ranch hand?"

"I think I'd like that."

"I have a ranch with two good old boys runnin' it for me. I'm gonna give you a job workin' on my ranch. You'll have to do everything they tell you the way they tell you how to do it. I'm gonna write you a letter to take to Curly. It'll explain everything to him. Pack your things up and head out in the mornin'. I'll tell you how to get there."

In the morning, the kid rides out of town headed for Jake's ranch. The mayor of the town sends for Jake, askin' him to come to his Office.

"Hello, Jake. I want to ask you if you'll take the job of Sheriff of this here town."

"Mayor, I'm honored that you would ask me, but I'm gonna have to decline the offer."

"I thought you had a Sheriff."

"We do, but there's trouble headed this way, and I don't think he can handle it. Maybe you'd take the job of deputy temporarily?"

"No. You see, I made a promise to someone that I'd never put my gun up for hire. Sorry, Mayor, I can't take the job."

"Tell me, what sort of trouble are you expectin'?"

"There's a mean bunch of men headed this way. When they hit a town, they do whatever they want, and it ain't good. Well, Mayor, like I said, I appreciate the offer, but I must turn you down."

Jake walks over to the Sheriff's Office and talks to the sheriff about the men headed for town. The sheriff tells Jake they're a ruthless bunch.

"Jake, I sure could use you as a deputy."

"Sorry, Sheriff."

Jake leaves the Sheriff's Office and walks over to the saloon and has a beer. The mayor and the sheriff are disappointed in the fact that Jake just doesn't care about the town.

A week later, the ruthless gang rides into town. They know they'll be met by the Sheriff. The sheriff has a reputation for bein' fast with a gun, so they send a man with a rifle up on the rooftop to gun down the sheriff when he stops them enterin' town.

The Sheriff walks into the street in front of the men, not knowin' the gunman is on the roof, pointin' a rifle right at him. A shot rings out and the man falls from the roof. At the same time, the men in the town come out of stores, alleyways, and appear on rooftops, all pointin' rifles at the gang in the street, sittin' on their horses.

The Sheriff looks around and sees Jake standin' on the porch in front of the saloon, puttin' his gun back into his holster. The sheriff tells the men to pick up the dead man in the street and ride out of town. The sheriff tips his hat to Jake by touchin' his hat with his gun barrel, then holsters his gun and walks into his Office.

Jake protected the town by organizing the men to back up the Sheriff. Later that afternoon, the sheriff walks into the saloon.

"Hey Jake, I don't know how to thank you. I was just a little nervous standin' out there alone in the street till you shot the man off the roof. When the townspeople started to appear from everywhere, I knew it was you that organized them."

"Well Sheriff, they can only expect so much from one man. It's their town—they need to help protect it."

The next day, a cowboy comes into the saloon, walks up to the bar, and orders a beer.

"Heard you boys had some trouble here yesterday. What happened?"

Being proud of themselves for protectin' the town, the men in the saloon tell the cowboy the story.

"Is this guy Jake in here now?"

"No, he's not. You couldn't miss him— a wearin' those buckskins and a black gun belt. Ya know, he's the fastest gun we ever saw."

"What's his last name?"

"Nobody knows. We asked him—he says Jake, just Jake."

"You should see him a sittin' tall on that big black horse of his."

"Well, that's some story. I gotta ride. See you boys another time."

The cowboy rides out of town to an old shack in the mountains where he meets the rest of his gang—the same gang that was gonna raid the town the day before. The man Jake shot off the roof was the gang leader's brother.

"What did you find out in town?"

"The gunman that killed your brother—his name is Jake."

"Jake what?"

"Just Jake. Nobody knows his last name. The men in the saloon said he's the fastest gun they ever saw."

"He wears buckskins. Does he ride a big black horse?"

"Yeah, that's what one of the men in the saloon told me."

"I've heard about this guy. They say he's the fastest gun anyone's ever seen. I found out when I was in town—he outdrew Big Red and shot him straight through the heart a few days ago, right in the saloon."

"If he outdrew Red, he's fast. Red was one of the fastest around."

"I'll get him for killin' my brother."

"We goin' to hit that town?"

"No, the townspeople are too well organized. We'd lose too many men takin' the town. We'll head south after I get this Jake."

"Shorty, go into town, get a room at the hotel, and keep an eye on Jake. Let me know if he leaves town."

"Jim, we gonna hang around here till he decides to leave town?"

Jim, very angrily, yells, "Yes, we're gonna hang around until I get Jake for killin' my brother."

"Okay Jim, don't get mad—I understand."

Shorty rides to town and hangs out in the saloon. He becomes friendly with some of the men. A few days later, Jake comes into the saloon.

"Well boys, I'm a headin' out of town in the mornin'. I got the urge to move along."

"Which way you headin', Jake?"

"West—to the first town I come to."

"Jake, it's been great knowin' ya. Thanks for savin' our town."

Shorty hears what Jake says. He walks out of the saloon and leaves town. He rides all night to the gang's hideout.

He tells Jim, "Boys, we're gonna gun him on the trail. Let's ride."

They get to a place on the trail where they can hide and ambush Jake.

In the mornin', Jake rides out of town. The townspeople are there to see him off. The crowd yells, "Goodbye Jake! Come back and see us again!"

"I will."

Jake rides to the edge of town, stops, and turns Big Black around. He rears his horse up and waves to the people in town. He then turns his horse and rides.

He rides for a few hours. The sun is in the western sky now, shinin' in Jake's eyes—it's just two hours past noon. All of a sudden, Big Black starts actin' up—he balks and jumps around. Jake knows there's danger ahead. He quickly turns Big Black behind a big boulder. A shot rings out from the rocks ahead—it misses Jake. Then several guns begin to fire at him.

"They seem to have us trapped here, boy."

Jake looks around and sees a space leadin' through a pile of big boulders.

"Look boy, through there—a way out."

Jake leads his horse through the opening and rides to the mountains to lose the gunmen.

Jake loses the gang in the mountains and then rides to the closest town. He knows it's the gang that attempted to raid the town days before. He rides into town wearin' trail clothes. Townspeople admire Big Black. Jake rides up to the hotel and ties his horse up to the hitchin' rail. An old man sittin' on the porch says to Jake:

"That's some fine lookin' horse ya got there, son."

"Thanks, old man."

"What's ya name?"Son,They call me Smokey."

"They call me Jake."

"Ya got a last name, Jake?"

"Just Jake."

"Say son, would ya like me to take care of your horse?"

"Sure. Don't try to ride him—he don't take kindly to people a tryin' to get on him."

"A one-man horse, huh?"

"Guess you could say that."

Jake walks into the hotel.

"Howdy cowboy, need a room?"

"I could use one."

"Sign this here register."

"Do you have a room overlookin' the main street?"

"I sure do."

"Ah, your name is Jake. No last name?"

"Nope. Just Jake."

"Number two—at the top of the stairs."

"Thanks. I'll put my things in the room and then go check on my horse."

"I saw Smokey leadin' your horse away. You don't have to worry about him if Smokey's takin' care of him. Old Smokey don't like people too much, but he sure loves horses."

"Thanks for tellin' me."

Jake, not worried about his horse, decides to clean up, put on his buckskins, and then check on Big Black. He comes out of the hotel and walks to the livery stable. Smokey has fed, watered, and is brushin' him down when Jake walks in.

"Smokey, he looks good."

"This here black horse sure shines when ya get all that trail dust off him. I cleaned up your saddle too."

"Well Smokey, let's go get us somethin' to eat."

"Nope. Don't like the people in that there eatin' place."

"Well, how 'bout a drink at the saloon?"

"Now you're talkin'."

"Say, you look pretty sharp in those buckskins. That's a fine lookin' gun and belt you're wearin'. Son, the way you wear that gun—strapped low and tied down—looks like you know how to use it."

"A little, Smokey. Let's go over to the saloon."

"Right behind you, boy."

Jake and Smokey walk into the saloon.

"Well lookie here, boys—old Smokey's got a friend."

They walk up to the bar and order a drink.

"Hey Smokey, who's your friend?"

"Jake. Meet the boys."

"Say cowboy, you're wearin' that shootin' iron like you know how to use it."

"A little, boys."

"There's somethin' about you. What's your last name?"

"My name is Jake—just Jake."

Sittin' over in the corner, a couple of cowboys are watchin' Jake.

One of them says, "Do you know who he is?"

"No, can't say that I do."

"You never heard of a fast gun named Jake that wears buckskins and rides a big black horse? He gunned down Big Red. He's the cowboy that'll let you draw against him shootin' beer mugs off a fence railin'."

"Wow!"

"That's him, huh?"

"Yup, sure is. I'd know him anywhere."

"Say, do you think he'll let me draw against him?"

"I don't know—why don't you ask him?"

"Think I will."

He gets up from the table and walks over to Jake.

"Hey partner, I heard about you lettin' men draw against you shootin' at beer mugs. Think we could do it?"

"In the past I've done that. It was to prove who was the fastest—it saved a few lives."

"Jake, I just want to see how fast you are and how slow I am."

"Friend, it'll cost you five dollars to draw against me."

"That's a lot of money, Jake."

"Yup, it is—but that's the only way."

"Okay, I'll do it."

Two or three boys say, "I'll pay you, Jake."

They just wanted to be able to say they drew against the fastest gun in the West—and lived.

Everyone in the saloon goes outside. Jake puts up four mugs, and they all line up. When one of the spectators drops the shot glass, Jake draws and fires, and puts his gun back in the holster before any of the three men get a shot off.

There's a buzz goin' through the crowd watchin'.

"He's the fastest gun we ever saw."

"I wouldn't want to be drawin' down on him."

The word of Jake drawin' against men shootin' beer mugs spreads throughout the West. Every town he goes to, there are men that want to draw against Jake—and pay the five dollars. The five-dollar fees support Jake and his travels.

One town he went to, a woman wanted to draw against Jake. She was one of the fastest with a gun that Jake encountered. There was talk that Jake slowed down his draw to make the girl look good. Jake denied this. He always said that if he did that, it would give the girl a false idea about her speed with a gun—and that might get her in trouble someday.

Jake rides out of town. He's on the trail for a few days before he gets to the next town. He's ridin' along and sees smoke comin' from town. He kicks up his horse and gallops toward the smoke. He stops his horse at the edge of town—the sight he sees is terrible. The church is burnin', women in the street cryin', and a half-dozen men lay dead on the ground. The smell of smoke and the sight of blood in the street angers Jake.

Jake rides up to a woman sittin' in the dust of the street, holdin' her husband, who's bleedin' bad. He dismounts and walks over just as the man dies in her arms. Jake consoles her and helps her off the ground. Then he picks the man up and carries him into a nearby buildin', layin' him on a table. He gets some of the women to tend to the lady who just lost her husband. Jake heads outside, lookin' for someone to tell him what happened.

He's told that Jim and his gang raided the town, robbed the bank, and set the church on fire— then they shot the men in the street. Jake rounds up some men to help pick up the dead. While doin' this, he notices one of the men lyin' on the ground is wearin' a deputy marshal's badge. Just then, the Marshal rides into town.

"Jake, what happened here?"

Jake explains it all to the Marshal and takes him to the deputy.

"Jake, that's my deputy, Rusty. I was on my way here to meet him. I gotta get up North—there's a problem I gotta tend to."

"Marshal, I'm goin' after Jim and his gang."

The Marshal reaches down and unpins the badge from Rusty's vest. He turns and pins it on Jake.

"I know you don't make money with your gun. I'm deputizin' you as a deputy marshal— without pay. I know Rusty wouldn't mind you wearin' his badge. This way, you can go after that gang legal-like, as a deputy marshal. This badge gives you the power to make arrests wherever you go. Be careful—Jim and his gang are a ruthless bunch. Jake, finish up takin' care of things in this town—I gotta ride North."

Jake always stays in touch with Curly, sendin' a wire to tell him he's headin' to Twin River after Jim and his gang. Jake rides out toward Twin River, lookin' for Jim and his band of cutthroats.

A few days later, Jake rides into Twin River, pulls up at the saloon, and ties Big Black to the hitchin' rail. He walks in, heads to the bar, and orders a beer. On the trail, Jake had taken off his deputy marshal's badge and stuck it in his shirt pocket. He asks the men in the saloon if they've seen or heard of Jim and his gang. One cowboy says he heard they were holed up in a town called Overlook.

Jake crosses the street to buy some supplies and ammunition. He grabs some feed for Big Black and rides out of town, headin' for Overlook.

On the way, Jake stops to bathe in a pond. He lays his clothes and gun belt on some rocks and dives in. Big Black steps into the water, takes a drink, then tilts his head, watchin' Jake splash around. Unknown to Jake, someone's watchin', lookin' to steal somethin'. The man climbs on a rock, pulls his gun, and aims at Jake. Just as he cocks it, Jake throws his knife, hittin' the man in the chest. Jake always keeps his knife handy when his gun belt's off. Two Arrows taught Jake how to throw a knife and use a bow and arrow when he was growin' up on Hank's ranch.

He buries the man and rides on toward Overlook. When he gets to town, he heads straight to the Sheriff's Office and asks about Slim also known as Jim and his gang. The Sheriff's mighty vague and don't seem keen on givin' Jake any useful information. Noticin' his attitude, Jake keeps quiet about bein' a deputy marshal. He leaves the Office and walks into the saloon across the street.

Jake knows older fellas in town are usually the best to talk to for information. He looks around and sees two old men sittin' at a table in the back. He orders three beers and walks over, settin' a mug in front of each of 'em.

"Why, thank ya, son. Take a seat."

"What can we do for ya?"

"I'd like a little information from you boys. I'm lookin' for Jim and his gang of outlaws."

"Shh… don't speak too loud. The owner of this here saloon is friends with Jim. We know the gang's holed up around here somewhere, but nobody knows where."

"Say, young fella—what's your name?"

"They call me Jake."

"No last name?"

"Nope. Just Jake."

"Say, do you ride a big black horse?"

"Yup, I do."

"Jake, it's a pleasure ta meet ya."

Jake says, "Thanks for the information. I'll be seein' ya around."

Jake gets a room at the hotel and lays down to rest. He lies there thinkin' the best way to draw out Slim and his gang is to let 'em come to him. He figures he'll let the saloon owner know he's lookin' for Jim—if the owner's friends with 'em, he'll pass word along.

Jake wakes from his nap. It's evenin'. He heads to the saloon, walks to the bar, orders a beer, and asks if anyone knows where Jim and his gang are hidin'.

The bartender goes into the Office. "Hey boss, there's a cowboy out here askin' about Jim and the gang."

"What's he look like?"

"He's tall, wearin' buckskins. His boots, gun belt, and hat are black. He wears his gun low and tied down."

"That's Jake—he killed Jim's brother. Send in one of the boys."

"Hey Mike, boss wants to see you."

Mike goes into the Office. "You want me, boss?"

"You see that cowboy out there wearin' buckskins?"

"Yeah boss, I did."

"Know who he is?"

"No boss. Never saw him before."

"That's Jake—the fast gun that killed Jim's brother. Head out and find Jim. Let him know Jake's in town lookin' for him. Take one of the boys with ya."

"Boss, it's a week's ride to the hideout."

"Guess you better get started then."

A few weeks later, Jim and his gang of ruthless outlaws ride into Overlook. They walk into the saloon and up to the bar.

"Hey boys, how ya been?" Jim asks.

"Where's Buckskins?"

"He ain't been in yet today—expect him anytime."

Jake walks down the sidewalk and spots five horses tied in front of the saloon. They're all lathered up—been ridden hard. Jake enters the saloon with caution. After goin' through the swingin' doors, he steps aside, outta the doorway. He sees four men standin' at the bar. One's missin'—there were five horses outside. Jake moves around the saloon, stayin' outta view from the windows.

Jim turns. "Hey fast gun, that was my brother you shot off that roof. You're gonna pay for killin' him."

Jake looks around for the fifth man. He knows how Jim operates— just like when he shot that dry gulcher off the roof.

"What are you gonna do now, fast gun? One against four?"

Just then, the saloon doors swing open. A lone cowboy walks in.

"No—it's two against four."

The cowboy glances in the mirror and outta the corner of his eye, sees the fifth man, gun drawn, standin' in the Office doorway. He turns, draws, and fires before the man can pull the trigger. Jake, surprised, looks at the cowboy for the first time.

The cowboy smiles and says, "Don't make it happen—just let it happen."

Jake gives him a questionin' look, noticin' how he wears his gun— looks like he knows how to use it.

Jake turns to Jim and his gang. "Y'all are under arrest."

"You can't arrest anyone!"

Jake pulls the deputy marshal's badge from his pocket and tosses it on the table in front of Jim.

"Either draw, or drop your gun belts."

Jim snarls, "They ain't gonna hang me." He draws, and the others follow. When the shootin' stops, Jake and the cowboy stand side by side. Four men lay dead on the floor.

"Curly, where did you come from?"

"Jake, when we got your last letter and you told us you were going after this gang, I headed out—thought you could use a little help."

"I guess I needed your help. That guy would've back-shot me if you hadn't got him."

"I knew that day when we rode to Randle's ranch and I saw you strap on that gun—you knew how to use it."

"Say, where did you learn to draw like that? You're almost as fast as I am. And who told you when you draw, not to make it happen—let it happen?"

"Jake, the same man that taught you how to use a gun taught me."

"I was Sheriff Hank's deputy when I was young."

"I quit after a few years—got tired of killing and took to prospecting till you came along and hired me to run your ranch."

"How come you never told me?"

"You never asked me."

They laugh and have a beer.

"Hey Jake, I almost forgot—I have something outside to show you. C'mon."

"Jake, look!"

Standing at the hitching rail is a big black horse.

"Curly, he looks just like Big Black."

"He ought to—he's Big Black's son."

"He sure is a beauty, Curly."

"Jake, this horse has bred a few mares. You got a fine string started."

"Curly, how's Bob and that kid I sent to you?"

"They're fine. The kid's a hard worker and wants to learn."

"Curly, I'm going to take the son of Big Black for a ride."

"Hold him tight—he likes to run away."

Jake takes the son of Big Black for a ride. Curly was right—the horse wants to run and he's not responding to the bit properly. Jake rides back to town. He tells Curly,

"The horse doesn't respond to the bit as he should. He needs to be worked with a long shank bit—gently."

Jake rides the horse to the livery stables and puts a long shank bit on the bridle. He begins to work the horse gently. It's easy to hurt the horse's mouth—the long shank puts a lot of pressure on it. Jake works the horse for a few days with the new bit, an hour each day. Soon, the horse begins to react to the bit as he should. Jake then puts the original bit back on the bridle. The horse responds properly.

"Curly, he's going to seem like a different horse. He responds like he should—you're in complete control."

"Curly, when are you going to head back to the ranch?"

"In the morning. On the way back I'm going to pick up a couple of mares to breed this horse to."

"Good idea, Curly."

"Hey Jake, those men are calling you."

"Jake, a few of us would like to draw against you—shooting at beer mugs."

"Jake, I'd like to try that myself."

"Come on, Curly, let's get a couple of mugs and a shot glass."

Word gets around and a crowd gathers to watch. Jake and Curly stand side by side. The shot glass is dropped. Two shots are heard—one a fraction of a second behind the other. Both beer mugs break.

"Jake, you didn't beat me by that much—but you beat me. You're the fastest with a gun I ever saw."

A few men challenge Jake and pay their five dollars. Most of the men never get their gun out of their holster before Jake draws, fires, and holsters his gun.

Following the shooting exhibition, Curly asks Jake about being a deputy marshal. Jake explains how he met the Marshal and became an unpaid deputy.

"I think I'll just keep this badge and work for the law unpaid. There are a lot of men that need to be brought to justice."

"Sam, that's quite a yarn. This Jake must have been some fast gun."

"Ya boys want some more coffee?"

"No thanks, Sara. Think we'll walk down the street and get a beer."

"Sam, what happened to Jake?"

"He rode the West, bringing in the worst outlaws and helping Sheriffs clean up towns. Whenever there was a reward on someone he brought in, the reward money always went to the poor people in that town."

"Let's head over to the saloon, and I'll tell you more about Jake."

The old boys walk to the saloon, sit at a table, and order beers. Sam continues to tell the men about Jake.

"Well boys, one day Jake hears about a town way out West that was having a lot of trouble. A group of men were in town taking it over.

They shot and wounded the Sheriff, killed the owner of the hotel, and took the hotel over. They kept the hotel owner's wife prisoner. They would go into the saloon, drink, and refuse to pay— often shooting the place up. They had everyone in town afraid to go out into the streets."

"Jake rides to the edge of town. There's nobody on the streets— the school's not even open. A couple of the outlaws see Jake riding in at the end of town. They knew who he was—Jake's fame had spread throughout the West. They called a couple more men out into the street."

"All of a sudden, Jake's big black horse comes walking down the street without a rider. Jake had dismounted when the two in the street went to the saloon door to call out the men. The four of them stood amazed."

"'Where did he go?' They drew their guns and looked around."

"Jake walks out behind them and tells them to drop their guns. They turn around shootin'. Jake kills all four. He ducks for cover, knowing the men inside would be coming out. Jake runs around the building and comes out behind them. He stands on the front porch of the saloon and says, 'Looking for me?'"

"One of the men draws his gun. Jake draws and fires. With a half twirl, he puts his gun back in the holster. He stands looking at the two men and says, 'Drop your gun belts—or draw.'"

They unbuckle their gun belts. One says, "We're not drawing against you."

Jake says, "You're under arrest. Head for the jail."

The deputy sheriff is in the street by now. Jake identifies himself to the deputy as a Deputy United States Marshal.

Jake says to the deputy, "Lock these boys up and hold them for trial."

Just as Sam finishes his story, one of the townsmen comes running into the saloon.

"Hey boys—Sara just took a heart attack and died."

The entire saloon becomes quiet. One man says,

"This town won't be the same without Sara and her General Store."

"Boys, raise your glasses to the memory of the finest woman we've ever known. Sara—we'll miss you."

A few days later, the entire town turns out for Sara's funeral. She is buried on her property next to the General Store. A few days after, the sheriff unlocks the door to Sara's store. He tells everyone she had said if anything happened to her, to open the store so the boys could sit around, talk, and have coffee.

The following morning, Sam and the other old men meet at Sara's store. They drink coffee and remember her.

"What did you put in this coffee? Tastes like it'll kill us!"

"It sure ain't like that fine coffee our Sara used to make."

Sam apologizes.

"Guess I put a little too much coffee in the pot. Boys, I'll do better in the morning. Be sure to be here—I got a yarn to tell you.

"We'll be here, Sam—bright and early."

In the morning, Sam is at the store just after sunup. Looking out the window, he sees the silhouette of the mountains with the sun rising behind them. The sky is light blue without a cloud in it.

"Good morning, Sam!"

"Good morning, boys. Coffee's on—it's better today."

"Sam, we're anxious to hear the yarn you're going to tell us today.

"Well boys it's a strange tail". "About Jake?" "No, it's about an unusual law man.

Just as Sam says that, they hear gunshots coming from the other end of town. One of the town members comes into the store and says,

"The bank is being held up—they wounded the Sheriff!"

Sam gets up out of his chair and slowly walks out to his horse. He opens his saddlebag and takes out a gun belt and a gun. He straps it on.

"Sam, where you going?"

"Just stay inside—under cover."

Sam slowly walks down the street. His gun is worn low and tied down.

"Never saw Sam wearin' a gun before."

"Me neither."

"What's he gonna do?"

Sam walks toward the bank and stops just outside the door. Two men come running out of the bank with the money in a sack. When they see Sam standing in the street, they point their guns and fire. Sam draws and shoots. Two men lie dead on the ground.

Sam puts his gun back into the holster and slowly walks to his horse. On the way, he takes off his gun belt. When he gets to his horse, he rolls the gun belt up and puts it back into his saddlebag. He walks back into the store.

"Sam, where'd you learn to draw and shoot like that?"

Sam doesn't speak—he just holds his hand up and shakes his head. The men say no more. Sam picks up a plug of chewing tobacco, cuts a piece off and puts it in his mouth. He pours another cup of coffee and sits quietly for a long while. Then he gets up, walks out, gets on his horse—without saying a word—and rides away.

The old boys in the store can't believe what they saw Sam do. One of the old boys says, "I can't believe that Sam could use a gun like that. He's so gentle and soft-spoken. He shot those men—they were dead before they hit the dirt."

"Yup, he sure was fast with that gun. I had no idea—never saw him wearin' a gun before."

Sam rides to his ranch and tells his ranch hands that he'll be back in a few days. He rides to the top of a hill and sets up a camp. His ranch hands could see the glow of his campfire against the night sky. Three days later, he rides back to his ranch. The ranch hands have heard about the shootin' in town. One of them tells the others that he saw Sam use his gun once before.

"We were camped out on the North Range havin' lunch when a rattler came up beside me."

"The snake was ready to strike. Sam drew, fired, and shot the head right off that snake."

"His draw was so fast I never saw him reach for his gun."

Sam rides up to the corral, gets off his horse, takes the saddle off, and walks to the barn. None of the ranch hands say a word until he speaks.

"Boys, round up those young horses out on the range and bring 'em in. Start breakin' them in the mornin'."

"Make sure you bring in that black stallion, or he'll run that herd to the next county."

"Okay, boss. We'll head out right after lunch."

"If they ain't branded, be sure to brand 'em."

"I'm goin' into town in the mornin'."

"See you boys when you get back."

The ranch hands ride out after lunch. They spot the black horse leadin' a half dozen horses. They took up the chase, knowin' it wouldn't be easy catchin' the black. However, they knew if they could catch him and bring him in, the others would follow.

The next mornin', Sam rides into town and up to the store. The old boys are inside drinkin' coffee. Sam walks in—they all become quiet.

"Pour me a cup of that there coffee and give me a piece of that chewin' tobaccey."

"Well, what are ya boys so glum lookin' about?"

"Go ahead, ask me the questions—I know you're dyin' to ask."

"Sam, we don't want to pry into your business or your life."

"I'll tell you my story. We're friends—you have a right to know."

"Remember when I was tellin' you about the kid Nevada that wanted to draw down on Jake, and Jake sent him to his ranch to learn ranchin'?"

"Yes!"

"Well, I was that dumb kid. I went to Jake's ranch and lived on it with Curly and Bob."

"Jake would come home every few months. He taught me to draw and shoot after he knew I had given up on those ideas of becomin' a gunfighter."

"See that horse out the window? He's the great-grandson of Big Black—Jake's horse."

"The brand on that horse is JJ. That was Jake's brand."

"What does the JJ stand for?"

"Don't laugh—it stands for Just Jake."

"Jake got up in the years and returned to his ranch to live out his days. Soon, Curly and Bob were gone. Then Jake died one night in his sleep as a very old man."

"He left his ranch to me—the very same ranch that Sheriff Hank Black left to him."

"Lookie here—this is Jake's Deputy Marshal badge that he proudly carried with him his entire life."

"With this badge and his gun, he brought more outlaws in than any other lawman and never got paid a dime for it."

"Most of the men he went after gave up—they wouldn't tangle with Jake's fast gun."

"Well, I'll be—Sam, we would have never known if we hadn't seen you draw down on those two bank robbers. You are some fast."

"I wasn't faster than Jake—nobody was. That's why Jake lived to be an old man."

"I drew against Jake, shootin' at a beer mug. He drew and broke the mug before I cleared my gun from my holster."

"Oh yes, Jake was fast—lightnin' fast."

"That sure is a fine-lookin' horse you rode in on this mornin'."

"He's a great cuttin' horse—he can spin on a dime and give you change."

"All our horses that descended from Big Black are top ranch horses."

"My ranch hands are roundin' up some of Big Black's offspring right now."

"There's a big black colt leadin' the herd. When he's broke, we'll brand him with the JJ brand and name him Big Black Junior."

As the years rolled by, Slim and the old boys turned Sara's store into the Western Feed and General Store. However, they kept the section where they sit, talk, spin yarns, and drink coffee just the same as it was when Sara was alive.

"Sam, do you have more stories about Jake?"

"Yes, I sure do—but I have a few other stories to tell ya first."

"I have a special story to tell you about Jake."

"Someday, I'll tell you That best story. The best story of all about Jake."

THE YELLOW ROSE OF TEXAS AND THE TEXAS RANGERS

"Sam, the Western Feed Company has grown so fast it's hard to believe."

"Yah Slim, I know it."

"Sam, tomorrow I have to leave for Stone City to open a new branch. I think that new man we trained to manage the store will work out just fine."

"Let's sit a spell while we have time and have us a cup a coffee. I got a yarn to spin for ya."

"Sam, before you begin, there's been a lot of interest in people wantin' to breed their mares to one of your stallions descendin' from Jake's horse, Big Black."

"If you wish, you could offer breedin' from a descendant of Big Black at our feed stores. Ranchers are aware of that great line of stock you have."

"That would be a good idea. However, the stud fee would be very high so the breed doesn't become too common."

"That line of horses is one of the finest in the country."

"Let's hear your yarn, Sam."

"The story begins with the state of Texas, before it became a state. Texas was a wild territory, and settlers were movin' in rapidly. They didn't have any protection from the Indians and ruthless outlaws.

About the year 1823, Stephen F. Austin organized ten men to protect six or seven hundred settlers. This was the beginnin' of the Texas Rangers."

"Say, Sam, where did the name Texas come from?"

"Well Slim, the story goes that the word Texas is a Caddo Indian word meanin' friend or allies."

"I guess there were a lot of different Indian tribes in that territory."

"Yes, there were. In 1835 the Texas Rangers became official, and by 1837 there were three hundred Rangers protectin' the citizens from Indians, murderers, and all types of criminals. In the year 1845, Texas entered the Union."

"My yarn begins in the year 1836. Robert McAlpin Williamson was the first major in charge of the Texas Rangers. Outlaw gangs were organizin' throughout Texas, and the Texas Rangers were increasin' their numbers."

One mornin' the Major was sittin' in his Office talkin' to one of his top Rangers when a young woman walked into his Office. She was tall, well built, and her long, flowin' blonde hair reached her shoulders. Her physical appearance wasn't the only thing they noticed—she was wearin' a gun belt and revolver on her hip.

"Hello there, young lady, what can I do for you?"

"I understand you need Rangers."

"Well, yes we do!"

"That's why I'm here."

"You mean you want to be a Ranger?"

"Yes, I do."

"What's your name?"

"Sandy Roberts, sir."

"Sandy, I don't think you understand. Rangers are all men."

"I don't understand that. I can ride and shoot as good as any man."

"You see, it's a rough life. Rangers spend weeks out on the trail, sleepin' under the stars, often alone."

"I'm used to doin' that. I have a fine horse, and I'm ready to be a Ranger."

"What have you been doin' with yourself?"

"I sing. I work in saloons and dance halls. I do have an old man that travels with me—he arranges for my appearances."

"You travel around makin' singin' appearances?"

"Oh, excuse me, this is Bob Lawson. He's a top Ranger."

"If you want to hear me sing, stop over at the saloon this evenin'. I'll be appearin' at eight o'clock."

"Well, young lady, I think you better stick to singin'. A Ranger's life is not the life for you."

"Well, I don't understand. I just want to be a Ranger."

"I'll stop over tonight. I'm anxious to hear you sing. If your voice is as lovely as you are, it'll be a treat."

She smiles as she turns away. "Why, thank you, Bob."

That evenin', Bob goes over to the One Horse Saloon to hear Sandy sing. A man walks out onto the stage and says, "We have a special treat for you boys—Sandy Roberts, a singin' sensation."

She walks out onto the stage wearin' a red evening gown slit up the side so her leg shows as she walks. The men in the saloon go wild, screamin' and yellin'. She begins to sing. The room becomes silent as everyone listens to her beautiful voice. Bob is very impressed. He thinks she looks like an angel and sounds like one too.

One of the drunken men in the room goes wild and starts shoutin' at her. She steps down off the stage and takes a few steps. The man is still yellin' at her. She reaches down and takes a gun out of one of the men's holsters and shoots the cigar out of the mouth of the loud, yellin' man.

"Nobody acts like that when I'm singin'."

She then shoots his hat off and runs him out of the saloon. She gets a loud applause as she returns to the stage.

"Start the music. Any of you boys have somethin' to say?"

No one speaks. She begins to sing again.

She spots Bob standin' by the bar. He motions for her to come to him. When she finishes her song, she walks over to him.

"Can I buy you a drink, Sandy?"

"No thanks. I seldom drink."

"That was some fancy shootin' you did."

"Bob, I just can't take it when someone tries to destroy my song."

"I don't blame you. You have a beautiful voice."

"Well, thanks, Bob."

That evenin', Sandy performs again at ten o'clock. Followin' her performance, she walks to the bar for a glass of water. She overhears two men talkin' about robbin' the bank later that night. She goes to her room, changes her clothes, and straps on her gun belt.

She goes out to look for the Rangers. It's too late—she don't have time to look for them—so she heads down the street towards the bank. Hidin' across from the bank, she can see the two men inside. She waits until they come out, then she steps out and says, "Hold it right there!"

They draw their guns. She draws hers and fires twice, woundin' the men. The gunshots wake up the townsfolk, and they come runnin' out into the street in their nightclothes with guns in their hands. Everyone stops all of a sudden when they see the two men layin' on the ground with the bank bags in their hands. Sandy is standin' over them with her gun on them.

"Get a doctor. These men need help."

"What happened?"

"They just robbed the bank. I couldn't find anyone in time, so I stopped them."

The townsfolk thank her and return to their beds.

When the Major of the Texas Rangers hears about Sandy stoppin' the bank robbery, he tells Bob to make her a Ranger.

"Bob, bring her into my Office—we'll explain to her."

The Major explains his idea to Sandy. Bob tells Sandy that she will report directly to him.

"When you're booked in to sing, no one will know you're a Ranger—except for me. Not even other Rangers will know. You'll be on the Ranger payroll and carry a Ranger's badge. You'll have complete authority, same as the other Rangers, if you need to use it in an emergency."

"It sounds okay with me. As long as I'm a Texas Ranger, I'll do whatever you want me to."

"One thing, Sandy."

"What's that, Bob?"

"No shootin' cigars outta people's mouths or shootin' hats off."

They laugh.

The Major says, "What was that?"

"Just a little habit she has."

"Oh, I don't think I want to know."

"Sandy, from time to time, you'll see me in town when you're singin'. Act like you don't know me."

"I can see why that could make sense, Bob."

"I'll find a way to contact you. No matter what I do, just go along with it. Sandy, you'll be our first undercover agent. By the way, your code name will be Yellow Rose of Texas."

"Oh, I like that."

The fact that the Yellow Rose of Texas was an undercover Texas Ranger is still a secret today.

"Sam, how'd you find out about her?"

"Jake ran into her durin' her service as a Ranger. She told him the story of how she became a Texas Ranger. She also told him some stories of her experiences as a Ranger."

"Hey Sam, we have to take a break from your story—we got a shipment of horse feed down at the rail head."

"Call the boys and send 'em down with wagons to pick it up. Send one wagon over to Stoneridge and have 'em put the rest in the warehouse."

"Okay, Slim."

"Sam, the feed is all taken care of."

"Back to the story of The Yellow Rose of Texas. The first town they sent her to was a wide- open town for outlaws. The leader of one of the most ruthless gangs of outlaws was someone in that town. The Rangers wanted to find out who he was. The local Sheriff was no help at all— he was part of the gang."

In the mornin, Sandy was sent by the Rangers to find out all she could. She worked in the saloon nightly, singing and getting to know the people in that town.

She became real popular with the men that attended the saloon, especially the owner.

"Sandy, I'd like you to stay on permanently. Your singing and good looks are great for business. I'll double your salary. Besides, I sure like havin' you around. Maybe someday I'll make you a partner."

She was hopin' for an offer to stay longer—she needed more time to work on her assignment.

One night, while singin', she notices two men goin' into the saloon owner's Office. She had seen them around before. She found them suspicious due to the fact that they never acted like saloon customers. They'd stop in from time to time and to visit the saloon owner's Office. They'd be in there a short while, then leave the saloon and ride outta town. There'd be other men outside, sittin' on their horses, waitin' for the two to come out, then they'd all ride off together.

While Sandy was on stage singin', a cowboy walks into the saloon—it's Texas Ranger Bob Lawson. She notices he ain't wearin' his Ranger badge. He walks up to the bar, orders a beer, turns, and watches Sandy sing. He thinks her voice is better than he figured.

"Hey bartender, what's a man gotta do to get that songbird to have a drink with him?"

"Why don't you try askin' her?"

"Well, just how would I go about doin' that?"

"Tell one of the girls workin' the floor to deliver a message. She usually responds to the invitation if the man's a gentleman."

"Suzy, take a message to Sandy for this cowboy—he'd like to buy her a drink."

"Well, cowboy, if she don't want to have a drink with you, I sure will."

"Thank ya, Suzy. If she won't, I'll take you up on that. How 'bout tomorrow night?"

"You have a date, cowboy. I'll give Sandy your message."

When Sandy receives Bob's message, she gives him a nod. When she finishes her song, she joins Bob at the table.

"Sandy, how are things goin'?"

"Fine, Bob. I was asked to stay on entertainin' for a while. That'll give me more time to figure out what's goin' on."

"I been watchin' the owner of this saloon. I think he's got somethin' to do with one of the outlaw gangs."

"I've spotted two men that come in and go into the Office. They're in with the boss for a short time and then leave. They never act like customers."

"Outside, sittin' on horseback, four or five men wait for the two to come out."

"I'm gonna be in town for a few days. I made a date with one of the girls for tomorrow night—see what I can find out from her."

"If those two come in while I'm here, give me a signal and I'll follow 'em."

A couple days pass, and Bob is leavin' town. He lets Sandy know and tells her,

"There's another Ranger comin' to town to watch and follow the gang you told me about."

"What's his name, Bob?"

"His name's Smokey."

"How will I know him?"

"He'll approach you. He should be here in the mornin'."

The next evenin', durin' Sandy's performance, a young cowboy walks into the saloon and sits at a table to watch her show. He nods to Sandy while she's still on stage. When her song's over, she walks toward the table. The cowboy stands and says,

"You are the Yellow Rose of Texas."

She says, "Smokey?"

"Yup, that's me, Sandy."

"Have you seen the two men you told Bob about?"

"No, not for a few days."

"When do they usually come in?"

"Always while I'm singin'."

"Sandy, that's when everyone's payin' attention to you. They won't be noticed. I'm gonna stay in town till they show up and I can follow 'em to see what they're up to. We need a signal. I'll start to yodel in my song when they walk into the Office."

The owner looks out and sees Sandy sittin' at the table with Smokey. He tells his right-hand man,

"She's been a sittin' with that cowboy too long—go break it up."

"Sandy, the boss wants to see you!"

"Oh? Well, tell your boss I'm busy."

"Hey cowboy, you been sittin' here a little too long. I think you better move along."

Sandy begins to stand and says,

"Who do you think you are?"

As she says that, the man pushes her back into the chair. Smokey gets up and punches the man in the mouth. The punch knocks him down. Smokey turns to see if Sandy's alright. The man on the floor draws his gun—he's fixin' to shoot Smokey in the back. Sandy reaches and draws Smokey's gun, shootin' the gun right outta the man's hand.

She says, "Go tell your boss I'll see him when I'm ready."

The men in the saloon applaud Sandy's shootin'. Smokey thanks Sandy and leaves the saloon.

The saloon owner's jealousy brings out his evil side.

"Sandy, I don't think you know how things work around here. In here, I'm the boss. From now on, you're my girl. I pay you, and I own you."

She gets up from her chair and walks to her room. The whole saloon goes quiet after the saloon owner's outburst. The patrons slowly get up and quietly leave.

The followin' evenin', Sandy is singin', and the two men come into the saloon and go into the boss's Office. She looks around—she don't see Smokey. However, she begins to yodel—the signal they agreed on. She looks toward the saloon doors and sees Smokey standin', lookin' in over the top of the swingin' doors, then he disappears. He follows the gang into the hills to their hideout. He recognizes three of the men waitin' at the hideout—they're wanted for murder and robbery. He rides to the nearest Texas Ranger outpost, rounds up a group of Rangers, and heads for the gang's hideout.

Followin' a fierce gunfight, two Rangers are wounded, three of the gang are dead, and two wounded. Three gang members give up. One of the wounded identifies the saloon owner as the leader of the outlaw gang. The Texas Rangers broke up one of the most ruthless outlaw gangs in Texas—thanks to the work of the Yellow Rose of Texas.

Sandy is in her room at the saloon when the owner knocks on her door.

"Who is it?"

"Open this door! I told you, you belong to me, and I'm comin' in to get what's mine!"

Sandy opens her suitcase and takes out her gun belt and straps it on. The saloon owner breaks down her door. He stops when he sees her wearin' a gun and holster.

"What do you think you're gonna do with that?"

"Put a hole in your chest if you don't leave this room."

"I ain't goin' anywhere."

"Then if you got a gun, you better draw it."

He draws his gun, thinkin' he'd outdraw her and hold his gun on her while he took what he wanted. She sees him reach for his gun—she draws and shoots, puttin' a bullet right in his chest. He stands there with his hand on his chest, looks down at the blood, then looks at her and drops to his knees.

"Who are you?"

"The Yellow Rose of Texas. Texas Ranger."

He repeats the word,

"Ranger…"

Then falls over on his face—dead.

"Well boys, that's the story of the Yellow Rose of Texas. She went on to do undercover work as a Texas Ranger, gatherin' information on corruption all over Texas."

"Hey Sam, how many people did Jake teach to draw a gun?"

"I don't rightly know. One thing's for sure—if Jake taught 'em, they were fast."

"Apache Rose and the Yellow Rose of Texas—the fastest gun women of the old Wild West."

"Sam, woes Apache Rose?" " Well boys that's another story, someday I'll tell ya all about her, it's a special story".

SLIM AND PEDRO

The old boys are sittin' around the late Sara's store drinkin' coffee and talkin'. The Western Feed and General Store has grown into a large company. With the exception of the cattle industry, the Western Feed and General Store Company is the largest company in the West.

"Sam, the ladies' apparel seems to be in big demand in our business locations. We don't have the space to dedicate to the line of ladies' products."

"I have an idea, Sam."

"What is that?"

"My idea is to open ladies' apparel shops in a separate location in each of the towns where we have our stores located."

"With the buying power we'll have buyin' for several shops, we'll be able to offer the ladies items at reasonable prices."

"If we have all the store's merchandise shipped here and then sent out on our wagons along with the freight to our feed and general stores, there won't be any additional fees for distribution."

"By havin' everything shipped to one location and then distributed by us, we'll save on the initial shipping as well."

"I think you got somethin' there. What would you say about puttin' Slim in charge of organizin' this branch of the business?"

"You mean Slim from the feed department?"

"Yes, he's got a good head for business. As he sets up a shop, he'll be able to choose a woman to manage the shop."

"I think your idea's a good one. Didn't you say he once was a deputy Sheriff and fast with a gun?"

"Yup, he was. He quit and put his gun away."

"No one's ever seen him wearin' a gun. He got tired of fast guns wantin' to challenge him, so he just put the gun away."

Sam and the boys talk to Slim about their idea and the ladies' apparel stores. He thinks it's a good idea.

"When do you want me to start?"

"As soon as you like, Slim."

"I'll head out in a couple of days."

"Sounds good."

A few days later, Slim rides out one morning for Jackson City to set up the first ladies' shop. When he reaches town, he goes straight to The Western Feed and General Store. He sits with the manager, and they talk about the idea of openin' the ladies' shop. He thinks it's a good idea.

"I can use the extra space in the store when the ladies' merchandise is moved to the ladies' shop."

"We have to locate a girl to manage the shop for us."

"Slim, I know just the girl—she's very bright, works part-time at the bank."

"I'd like to meet her."

"I'll set up a luncheon date with her for tomorrow."

"Sounds good. I'll see you in the morning."

The next day, they all have lunch together.

"Slim, this is Julie, the girl I told you about."

"Hello, Julie."

They discuss the ladies' apparel shop. Julie is delighted with the idea.

"Slim, there's a store for sale right on Front Street. It'll be the perfect spot."

"Okay Julie, we'll go look at it after we're done with lunch."

"Miss, could we have some more coffee please?"

"Be right with you."

As they're finishin' their coffee, gunshots ring out in the street. Slim looks out the window and sees two men shootin' at a young Mexican man's feet, makin' him dance. The Mexican's clothes are old and torn. He's wearin' a straw sombrero.

"Julie, what's goin' on with those two men shootin', makin' the Mexican dance like that?"

"Who are those two men?"

"They're part of a gang that works for Jackson—he's a big rancher that everyone says is crooked."

"Oh look!"

"They're talkin' to the two men dressed in Eastern clothes now."

"Do you know who they are?"

"No, Slim, they've only been in town a few days."

"Strange those two cowboys would be talkin' to them."

"Slim, let's go back to the feed store."

"Okay, Bob."

"There's somethin' we have to talk about."

Returnin' to the store, Slim and Bob sit down to talk.

"Slim, there's somethin' goin' on in this town. I'm not sure what it is, but the townspeople are not happy with Jackson."

"They seem to think those two Easterners are involved."

"I'm sorry to hear that, Bob."

"I'm gonna keep my eyes on 'em."

"Slim, every time Jackson's gang comes into town, there's some type of trouble. They're a ruthless bunch."

"Now the small ranchers are havin' their stock rustled and other problems. They think Jackson is behind it all."

"What about the Sheriff?"

"He's no help. Everyone thinks he's on Jackson's payroll."

"The townspeople sent a rider to get a Marshal. Neither the Marshal nor the rider ever showed up back in town."

"They're always pickin' on Pedro because he can't fight back."

"That's the way bullies are. They pick on the weak—they're afraid of anyone else."

"Pedro is quite a character. Along with his pet donkey, he loves to entertain the children. In doin' so, he entertains the adults as well."

"He's sort of a clown. Some think he's a little slow, if you know what I mean."

That evenin', Slim walks into the saloon. The same two men are tryin' to get Pedro to drink whiskey. One man is holdin' Pedro, the other tryin' to make him drink.

"Drink this whiskey!"

"No! No! I don't drink whiskey."

"I said drink it."

Slim says, "Why don't you drink it yourself!"

The people laughin' inside the saloon all become quiet.

"You talk pretty big for a man not wearin' a gun."

"I don't need a gun."

"What do you mean by that?"

When the man asks that, Slim punches him and knocks him out. The second man goes for his gun. Slim reaches out and takes the gun away from him, then points it at him and tells him to pick his friend up and get outta there.

Slim asks, "What are their names?"

"Pete and Ray."

"Would you like a beer, Pedro?"

"No thank you, Señor. I just came in to clean up."

Saturday mornin', Slim walks out of the hotel. He hears laughin' and cheerin'. He sees the children gathered all around Pedro and his donkey. The donkey is sittin' on his hind end. Pedro is pullin' on the rope; the donkey won't get up. All of a sudden, the donkey quickly gets up, and Pedro sits down in the dirt. The donkey lets out a loud hee-haw. The children all laugh and applaud.

One of the kids says, "You need a horse."

One of the townspeople who knows what Pedro is gonna do says, "You can use my horse."

Pedro pats the horse and slips him a lump of sugar.

He asks the children, "How do I get way up there?"

"Put your foot in the stirrup and swing your leg over the saddle."

Pedro puts his foot in the stirrup. The kids start yellin', "The other foot!"

Pedro swings up onto the horse facin' backward.

"This horse is backwards," he says.

Laughin', the kids say, "No, you are!"

"How do I get down?"

"Put your foot in the stirrup and swing your leg down."

He puts his left foot in the stirrup and swings his leg down.

"Where did everyone go?"

"We're on this side! You used your wrong foot again!"

He gets down on his hands and knees and looks under the horse.

"Oh, there you are!"

He crawls on his hands and knees under the horse and gets up on the other side.

"Pedro, put your left foot in the stirrup and swing your right leg over the horse."

He gets halfway on the horse and says, "I'm stuck, give me a push."

He yells, "Not so hard!" as he goes up and over the horse and falls on the ground.

He lays there and says to the kids, "I don't know how to ride a horse anyway—I give up."

The kids, all laughin', help Pedro get up off the ground. A loud applause breaks out from the townspeople.

Slim walks over to Pedro.

"You sure are great with those kids. You put on a great show—not only do the kids enjoy your act, so do the adults."

"Gracious."

"Come on Pedro, I'll buy you a drink."

"Soda pop?"

"Yes, Pedro, a soda pop."

They sit at a table talkin' for a while.

"Slim, why do those men pick on me? I never bother anyone."

"I don't know, Pedro."

"Where do you sleep, Pedro?"

"I sleep outside. The sky is my blanket. I count the stars to go to sleep."

"I have an idea," Slim tells him about the ladies' apparel shop and asks him if he'd like to work helpin' Julie.

Slim speaks to Julie about Pedro. She likes the idea.

"Maybe he could set up a bunk in the back room and sleep there?"

"Sure thing, Slim, that's a great idea."

A few weeks pass and Julie, with Pedro's help, get the store open.

The store has been open for a couple of weeks when the two Easterners walk in.

"Hello boys, may I help you?"

"Well I think—maybe I'll rephrase that—you will help us."

"What do you mean?"

"There are things that are bad that can happen to you and your shop that we can prevent."

"Now, there's a small fee for our protection. I see your business is already successful."

"I'm sure you don't want anything to happen to your business."

"What on earth are you talkin' about?"

"Ten dollars a week or your business will be closed."

She tells them to get out of her shop or she'll get her rifle.

"I see you're gonna need some persuasion."

They leave the shop.

"Pedro, go get Slim. Tell him I need him right away."

Pedro comes back with Slim in a matter of minutes.

"Julie, what happened?"

She explains to him what happened.

"They want money for protection—protection from them."

"What kind of a racket are they operatin'?"

Slim leaves the shop, and he's not happy. He speaks with other merchants in town.

He finds out they're payin' for protection every week.

He asks them if they've told the Sheriff.

"Slim, the Sheriff works for Jackson. It's his men that come into town and collect the money."

Two ranchers come racin' into town and start yellin' in the street outside the Sheriff's Office.

"Sheriff, both our herds were rustled last night. Two of our hands were shot down in cold blood. You've got to do somethin' about this gang of outlaws!"

"What do you expect me to do? Whenever I go after them, they disappear—along with the cattle."

"Jackson and his gang are behind the rustlin'—you know that. Why don't you send for help?"

A week later, another rancher rides into town. He walks into the saloon.

"My ranch was raided last night. Two of my men were wounded. They ran off my stock and burnt my barn down."

"Somethin's gotta be done."

"Jackson is tryin' to run all the small ranchers out and take over the town." "We could form a posse and go after them."

"Slim, they vanish like they were ghosts."

That night, a half-dozen men wearin' kerchiefs over their faces raid a small rancher. His herd is grazin' near his ranch house. The rancher's name is Clem. He begins shootin' out the window at the raiders. One of the raiders is ridin' with a torch burnin', headin' for the barn. Clem sees him and is about to shoot when a shot rings out and the man falls off his horse. The torch burns out on the ground. Two more men fall off their horses. Clem wonders who's shootin' them. Just then, a man on a white horse appears in Clem's view. He's wearin' a blue shirt and a blue hood. The silver decorations on the black leather saddle shine in the moonlight.

The three remainin' raiders ride off. The hooded man takes out his rifle and shoots one of them off his horse.

The next day, Clem goes into town to buy a wagon load of feed from the Western Feed and General Store. He tells the manager what happened the night before.

"I wonder who that hooded man is. He sure can shoot. He's some sight on that white horse with the moonlight shinin' on him."

Slim goes into the saloon and listens to the men talkin' about the Blue Ghost and how he's been seen now and then ridin' the prairie. No one knows who he is or where he comes from. Slim orders a beer, sits down, and tries to figure out what's goin' on in this town. Whatever it is, Jackson's behind it all.

The next mornin', Pete and Ray ride into town and up to the Western Feed and General Store. They get off their horses and walk into the store. They tell the manager it's time he started payin' for protection. He disagrees and gets beaten. They take twenty-five dollars and tell him that's his fee for protection. They make a mess of the store so he'll remember and then walk out. Pedro's standin' in the street when they come out. They knock him down and join six other gang members. They go about collectin' protection money from the rest of the merchants in town. The eight men ride out.

When they get to the pass, Pete warns the men, "This is where he held us up. Be ready—he'll be hidin' on the other side." They take their guns out, ready to meet the man on the white horse. As they get into the pass, a voice comes from above in the boulders.

"Hold it right there, drop those guns."

They turn to fire, but they don't see him. He shoots two men off their horses and tells the others to drop their guns.

"Get off your horses and lead 'em out of the pass."

The Blue Ghost tells the men to drop the money. One of 'em has another gun and draws it. The Blue Ghost puts a bullet right in his forehead. Pete drops the money.

"Now take off your boots, get off your horses. Now run 'em off and start walkin'."

They walk a short way, then turn back for their boots and guns.

"Look for that ghost. He's got to be here somewhere."

"There's no sign of him anywhere—vanished, just like a ghost."

"Let's ride to the ranch, round up those horses."

When they get to the ranch and tell Jackson, he yells,

"Get my horse and round up the entire gang. We're goin' to town to settle this once and for all. They'll pay this time, and they'll pay big."

The Blue Ghost expects somethin' like this to happen, so he dynamites the pass closed. He stays on Jackson's ranch side of the pass. He's watchin' the ranch. When Jackson and his gang ride out, the Ghost raids Jackson's ranch. He turns the livestock loose and runs off his herd of cattle. Then he rides into the ranch yard and sets the barn on fire. A couple of hands left behind shoot at the Blue Ghost. He returns fire and kills one of them. The other man mounts his horse and heads for the pass.

At the pass, the gang's cleared just enough rubble for a horse to get through. Jackson takes three men and rides for town, tellin' the others to finish clearin' the pass and join him later.

The Blue Ghost knows a path through the mountain range and rides for town. Jackson and his three men reach town, go into the saloon, and drink beer, waitin' for the rest of the gang.

Slim walks into the Western Feed and General Store and finds the manager cleanin' up. Slim's about to ask what happened when he sees the bruises on the man's face from Pete and Ray.

"Who did this?"

"Pete and Ray. They wanted protection money."

Slim walks into the back room, takes his gun belt and gun out of his saddlebags. He straps it on, checks to see that the gun's loaded, and walks out. He heads for the saloon. When he walks in, he sees who he's lookin' for—Pete and Ray. He's surprised to see Jackson standin' at the bar drinkin'.

Slim says, "Turn around."

"Look, Pete, he's wearin' a gun."

"Now what do you think you're gonna do with that? You're only one against four."

Then one of Jackson's men comes runnin' in.

"Jackson, that Blue Devil raided the ranch and burned the barn!"

Two of Jackson's men draw their guns. A series of gunshots ring out. Gun smoke fills the air. When the shootin' stops, two men lay on the floor. Jackson is so angry he loses all sense and draws his gun. Slim outdraws him. Jackson lies dead on the floor.

Slim runs the rest of the men out of town. Julie runs into the saloon and tells Slim, "The two men from the East just left town on the stage!"

Slim says, "I'll chase the stage and bring them back."

Slim rides out to catch the stage.

Slim catches up with the stage. One of the men from the East shoots at him. Slim returns fire and wounds the man. He catches up with the stage and turns it back to town. He locks the two men up and walks into the saloon. The men inside sit around in amazement.

Pedro is sittin' in a chair, playin' a guitar and singin'—but that's not what amazes them. Pedro is wearin' a blue shirt and two pearl-handled guns. A blue hood is sittin' on the table.

Slim says, "Pedro, you are the Blue Ghost."

"I prefer you call me U.S. Marshal Randell Jones."

"Slim, I heard about you outdrawin' Jackson and two of his men."

"Well, I was just a little faster, Marshal."

"I heard you were a lot faster. Where did you learn to shoot like that?"

"Years ago, an old gunfighter taught me how to draw."

"Who was that, Slim?"

"His name was Jake."

"'Slim, don't make it happen, let it happen'—that's what Jake taught me."

"Marshal, where did you hear that?"

"Well, Slim, years ago I knew Jake. I was outdrawn in a gunfight and wounded."

"When Jake heard about it—and knowin' I was a Marshal—he taught me how to draw."

THE MOST RUTHLESS GANG OF OUTLAWS OF THE OLD WILD WEST

"Hey Sam, do you have a story to tell us today?"

"I sure do. I'm gonna spin a yarn about the most ruthless gang of outlaws that ever rode in the Wild West."

"First, we need some coffee and a plug of that chewin' tobaccy. Sit down and make yourself comfortable."

"I know you've heard about the outlaws terrorizin' the old West. I'm gonna tell ya about the meanest, shootin'est bunch of hombres that ever lived."

"The name of the gang was the Clancy Brothers—Tom and Mark. These two brothers started out bad from an early age."

"Boys, let me point out that this story could be called 'Pedro,' or 'Marshal Randolf Jones.'"

"Sam, the same Pedro that cleaned up the Jackson gang you told us about?"

"Yup, the very same. This yarn is about the Clancy Brothers and how Marshal Jones eventually put a stop to the gang."

"Sam, guess he was a pretty tough Marshal."

"Back in those days, a Marshal had to be tough—and as ruthless as the outlaws. He was one of the most ruthless men that ever carried a badge. It's a good thing he was on the side of the law, or he would've terrorized the entire West."

"Why do you say he was so ruthless? What did he do?"

"Remember how I told you he goaded outlaws into a fight, then he killed 'em? He burned down Jackson's barn and even got the Sheriff to draw against him just so he could kill him.

He believed in the old sayin', 'Fight fire with fire.' Maybe he's the one that started it.

He'd often say, referin' to gang leaders, 'If you wanna kill a snake, you gotta shoot his head off. Kill the gang leaders, and the rest of the gang dies.'"

"Before I tell the story, I'm gonna let you in on a little secret. Jones wasn't his real name. Due to the methods he used, his name was kept a secret.

The government was completely aware of him—however, they denied any such person existed due to his methods.

They denied he was a Marshal.

Truth is, the government knew exactly who he was and that he was a U.S. Marshal.

They just didn't want any association with him as far as the public was concerned."

"He always appeared in problem areas as Pedro, the silly clown.

Due to his act as Pedro, it was easy for him to get to know the people of a town and what was goin' on.

In saloons, men would talk right in front of him, payin' him no attention.

He'd just show up in town as Pedro."

"One day, Marshal Jones just disappeared. However, the Blue Ghost would be seen from time to time."

"How did that happen, Sam?"

"He stopped bein' a Marshal and takin' government assignments when war profiteers started makin' money by escalatin' the American Indian wars.

He found out the people makin' money off the wars were folks in Washington—members of the government.

He made a war of his own against such people operatin' in the West."

"Sam, hold onto your yarn. We've got a customer that needs twenty bags of horse feed. I'll take the order and have the boys load his wagon."

"Oh, by the way, Slim sent a telegram. He put Julie in charge of all our lady's apparel shops.

They've opened shops in six towns. She's done a fine job for The Western Feed and General Store Lady's Apparel Division."

"Sam, Slim wants to name the lady's shops after our late Sara."

"That's a fine idea—after all, it all started when she left this store to us."

"Well boys, back to the story about the outlaw gang.

They robbed banks, trains, killed people, and ran ranchers off their lands.

There wasn't nothin' they wouldn't do for money. They even rustled cattle.

They were mean and brave—it was gonna take someone just as mean and brave to stop them."

"It all started when the Clancy brothers were only fourteen and sixteen years old.

They ran away from home 'cause they felt their father was workin' them too hard.

They were lazy and didn't want to work.

When they ran off, they stole their father's horse and his gun.

Mark, the older brother, had all the ideas. His younger brother Tom followed him and did whatever Mark said.

They wandered from town to town, livin' on handouts and stealin' from townsfolk."

"Mark decided they needed another horse.

They came upon a small ranch with two good horses in a corral.

They watched the ranch for a while, then went down to the corral to steal both horses.

Inside the house, they could hear a dog barkin'. The old rancher came out with a rifle.

Mark shot and killed him."

Tom said, "What are we gonna do now?"

Mark said, "Don't worry about it. Let's see if there's anyone else in the house."

"Enterin' the house, they could tell the old man lived alone."

"Tom, do you know what we got here? Look—food and a place to hole up.

We can stay here a long while. I'm goin' out to get rid of the body. While I'm gone, rustle up some grub."

"Mark takes the body up to the edge of the mountains and hides it in some boulders, then covers it with stones.

He notices a trail through the mountains—thinks it's perfect if they need to get away quick from the main trail."

"While Mark's out, Tom spots a gun and holster hangin' on the wall.

He takes it down and straps it on. He wears that gun all day, every day."

"Sam, those boys were bad right from the start."

"Yup, they were two mean kids."

"How 'bout some more coffee before you continue your story?"

"Good idea. I'll get the pot."

After they have their coffee, one of the men lights his pipe, and they all sit back to listen to Sam's story.

"Those boys held up at that ranch for a few months."

"Mark, we're gettin' low on food. The horses need some feed too."

"We got no money. What are we gonna do?"

"I got an idea, Tom. Remember that town we passed through?"

"The last one?"

"Yep."

"Oh yeah, that's where the lady fed us and gave us food to travel with."

"Well, we're gonna rob the bank."

"How we gonna do that?"

"Very simple. We'll ride into town. You stay outta sight. I'll go into the bank and rob it."

"Why can't I go into the bank?"

"I don't want anyone to see you. If they do, they'll know we're just kids."

"I'm big enough—and if I wear the old man's clothes, keep my hat down, and wear a bandanna over my face, no one'll know I'm a kid."

"The Sheriff'll be lookin' for men."

They ride for town and hide around the corner of the bank. Mark goes into the bank.

"This is a hold-up! Nobody move!"

The girl behind the counter puts the money into a bag.

Just then, the bank manager comes outta his Office, unaware a robbery's takin' place.

Mark shoots and kills the manager, then runs outside, gets on his horse, and they race outta town.

They ride in the opposite direction of their ranch hideout.

They keep ridin' until they reach the mountains, then turn off, ridin' over rocky ground and up into the hills.

The Sheriff, leadin' a posse, tries to trail them but loses the trail.

The boys double back and return to their hideout.

Their outlaw rampage begins—at the ages of fourteen and sixteen.

"Sam, did the bank manager die?"

"Yes, he did. As teenagers, they were already wanted for murder and bank robbery.

In the years that followed, they terrorized the West—robbin' banks, stagecoaches, trains, and rustlin' cattle.

They'd kill anyone who resisted."

"Sam, you said it was a gang of outlaws?"

"Yes. As time went on, they grew in numbers.

The members of the gang were as ruthless as the Clancy brothers.

Some real mean hombres joined up with 'em."

"Mark ruled the gang with an iron thumb.

Tom, the fastest with a gun, made sure everyone did what his brother said—without question.

The number of gang members grew to eight men, ruled by Mark."

"The Clancy gang rode for several years.

No one could catch 'em.

Sheriffs and posse members were killed if they got too close.

The government got concerned—especially when the Clancy gang rode into a town and completely took it over."

"Marshal Randell Jones was sent to break up and arrest the gang by his government contact."

One day, Pedro and his donkey wandered into the town the Clancy gang had taken over.

The gang paid little attention to Pedro—after all, he seemed a little simple.

Pedro entertained the children.

He got a job in the saloon sweepin' and cleanin' up.

He always tried to get a job in the saloon in any town he rode into.

Workin' in the saloon, he got to know everyone, and he could overhear what was goin' on in town.

"Sam, I wonder if Jake would've approved of the Marshal's methods?"

"Most likely not. However, Jake taught him how to use a gun—and he sure cleaned up a lot of outlaws with that fast gun.

He saved a lot of lives.

One day Pedro overheard Mark talking to a couple of the members of the gang.

"I want you to go over to Cactus Falls and scout out the bank and look the town over."

This is what Pedro wanted—to get members of the gang separated.

The two men ride out of town. When they get to a sharp bend in the trail and have to slow down, a man rides out from under cover and stops them. He's wearing a blue shirt and a blue hood, riding a white horse.

"Hold it right there, your days of being outlaws are over."

They draw on the Blue Ghost. The Ghost kills one and wounds the other. He tells the wounded man to put the dead man on his horse and head back to where he came from.

"Tell the Clancy brothers that the Blue Ghost is after them."

Back in town, the wounded man tells Mark Clancy what happened.

"Who is this Blue Ghost?"

"I don't know, but I'll tell you—I never saw anyone so fast with a gun."

"I think he only wounded me so I could deliver the message to you."

Pedro walks into the saloon, starts sweeping the floor, and listens to what is going on. Mark Clancy sends four men out looking for the Blue Ghost.

"How will we know him if he's not wearing a blue hood?"

"Do I have to do all your thinking for you? Kill anyone you see riding a white horse."

"Oh yeah boss, I didn't think of that."

They ride out of town. Pedro is listening to and watching the three gang members that stayed in town.

The four ride to the spot where the Blue Ghost stopped the two men.

"Here's where he stopped the boys. Look, there are no tracks leaving the area."

"It's as though he disappeared. Maybe he is a real ghost."

"We killed a lot of men. You think the ghost of one of them is after us?"

"Don't be foolish, there ain't no such thing as a ghost."

They ride around in the high country, looking down into the lowlands. There ain't any sign of a man on a white horse. They ride back to town.

"You four boys rest up and then go out for a few days and look for this ghost. I want him dead."

The next morning, the four men ride out looking for the Blue Ghost. They ride around a couple of days. There is no sign of the ghost. Headed back to town, they look up on top of a hill—the Blue Ghost is sitting on his white horse, looking down on them.

They start up the hill after him and begin shooting at the Ghost. He returns gunfire. One falls off his horse. The Blue Ghost rides away and disappears. When the three riders get to the top of the hill, there is no sign of the Ghost. There are no tracks to follow.

"He just disappeared—vanished like a real ghost."

"That must be why they call him the Blue Ghost."

The Blue Ghost rides hard, hides his horse, and walks into town.

Just as Pedro is walking into the saloon, the three ride into town, leading a horse with the dead man across the saddle.

Pedro yells, "Mr. Mark, your men are back, and one is over the saddle."

Mark and Tom run outside.

"What happened?"

They tell Mark and Tom how the Blue Ghost was on the hill and shot the gang member.

"Then he just disappeared, leaving no tracks!"

"Get your horses—we're goin' and get this blue devil!"

They ride out looking all over the countryside. There is no sign of the Blue Ghost. Heading back to town, the gang of outlaws spot the Ghost. They begin to chase him.

The Blue Ghost runs—this is just what he wanted. He gets to a bend in the trail, pulls up his horse, takes out his rifle, and rides out of cover. The outlaws start shooting at him. He is out of pistol range. He takes his rifle, aims, and fires—one more of the outlaws is dead. The Ghost turns his horse and races away, still carrying his rifle in his hands. He disappears.

Mark and Tom are furious. Tom says, "He's not a ghost—he's a demon. I don't think we'll ever catch him. We are always chasing shadows."

When the gang of outlaws get back into town, Pedro is in the saloon sweeping the floor. As they are walking into the saloon, Mark is telling Tom to take two men and ride to Cactus City and scout out the bank.

"Tom, let them ride way ahead of you. If the Blue Ghost goes after them, you'll be far enough behind to get a shot at him."

"Mark, he'll get them."

"Yes, but you'll get him. I want him dead at any cost."

Pedro listens to the conversation between Mark and Tom. He leaves the saloon. He goes, gets his white horse, rides out on the trail, hides, and waits. He lets the two riders go by, then waits for Tom to come along.

When he gets close to Pedro, the Blue Ghost rides out from cover and stops him. Tom draws. The Blue Ghost outdraws him and kills him.

The two riders riding ahead of Tom hear the gunshots. They turn their horses around and race back down the trail. They see Tom lying in a pool of blood. His horse is standing over him.

"What's Mark going to say?"

"Let's take Tom back to town and then get out of here before that Ghost kills us."

They slowly ride into town. One of the gang members sees them coming. He calls Mark outside.

Pedro goes outside to listen to what they have to say. Mark is very upset. It's okay for them to go around killing people, but it's not okay when their men are being killed.

Mark says, "There's only four of us left, and Lefty is wounded."

Sam says, "Well boys, it's time to close the store. Be seein' you in the morning."

"Sam, the Marshal gets the rest of the gang, doesn't he?"

"That's a yarn for the mornin'. See you then."

"Okay, Sam. Don't sleep all day."

"Oh, you just think you're funny."

[Next morning:]

The next morning, the Old Boys are in the store early, waiting for Sam. When Sam walks in, the coffee is already made.

"Here's your coffee—hot and just the way you like it."

"Howdy, boys!"

"Sam, you're still calling us boys. We're old men now."

"As long as we live, we'll still be our Sara's boys, rest her soul."

"I guess we will be, Sam."

The sun has been rising for about two hours and it's hot already.

"Guess it's gonna be a hot one today."

"Yup, it already is getting hot. Good day to stay in where it's shady."

"Ya know, Sam, I was a-thinkin'—after all these years, I still miss dear old Sara."

"Me too."

"I would love to have seen her when she was young. Bet she was pretty."

"Well, I've heard she was a fine figure of a woman in her younger days."

"Sam, how about finishing your yarn this mornin'?"

"Okay boys, let's see... where did I leave off?"

"The Blue Ghost just shot and killed Tom."

"Oh, I remember."

"Well boys, remember I told you he was ruthless? He wanted to get one of the Clancy brothers alone—finally he did, and he killed him. He would always say, 'If you want to kill a rattler, you gotta shoot his head off.' He considered the gang a rattler, and the leaders the head of the snake."

"Now there were only four members of the gang left, and Marshal Jones had only been in town for three weeks. It was still too dangerous to take on all four at the same time—not only for his safety, but for the safety of the town. All those bullets flying around, someone would be hurt."

Pedro stands outside listening to Mark and the two men that brought Tom's body back. The two men tell Mark that they are leaving before the Blue Ghost gets them.

Mark says, "You're not going anywhere."

"I tell you Mark, he's gonna kill us all."

"He knows whenever one of us leaves town, he's out there waiting. Someone must be telling him what we're doing—either that or he is around here watching us."

"We're getting out of here!"

"If you do, he'll be waiting out there for you. You don't have a chance—he's too fast with a gun."

"We will not leave town. We'll wait till he comes for us."

"He'll still kill us all, Mark."

"I have a plan. When he rides into town, one of you boys will be across the street waiting. When he shows himself, the one in the alley will kill him."

"That's fine, but we don't know when he's going to come after us."

"I know that. We'll take turns waiting in the alley. Another of you boys will get up on the water tower—you'll see him coming from miles away. When you see him coming, signal from the tower to the man in the alley. The tower is close enough to the alley that your signal—a whistle—can be heard."

Pedro is listening to all this. Once again, there will be a gang member alone in the alley.

One of the gang members walks across the street and into the alley carrying his rifle. He waits there for three hours. Then there is a sound behind him. When he turns around, Pedro is standing there.

"What do you want?"

Pedro is not acting as the simple Mexican. Pedro answers him,

"I've come to arrest you. You see, I am Marshal Jones. You might know me as the Blue Ghost."

Pedro knows he's going to draw on him. He is ready. When the man draws, Pedro throws a knife. The knife pierces the man's heart. He is dead.

Jake had taught him how to throw a knife the way the Indian taught him, as well as how to draw his gun.

In the saloon, Mark tells one of the gang to go over to the alley and relieve the one watching for the Blue Ghost. When he walks into the alley, he doesn't see his fellow outlaw anywhere.

He calls for him.

"He's not going to answer you."

When he looks up, he sees the Blue Ghost standing at the end of the alley.

"Draw or surrender and hang."

"Ain't nobody gonna hang me!"

He draws—and dies in the alley.

The Blue Ghost heads in the direction of the water tower. He thinks the man up on the tower will come down when he hears the gunshot. He was right.

The man comes down the ladder. Reaching the ground, he takes his gun out and starts for the saloon. Then he sees the Blue Ghost standing by the corner at the back of the building.

He starts shooting at the Blue Ghost. The Blue Ghost shoots back—hits and kills the man.

The two members of the outlaw gang left run out of the saloon and head for the alley. When they enter the alley, the Blue Ghost steps out from behind the building. Mark and the gang member draw their guns. The Blue Ghost draws and fires two shots before they can get a shot off. They fall and die in the alley.

While Mark is dying, the Blue Ghost walks up to him.

"Who are you?"

The Blue Ghost takes his hood off and stands looking at Mark without saying a word.

"No! No! It couldn't be you..."

With that, he gasps and goes limp. The Blue Ghost says,

"The head of the snake is dead."

He disappears, and the men come out when they hear the gunshots and return to the saloon.

"It was the Blue Ghost—I saw him!"

"So did I."

"Yeah, me too. Wonder where he went?"

"He just disappeared."

"That's why they call him a ghost... the Blue Ghost."

Pedro walks into the saloon.

"Hey Pedro, your donkey just ran up the street, headin' out of town."

"Guess he's ready to leave town—see you later."

"Look!"

"Pedro's tryin' to catch that donkey. He can't run in those baggy pants!"

They all laugh as Pedro falls down, tripping over his pants. Then his sombrero falls off, he stops to pick it up, and trips over his pants again. He runs, pulling his pants up.

Everyone in town is laughing and yelling,

"Goodbye Pedro!"

The people of that town never saw Pedro or the Blue Ghost again.

JAKE RIDES AGAIN

"Sam, did Jake ever leave his ranch after he retired, and ride out with his gun?"

"Well, that's another story."

Not too far from where Jake lived, there was a small ranch. Next to it, there was a large spread. The owner of the large ranch wanted the small ranch, due to the fact that the small ranch had control of the water in the valley, and it had good grazing land for his cattle. He offered to buy the land on many different occasions. The rancher refused to sell.

The owner of the large ranch sent his men to raid the small ranch. They rode in shootin' and yellin' one night. They weren't supposed to hurt anyone, just scare 'em and threaten to light the house on fire.

In the ranch house, a man, his wife, and twelve-year-old son were hidin'. A stray bullet entered the cabin and struck the boy. The raiders rode off. The boy's father put him in a wagon and raced to town.

He takes his son to the doctor's Office and bangs on the door.

"Doc, get up! Open the door, hurry!"

The door opens and the doctor says, "Quickly, put him on the table." As the doctor begins to work on the boy, he asks, "What happened?"

The boy's father explains.

"Where's his mother?"

"She's out in your sittin' room. You didn't see her—she was behind me and the boy."

The boy was near death. The doctor says, "It's a good thing you got him here, he has a chance. How slim his chance is, I can't say. I have to tell you, he may not make it. Go out in the sittin' room. I'll take care of the boy the best I can. You take care of your wife—she needs you now more than ever."

The doctor comes out of surgery and says, "I got the bullet out. If he makes it through the night, he'll have a good chance."

The next morning, the doctor comes out to see the boy's parents. He's solemn.

"I think he's going to live."

"That's great news, Doc. Why so serious?"

"The bullet entered near his spine. I'm not sure if he'll ever walk again."

"Oh my God, my poor son."

"Calm yourself, dear. The doctor will do what he can. Right now he's going to live, and that's the most important thing."

The sheriff walks into the doctor's Office and asks what happened. The rancher explains to the Sheriff.

"You think it was Stevenson's men?"

"I can't be sure, Sheriff. Who else could it be?"

"When your boy's ready to travel, I think you better take him back East to be looked at by a specialist. They have some very fine doctors in the East."

"Where will I get the money, Doctor?"

"I'll have to sell my ranch to Stevenson."

The boy's father rides to Stevenson's ranch and talks to Stevenson. Finding out how desperate the man is, Stevenson offers him less than half the value of the land. The offer is refused. The boy, his mother, and father return to their ranch.

As time goes by, the boy doesn't make any improvement. His bullet wound heals, but he still can't walk.

Stevenson wants the small ranch more than ever. He sends his men to raid the ranch again. He tells his men, "No shootin'—burn the barn down."

They ride in yellin', carryin' torches, and light the barn on fire. The glow of the fire can be seen for miles in the night sky as the barn burns to the ground.

The next day, a horseman passin' by rides into Jake's ranch and tells him about the fire. Jake tells his foreman, Bob, "Saddle up Big Black."

"Jake, what's up? You haven't ridden Big Black in months."

Jake walks into the house. He comes out wearin' old buckskins and his gun. Jake says, "I'm gonna take a ride. I'll be gone for a few days." He's wearin' his black boots and hat, gets on Big Black, and rides off. The ranch hands all stand around, speechless, wonderin' what's goin' on.

Jake rides to the nearby ranch and rides in through the gates. He stops his horse and looks at the burned-down barn, then he kicks his horse up and rides to the ranch house. They see him comin' and go out to see who he is.

"Why, it's you, Jake. You look rather handsome sittin' up on that big black horse in those buckskins."

"Why, thank you, ma'am."

They hear a noise from the porch. The boy is tryin' to get up—he wants to see the big black horse. His father helps him over.

"Wow, mister, he's the prettiest horse I ever saw—and he's big."

"His name's Big Black. I have a few more that look just like him. What's your name, son?"

"Johnny, sir."

"Well, Johnny, maybe I'll be back and take you over to see the black horses."

"Oh, I couldn't—I can't walk, you see."

"Johnny, we'll figure it out someday."

"Jake, are you fast with that gun?"

"A little, son."

Jake gets down off his horse.

"I'm gonna look around by the barn and see if I can find horse tracks left by the raiders."

As he's walkin' around, he spots somethin' shinin' in the sunlight. He walks over and picks it up—it's a silver concho that fell off one of the raiders' saddles. Jake puts the concho in his pocket.

Jake says goodbye to the family, mounts Big Black, and rides to town. When he gets to town, he ties up Big Black in front of the saloon and walks in. He's no sooner through the swingin' doors when everyone notices him. Jake is a tall man who stands straight. He wears his gun low and tied down. A few of the old men in the saloon recognize him; the others never saw him before.

As usual, there's always a gunman that's had too much to drink. He sees Jake and says, "What do we have here?"

Jake figures he'll end this all before it starts. He draws and shoots three beer mugs off the bar, right next to where the man is standin'.

Jake says, "You were about to say?"

The man puts his hands up and says, "I wasn't goin' to say anything," then turns around and picks up his beer.

"Did you see how fast that old man was?"

"Well, son, let me tell you who he is. His name is Jake. He's the fastest man with a gun that ever drew one."

"What's his last name?"

"He answers that question by sayin' Just Jake."

"Wonder what he's doin' in these parts?"

"They say he has a ranch not too far from town. He's been stayin' on the ranch the past few years."

Jake tells the men in town that he's gonna have a barn raisin' and a barbecue. He tells the men where the ranch is and when he needs their help. He then goes out and orders the lumber. Returnin' to the saloon, he tells the men the lumber will be delivered in the mornin'.

The next day, the men with their tools and wagons meet the lumber wagons on the way to the ranch.

"Look, Dad! Here comes a lot of wagons."

They pull the wagons into the ranch. Jake is ridin' his horse ahead of the wagons. Jake rides up and sees the boy sittin' on the porch.

"Hey Johnny, how you doin'?"

"I'm doin' okay, Jake. What's goin' on?"

"We're here to build your dad a new barn. It's gonna be bigger and better than the one that burnt down."

The men unload the wagons. Some of the men begin cleanin' up the burnt debris, others start the barbecue.

"Jake, I can't believe what these men are doin'. I don't know how I'll be able to pay for the lumber."

"The lumber's all paid for."

A few days later, the new barn was up and finished.

Jake rides into town and looks for a saddle with a concho missin'. He finds what he's lookin' for—a horse wearin' a saddle with a missin' concho. A man comes out of the gun shop, gets on the horse, and rides down the street to the saloon. Jake follows him. Inside the saloon, Jake watches the man. When he leaves, Jake asks the bartender who he was.

"He's called Smitty. He works for the Stevenson Ranch. He's a mean hombre. Actually, most of the men workin' for Stevenson are tough guys."

Jake is sure now it was Stevenson's men that raided the ranch and wounded young Johnny. He takes the concho out of his pocket and thinks, These are the men I'm after. Jake rides to the top of the hills and looks down into the valley. He can see the importance of controlin' the water. He spots a small ranch at the edge of the valley. He decides to ride down and talk to the rancher.

He rides up to the gate. The ranch is called the Circle M. While he's sittin' at the gate, the rancher looks up and sees Jake. He waves him in. Jake rides up to the ranch house.

"Boy, that is a fine lookin' horse."

"Thank you."

"What can I do for you, old timer?"

"My name's Jake. I'd like to talk to you about what's goin' on in this valley."

"Well, climb down off that horse. Come on in and sit a spell. The coffee's on."

They walk into the house and have coffee. While they sit drinkin', Jake asks Martin what seems to be goin' on with the small ranchers.

"It's that Stevenson. He wants all the land in the valley. He's tryin' to drive the small ranchers out. He offers to buy the ranches way below market value. See what he did to Jameson's ranch? Burnt his barn down, and his son Johnny got shot in the raid."

"Yes, I know what happened to poor Johnny."

"How do you ranchers know it's Stevenson behind all this?"

"Well, he's the one tryin' to buy all the land—who else could it be?"

"I see what you mean. It has to be Stevenson that's behind all the trouble."

"Gettin' late, I better get ridden."

"Jake, stay here tonight. There's plenty of room in the bunkhouse."

"Sounds good to me. I'll see you in the morning."

Jake walks to the bunkhouse.

"Howdy boys, guess I'll be bunkin' with you if you don't mind."

"Come on in, there's a fresh bunk right over there."

Jake takes his gun belt off and hangs it on a hook on the wall with the rest of the gun belts.

"Hey old timer, that gun belt's a little worn—guess you been wearin' it for years."

"You might say that."

"Know how to use it?"

"You might say that too."

"I'm goin' out to bed down my horse."

"By the way, what's your name?"

"They call me Jake, just Jake." Then he walks out.

"Hey boys, I heard of a gunfighter named Jake—rides a big black horse and dresses in buckskins. He's supposed to be the fastest gun in the West."

"Do you think he's him?"

"Must be. I thought the story of him was just that—a story."

"Well, can you imagine that? He's right here under our roof."

Jake spends the night and rides out in the morning. He heads for town and goes to the doctor's Office. He talks to the doctor about young Johnny's physical condition.

"Jake, the boy needs an operation. I'm sure he could walk again."

"The only place the operation can be done is back East by highly skilled surgeons."

"Doctor, how much would this operation cost?"

"Thousands of dollars."

"More than ten thousand?"

"Oh no, around four or five thousand. But there's the time he'd have to spend in the hospital, and travel expenses. I'd say no more than six thousand dollars."

"I see. Thank you, doctor."

Jake leaves the doctor's Office and spots the horse with the saddle that has the missing concho—it's tied in front of the saloon.

Jake walks up to the saloon, thinkin' about how his family was murdered and his home burnt when he was a kid. Thank goodness the boy didn't lose his parents. Jake has mixed feelings— sorrow and anger. He stands outside the saloon, calmmin' himself, then slowly walks in.

"Smitty, is that your horse tied up out front?"

"You talkin' to me, old man?"

"If your name's Smitty, then I'm talkin' to you. Now answer my question—is that your horse tied out front?"

"Yes it is. What of it?"

"I guess this is yours." Jake tosses the concho on the floor in front of him. "It came off your saddle."

"What of it?"

"The fact is not that it came off your saddle. The issue is where it came off."

"What's so important about that?"

"There's a small ranch near here. One night the barn was burnt to the ground."

"What of it?"

"The next day your concho was found on the ranch near the barn. I'm takin' you to the Sheriff."

"Old man, you ain't takin' anybody anywhere. You wear a gun—do you know how to use it?"

"A little. I've had to use it on occasion."

"Say, in case I have to use it today, why don't you tell us the name you want on your grave marker?"

"Why, you arrogant old man."

"Smitty, either take off your gun belt and come with me—or draw."

Smitty reaches for his gun. Jake outdraws him and puts a bullet into Smitty's chest.

There's another man in the saloon who says, "He didn't have a chance—you're so fast."

"I gave him a chance to surrender or draw. He chose to draw—now he's dead."

Jake says, "The options will be given to the rest of Stevenson's men. Tell him he's all done threatenin' the small ranchers in the valley. He'll never get their land. I'll be comin' for him."

A rider races to Stevenson's ranch and tells him what happened.

"What does he think he's gonna do? He's just one man!"

"I know, boss, but he's the fastest man I ever saw with a gun. Smitty reached for his gun first— he never got it all the way outta his holster before he was shot dead."

"Who is this guy?"

"I don't know. But he's an old man—rides a big black horse and wears buckskins."

"If he's that fast, I'm gonna send for Rusty. I want you to ride over to Silver City and get him."

Reaching Silver City, the cowboy locates Rusty. He tells Rusty what Stevenson wants him for.

"What does this guy look like?"

The cowboy explains what Jake looks like.

"You say he wears buckskins, rides a big black horse, and he's fast with a gun?"

"You don't know who he is, do you?"

"No, I never saw him before."

"Well, I know who he is. And if I go after him, I'll be dead before I get off a shot."

"Well… you could dry-gulch him."

"That's not the way I work. You ride back and tell Stevenson I don't want the job. Also tell him if this guy is after him—he's as good as dead."

The cowboy rides back to Stevenson's ranch and tells him what Rusty said.

"If this Jake is faster than Rusty, he must be like lightnin' with that gun."

"Tell the boys not to draw against him. If they run into him, tell them to do exactly what he says. If he locks them up—I'll get them out."

Jake rides to a hill overlookin' Stevenson's ranch. He sits on the hill all morning watchin'. He does this for a few days—he's tryin' to upset Stevenson and his men, he does. Stevenson gets angry and offers a five-hundred-dollar reward to any of his men that kill Jake.

One of the men gets up early and rides up onto the hill, waitin' for Jake. He figures when Jake shows up, he'll back-shoot him. Jake doesn't know about the reward, but he knows how outlaws think. He figures someone would be waitin' for him.

The outlaw waits for two or three hours. Then he hears a voice behind him—

"Lookin' for me?"

The man has his gun out and turns. Jake shoots him. The gunshot echoes through the valley.

Jake puts the dead man across his saddle and turns the horse loose. The horse slowly walks down the hill into the ranch. Jake rides to the top of the hill, lets Stevenson see him, then rides away.

The next day Stevenson sends four men into town. He tells three of them to go into the saloon and for one to wait outside.

"When Jake goes into the saloon, you follow him and shoot him in the back. I want him dead."

Jake is watchin' from a place where he can't be seen. He sees three men ride up to the saloon, get off their horses, and walk in. Once again, Jake knows how outlaws think. He wonders where the fourth man is.

Jake comes out into view and sees the three horses were ridden hard—they're all lathered up. He never rushes into a gunfight. He walks around town. At the other end of town, he sees a horse tied to a hitchin' rail—it's all lathered up. He knows this is the fourth man's horse. He looks around at the men standin' around town. He decides to let him come to him.

Jake walks into the saloon. He moves away from the door and stands with his back against the wall, out of view from the windows.

"You three boys—drop your guns. You're under arrest."

Just then, the fourth man comes in through the swingin' doors, thinkin' he'll be behind Jake. He has his gun out. He sees Jake and turns to shoot. Jake draws and shoots the man. He then turns and says—

"Don't think about it. Now drop those guns. Come with me—we're goin' to the Sheriff's Office."

Jake walks in with the three men. He shows the sheriff his marshal's badge and asks the sheriff to lock them up.

"Sheriff, when word gets back to Stevenson, he's gonna send his men to break them out of jail. They'll come at night and try to do it quietly, thinkin' we're asleep."

"I want them to try it. I think we can put a stop to this gang if they do. I don't think they'll come tonight—it's too soon. Tomorrow night would be the night."

"Sheriff, I don't want you to stay in the Sheriff's Office at night until the attempt is made—it's too dangerous for one man alone. We'll watch from across the street from the alley, where we have good cover."

"How many deputies do you have?"

"Two."

"We'll put them upstairs in this building, watchin' out the windows."

"Sheriff, tell your deputies not to expose themselves just to get a shot at an exposed target. If they do, someone'll see 'em. You remember that too, Sheriff."

"Okay, Jake."

Nothing happened that night.

The following night, Stevenson's men ride into town up behind the Sheriff's Office. One man stays with the horses.

"Sheriff, do you think you can sneak up and get the one on the horse, then drive off their horses? You'll have to hurry."

The sheriff runs across the street, down an alley, and up behind the horsemen.

"Hold it right there."

The man reaches for his gun.

"Don't do it!"

"Get down off that horse."

The sheriff scatters the horses.

Inside the Sheriff's Office, the men get the three prisoners out of jail.

"Something's wrong. It's all too quiet and easy. Where's the Sheriff?"

When they start to come out, Jake fires a shot, driving them back into the Office. They start shooting in Jake's direction. No one shoots back—Jake told his men not to shoot unless they try to come out.

The sheriff is watching the back door. When they try to come out, he shoots at them. Jake, the Sheriff, and the two deputies just watch the Sheriff's Office. They only shoot when one of them tries to come out.

A few hours pass and the sun is starting to rise. Jake yells to the men inside,

"You have no place to go. You got no horses. You might as well give up."

One of the men inside runs out of the Sheriff's Office shooting. Jake shoots and wounds the man.

"Jake, we are coming out."

"Drop your guns inside the Office and come out one at a time and lay down on the ground."

They follow Jake's instructions. Jake knows there's always a stupid one—he watches them close. He knows if they try something, it'll be him they try to get.

One of the men has hidden his gun in his shirt. He takes it out and aims at Jake. Jake draws and fires—he only wounds the man.

"Sheriff, they're all yours. Lock 'em up."

Later, they would be tried, found guilty, and sentenced to twenty years in jail.

The next morning, Jake is getting ready to leave.

"Leavin' town, Jake?"

"It was a pleasure workin' with you, Jake."

"Say, what's your last name?"

Jake swings up onto Big Black and says,

"My name's Jake. Just Jake, Sheriff."

He turns his horse, touches the rim of his hat, and rides out of town.

With all Stevenson's men in jail, with the exception of a couple, Jake rides to Stevenson's ranch. They see him ridin' in and start shootin' at him. He fires his gun from horseback and kills both men. Stevenson runs into the house and starts shootin' at Jake.

Jake dismounts Big Black and hides behind the well. He sits there with his back leanin' against the well and lights his pipe. Stevenson can't figure out what Jake's doin'. He can see the smoke risin' from his pipe—Jake ain't shootin' back.

Stevenson yells out to Jake, "What are you waitin' for?"

"For you to come out."

"I ain't comin' out. You'll have to come in to get me."

Jake sees a wagon near the well. He knows he can sneak to the back of the house, hidin' behind the wagon without bein' seen. He takes a piece of paper from his pocket and stuffs it into his pipe so smoke will keep risin' for Stevenson to see. He sets his pipe on a stone and sneaks around to the back of the house.

He enters through an open window, walks up behind Stevenson, and says,

"You told me to come in and get you—here I am."

Stevenson turns and fires. Jake's behind the door casing.

"Drop your gun. You're under arrest."

"You'll have to come and get me."

Jake steps out into view, his gun still in the holster. Stevenson starts to shoot. Jake draws and shoots him.

Jake stands over him and says,

"You won't be sendin' your men to burn out any more ranches."

Jake rides to his ranch, rides in, and gets off Big Black. Bob is there to take Big Black for Jake.

"What's the matter, Jake, you're limpin'?"

"I spent a lot of time in the saddle these last few weeks. I ain't no kid, you know—I'm a little sore."

Jake walks into his house and lies down on his bed. Within a few minutes, he's asleep.

The next morning at breakfast, he tells Bob he'll be ridin' out again in the morning. The next morning, he rides to see Johnny's parents.

"I've talked to the doctor. All arrangements have been made for Johnny to go back East for surgery."

"Jake, we don't have the money."

"It's all paid for."

Johnny's mother begins to cry.

Johnny's father asks,

"Why, Jake? We hardly know you."

"I wish it had been this easy when I was a kid."

"What do you mean, Jake?"

"Oh, nothin'. I was just mumblin'."

A week later, Johnny and his parents leave for back East and Johnny's surgery. A few days later, Jake rides into town and visits with the doctor. The doctor tells Jake he got word that Johnny's operation went well—he should be home in a month. Jake rides home for a well-deserved rest.

A month later, Jake rides Big Black over to see Johnny. The doctor is visitin' Johnny.

"Howdy, Doc."

"Jake, how you been?"

"Well, Doc, I ain't kicked the bucket yet, so I guess I'm okay."

"Hello there, Johnny. How you doin', boy?"

"I still can't walk," Johnny answers with tears in his eyes.

Jake looks at the doctor. He shakes his head and asks Jake to step out.

"Jake, there's no reason why Johnny can't walk. The operation was a complete success. It's all in his mind—we don't know what to do."

Jake sits down alone for a while. Then he says somethin' to the doctor and Johnny's parents. Jake walks outside. Soon, gunshots can be heard inside the house.

Johnny says "what's that?"

"Jake is takin' some gun practice."

"Dad, help me out on the porch so I can watch him."

Johnny's father picks him up out of bed and takes him out on the porch to watch. When Jake finishes his practice, he walks over to Johnny.

"Jake, you hit the target every time! You draw so fast I could hardly see your hand move!"

"Johnny, over the past years I taught a few people to draw and shoot just like that—maybe not as fast, but darn near it."

"Boy, I wish I could shoot like that."

"Well, Johnny, if your folks let you come and stay with me a few days, I'll teach you."

"Oh boy! Dad, could I please—oh, I forgot, I can't walk."

"That's alright—I can teach you to shoot."

"Mom? Dad?"

"I guess it'd be alright."

"I'll be by and pick you up in the mornin'."

Jake rides home.

The next morning, Jake has Curly round up one of the smaller black horses. The horse was smaller than Big Black, but still a good-sized horse.

"Curly, saddle that horse and Big Black for me."

Jake rides out, ridin' Big Black, leadin' the other horse.

Jake rides into Johnny's father's ranch, leadin' the black horse. Jake goes into the house,

"Johnny, you ready?"

His mother says,

"He's been ready since sun-up."

They all laugh.

"Come on, Johnny, we got a long ride to get to my ranch."

They go outside—Johnny's father is carryin' him.

"Where's the wagon, Jake?"

"I brought a horse for you to ride."

"Jake, I can't—my legs."

"Johnny, all you gotta do is sit there. We'll go slow."

"I think you better ride him, considerin' he's your horse."

"Did you say my horse?"

"Yes, Johnny, he's all yours."

"Gee, he's beautiful. Can I call him Big Black like your horse?"

"Sure you can, Johnny."

Jake helps his father puttin' him on the horse. Jake says,

"Relax. Put your feet in the stirrups."

"I can't—they won't move."

"Okay, I'll put 'em in for you. Now, when you ride, just push with the balls of your feet to keep your balance."

As they ride, Jake notices that Johnny is usin' his feet without realizin' it. When they get to the ranch, Johnny says,

"Gee whiz, I never saw a ranch so big. Look at all the black horses!"

"We got a few around—we breed 'em here."

"Jake, I thought horses could be other colors when born, not just black."

"You're right, son. We've bred a lot of horses over the years. We only keep the black ones— we sell the rest. Our horses are in big demand and bring a good price."

"Let's go into the house. I'll show you to your room. You need a rest—I'll wake you for supper. Maybe in the mornin' we'll take a ride around the ranch—they do this every day."

Each day, Johnny is usin' his feet a little more while ridin'.

"Jake, when are you gonna teach me how to use a gun?"

"When you can stand up on your own."

"Oh, okay Jake."

That night, Jake hears a sound from Johnny's room like someone falling. Jake goes to Johnny's room and peeks in. Johnny is on the floor trying to get up; eventually, he gets back on his bed. Jake walks away.

The next day, Jake is outside taking target practice. Bob and Curly help Johnny into a chair out on the porch.

"Hey boys, help Johnny to come over here."

Bob holds Johnny up while Jake straps a gun belt on him.

"That's your own gun, Johnny. Do not take it out of the holster. I just want you to get used to wearing it."

"Bob, let's see if Johnny can stand on his own."

Bob lets Johnny go and stands close to him. He is able to stand on his own for a few minutes, then he begins to fall. Bob and Jake catch him and stand him up and let go of him again.

"Johnny, if you are gonna learn to use a gun, you must be able to stand on your own. A gun is not a toy, it is very dangerous. You must be able to stand on your own before you will be able to shoot it."

"I understand, Jake. I have to have control of myself first so I will have control over the gun."

Johnny is standing on his own as they talk.

"Okay, Bob, take him back to the porch so he can sit down."

The next day, Jake and Bob with Curly help Johnny over to the hitching rail and stand him holding onto the rail.

"Johnny, use the rail for help. Try to stand on your own. If you feel as though you're gonna fall, grab the rail, get your balance, and then stand without holding on. We have work to do. If you need help, give us a call—we'll be nearby."

"Okay Jake, I think I'll be fine as long as I have the hitching rail to help me."

Jake and the boys walk away. They bring Johnny's horse out and put him in a corral where Johnny can see and watch him. Standing by the hitching rail watching his horse, Johnny stands longer and longer.

Jake has Johnny stand at the hitching rail every day for several days. His balance gets better and better. One morning, Jake walks over to the hitching rail.

"Johnny, turn around so the hitching rail is behind you. It's time you began to learn to draw your gun. Johnny, take your gun out of the holster. This is how you check your gun to see if it is loaded. See, it's not loaded. Now put it back into your holster. Now stand there and take your gun out and put it back into the holster. Do it over and over. Don't try to draw it—just take it in and out slowly."

Jake begins to explain the gun and how and when to use it, just like he did with others he taught to use a gun.

"Johnny, you will get fast with that gun. You must promise me—you will never put your gun out for hire, never make money with your gun."

"I promise, Jake."

Jake would repeat those words to Johnny every day.

Johnny's balance grew better every day as he practiced his draw. He was getting faster with his gun.

"Johnny, I want you to take a step."

"Jake, I can't, my legs."

"Johnny, your feet and legs are fine. You've been using them every day when we go riding. If you weren't, you'd fall off the horse."

Jake stands in front of Johnny and holds out his hands.

"Take my hands and take a step. Make believe you're riding your horse. Relax and use your legs."

"I'll try, Jake... I can't."

"Johnny, when I take you home, if you wish to practice shooting, you'll have to be able to walk to set up targets."

Jake pulls a little on Johnny's hands. He takes a step. Then another. And another.

"See Johnny, your legs work just fine."

"Yes, Jake! They do, but I feel like I'm gonna fall."

"You have to gain control over your balance and strengthen those legs. Besides, if you fall down, get up and brush yourself off."

Each day, Johnny is getting stronger. He is able to walk on his own.

Johnny practices with ammunition. He gets faster and accurate with his gun.

"Johnny, it's time for you to go home and see your parents. They will be very pleased to see you."

Jake and Johnny's black horses are saddled and ready to go. They mount the horses and ride out.

Curly says to Bob, "I'm gonna miss that kid. He was a pleasure to have around. It sure did my heart good to see him walking."

"Me too, Bob."

Jake and Johnny ride into the ranch. His parents hear them coming—they come outside.

"Hi Mom, Hi Dad."

Neither Jake nor Johnny say anything about his being able to walk. His mother says,

"Johnny, you sure look handsome sitting up on that black horse, wearing those new clothes and that gun."

His father starts to walk over to Johnny's horse.

"Let me help you down, son."

Johnny holds his hand up, gets down off the horse, turns, and walks to his parents.

His mother starts crying.

"Johnny, you can walk?"

"Yes, Mom, I can walk just fine."

Johnny's father says,

"Jake, I thought you were going to teach him how to use a gun to help him—I had no idea it would help him this much."

"Oh, he can use a gun alright."

His mother says,

"Thank you so much, Jake. We owe you so much," as she gives Jake a hug.

"The only thanks I would like is for you to let Johnny come and stay a week or two at my ranch once in a while."

"Of course, Jake. Anytime he wants."

Jake gets on his horse. Looking down at the family all hugging each other, he wipes a tear from his eye, turns his horse and says,

"See you again soon."

Jake rides out on Big Black and heads for home.

SAM AND SLIM HAVE TO STRAP ON THEIR GUNS ONCE AGAIN

"Sam, where's the rest of the Old Boys?"

"They've taken a wagon of supplies over to Marksville, to our store there."

"Sam, I understand there are some people in Marksville tryin' to start up a feed store."

"Well, that's alright, there's enough business for all of us. They might cut into our sales a bit."

"We have a big company with stores in many different towns."

"The West is growin' so fast, the ranchers and farmers need supplies."

A rider comes racin' into town and up to Sam's store. He gets off his horse without takin' time to tie him up and runs into the store.

"Sam, your wagon was attacked! Pete was wounded!"

"The wagon was burnt, and the supplies were destroyed!"

"Your men caught the horses and rode them into town. When I left, Pete was at the doctor's—he was shot in the shoulder!"

"When did this happen?"

"Yesterday mornin'. I work for your company in Marksville—the manager sent me to tell you about the incident."

"Well, this is the first time we've had a problem like this. I don't like our men bein' shot."

"I'm gonna ride over to Marksville and find out what's goin' on."

Sam takes a bedroll and other items off the shelf, walks out to his horse, and takes his gun belt out of his saddlebags and buckles it on. He gets on his horse and races out of town.

"Look, there goes Sam—and he's wearin' his gun. It's only the second time I've seen him wearin' a gun."

"The first time, he outdrew and gunned down two outlaws in the middle of the street."

"Somethin' serious is goin' on to make him ride like that wearin' his gun."

"He says he doesn't like to wear his gun—every time he does, someone dies."

"He is very fast on the draw. Jake taught him how to use his gun, so you know he's fast."

Sam sends a rider to the town where Slim is workin' to tell him about the attack on the wagon and Pete bein' wounded. The rider tells Slim that Sam rode out, headed for Marksville.

"Slim, he was wearin' his gun."

When Slim hears that Sam was wearin' his gun, he knew Sam expected trouble.

Slim packs up his gear, straps on his gun belt, saddles his horse, and rides to Julie's Lady's Apparel Shop. He tells Julie that he's headed for Marksville and explains what happened.

"Sam is wearin' his gun. He doesn't like to."

"Neither do you, but you're wearin' yours."

"Julie, I'll be in touch."

"Be careful, Slim."

"Why Julie, I didn't know you cared. Why didn't you tell me before?"

"Get outta here, I'm old enough to be your mother."

"Oh, goodbye Mother."

She swats him with a newspaper. He leaves.

Sam approaches Marksville. He sees a fire burnin' in town. It looks like the Western Feed and General Store. Rememberin' what Jake told him—never hurry into the sight of trouble—he slows his horse to a walk and rides into town.

The Western Feed and General Store is burnin'. The sky is red as the flames reach up. People are rushin' around tryin' to put the fire out. Men are loadin' the feed into wagons to take to the livery stable and put under cover.

Sam rides up and asks, "Was anyone hurt?"

"No, the manager became overcome with smoke. He's doin' okay now—he's sittin' right over there."

Sam rides over to where the manager is sittin'.

"John, are you okay?"

"Yes, Sam, but the store..."

"Don't worry about the store. We can rebuild it."

John begins coughin'. Sam says, "Here, take a drink of water."

"Sam, where'd you come from?"

"I headed out as soon as your messenger brought the message to me about the attack on the wagon. By the way, how is Pete doin'?"

"He's doin' fine. He's recuperatin' at the doctor's Office."

"If you're okay, I'm gonna see Pete."

"I'm fine, Sam. The doctor's Office is at the end of town on the right."

"I'll see you later. Take care of yourself—don't worry about the store."

Sam gets on his big black horse and rides down to the doctor's Office.

When Sam reaches the doctor's Office, a man comes up to him.

"Hey, ain't you Sam—the owner of the feed and general store?"

"Yes, I am."

"I thought so when I saw you ridin' down the street on that big black horse. He sure is a good- lookin' horse."

"Well, thank you. He is a good horse and serves me well."

"Sam, the reason I stopped you—I saw a man runnin' from the back of the store just before the fire started."

"What did he look like? Do you know his name?"

"No, I don't know his name, but I recognized him as one of the men from that new feed company."

"Thank you for the information."

"Sam, I'll point him out to you down at the saloon when he comes in."

"Okay, that'll be a great help."

Sam goes in to see Pete.

"Hey Pete, how you doin'?"

"Sam! Where'd you come from?"

"I just rode into town."

"Did they get the fire out?"

"No, it's still burnin'. The store is a complete loss."

"That's not the issue. The issue is how are you doin'?"

"I'm fine, except that this sore shoulder won't let me get outta bed."

The doctor laughs and says, "Pete, you lost a lot of blood. Your partner got you here just in time. You gotta stay in bed a few days to get your strength back."

"Pete, you lay there and recover. Don't worry about anythin'. You'll be up in a few days."

"Okay, Sam. After all, you are the boss."

"Pete, before I go, tell me what happened on the trail."

"Three men rode up, shot me, told us to get outta the wagon, then they set it on fire."

"Jess was able to hold the horses and unhitch 'em from the wagon, savin' them."

"It's a good thing he did, Sam, or Pete would've died out there on the trail."

"Yes, doctor, it is a good thing."

"Pete, where's Jess now?"

"He went to help with the fire."

"You get some rest—I'm gonna see Jess."

Sam rides back to the other end of town and looks for Jess.

"Anyone know where Jess is?"

"Yeah, he's down at the livery stable storin' the feed."

Sam rides to the livery stable to find Jess.

"Jess, how you doin'?"

"Not bad, Sam. I heard you were in town."

"Jess, what can you tell me about the ambush on the trail?"

"Three riders came up, they shot Pete and set the wagon on fire, then rode off."

"Pete and I rode the horses into town."

"Can you tell me about the three men?"

"Yeah, they looked like professional gunmen. One thing I noticed— the one that shot Pete had his little finger missin' on his gun hand. He was right-handed."

While Sam is at the livery stable, he has his horse fed and put up for the night, then he walks to the hotel and gets a room.

The next mornin', the fire has burnt itself out. The town has settled down. There's nothin' left of the burnt-out buildin'. Sam walks across the street to get coffee and breakfast. While he's eatin', John, the store manager, walks in.

"Good mornin', Sam!"

"John, good mornin'."

"Sam, the fire started in the back room of the store. Someone tossed a torch in through the window. By the time I knew it, the fire was burnin'. I tried to put it out, but the flames had already reached the walls and they started to burn outta control."

"That goes along with what an old-timer told me. He said he saw someone runnin' from the back of the store just before the fire started."

"Did he know who he was?"

"Not exactly. However, he recognized that he hung around with the people from the new feed store."

"John, I'm headed for the saloon. The old boy told me he'd be in the saloon and point the man out to me when he comes in."

"Maybe I'll see you there later."

"Okay, John."

That afternoon, Slim rides into town. He slowly rides down the street and sees the Western Feed and General Store burnt to the ground. He thinks there's more goin' on than just an attack on the wagon. He rides up to the saloon, gets down off his horse, and walks inside. He spots Sam sittin' at a table. When he looks at him, Sam shakes his head and gestures not to say anything. Slim walks to the bar, orders a beer and says,

"Looks like you had a fire up the street."

The bartender says, "Everyone thinks there's somethin' suspicious about it."

"You mean people think it was set?"

"I don't know." Then he walks away to wait on another customer.

Sam walks up to the bar.

"How 'bout another beer."

He whispers to Slim, "At the hotel."

Sam finishes his beer and walks to the hotel. A short while later, Slim does the same. Inside the hotel, he asks for a room. While walkin' to his room, he meets Sam in the hallway.

"Come in here, Slim." Sam tells him what's been goin' on.

"Slim, they know who I am in this town. I don't think they know you. Let's keep it a secret that we know each other and that we're workin' together."

"We have to find out what's goin' on in this here town."

"There's gonna be trouble—big trouble. Remember everything Jake taught you."

"The burnin' of the store proves that the attack on the wagon wasn't a random act."

"All the evidence points toward the new feed company. I expect trouble in other towns where we've got stores."

"I'm sendin' the men that worked here to other towns to warn them."

"We have to stop them before one of our men gets killed."

"The best place to see who knows who is in the saloon. We're mainly lookin' for the man with the missin' finger. When we spot him, we'll see who he's associated with."

"We must be quiet about what we know—we don't want them knowin' we suspect 'em."

A few days later Pete walks into the saloon. Sam calls him over to where he is sitting.

"Pete, we don't want anyone to know that Slim and I know each other, don't speak to him."

"Okay, Sam, I understand. Looks like you expect trouble—you're both wearin' guns."

"I'm afraid so, Pete."

"Pete, how's that shoulder doin'?"

"It's still a little sore. I can't move my arm much yet."

"Pete, when the doctor says you can travel, I want you, Jess, and John to take the stage to my ranch and stay there a few weeks and rest up. You boys deserve a vacation."

"That sounds like a good idea. I'll check with the doc and see when I can travel."

"Pete, leave as soon as you are able. The men that stopped you on the trail know who you are. I don't want anything to happen to you or Jess."

While Sam is sitting in the saloon, he spots a man drinkin' his beer—his hand is missin' a little finger. Later, in the hotel, Sam tells Slim what he looks like and the horse he is ridin'.

Later that day Slim notices two men ridin' up to the hitchin' rail in front of the saloon. The horses are packed for travelin'. Slim notices that one of the horses is the one described by Sam, and they look like they're leavin' town, not just arrivin'. The horses are dry and clean.

Slim follows the two men into the saloon. He sits and watches them. He thinks they are the men he's lookin' for. The two men drink up their beer and walk out of the saloon, mount their horses, and ride out of town. Slim waits a few minutes and follows them.

The two men are headed for a town where there's a location of The Western Feed and General Store. Slim follows them into town, stays outta sight watchin' the men. They tie their horses up in front of the saloon, then they casually walk down the street toward the feed store. They stand across the street and look the store over from a distance. Then they turn and walk back to the saloon. Slim keeps his eye on 'em the rest of the day and into the night.

In the cover of darkness, they come out of the saloon and walk down the street toward the feed store. Slim follows, stayin' outta their sight. The two men walk down an alley that takes them behind The Western Feed and General Store. One of the men makes up a torch out of an old piece of wood and a rag he had in his pocket. When he lights the torch, Slim speaks out, "Drop that torch, drop your guns."

The men look at Slim. In the moonlight, they can see his gun is in his holster. They draw their guns—one dies and the other is wounded. Slim walks over to the wounded man, takes his gun, and checks the dead man. He sees that he's got a finger missin' on his right hand.

The wounded man is cryin' out, "Get me help, I'm bleedin'."

Slim puts his gun back into his holster and says, "Who sent you?"

The man cries for help.

"I asked you who sent you. If you want help, start talkin'."

Hearin' the gunshots, the sheriff runs up to the scene. He stops and listens to Slim question the man. The Sheriff can tell what was goin' on, seein' the torch on the ground still burnin'. He sends a bystander to go and get the doctor.

"Help, I'm bleedin' to death!"

"I told you, if you want help, start talkin'. Who sent you?"

"All right, it was Colter."

"Who is he?"

"He owns the feed store."

"The new one in Marksville?"

"Yeah. He wants to run you outta business."

"How many men does he have workin' for him?"

"Three gunmen and a few work hands."

"Okay, Sheriff, he's all yours."

The doctor arrives and takes care of the wounded man. Slim heads to the hotel for a night's sleep—he's gotta return to Marksville in the mornin'. He has trouble sleepin'. He don't like havin' to use his gun. Eventually he falls asleep.

When he awakes the next mornin', the sun is already up and the town is buzzin'.

Slim walks to the Sheriff's Office and asks him to send a telegram to the sheriff in Marksville tellin' him that one of Colter's men is dead and the other is wounded in jail.

"Ask the Sheriff to notify Colter, but don't tell him why or what happened."

"Okay, Slim, I'll go do it right now."

"Are you leavin' town, Slim?"

"Yeah, just as soon as I have a cup of your coffee and wake up."

When Slim reaches Marksville, he goes right into the saloon, sees Sam sittin' in his usual spot, walks over, sits down with him, and tells him where he's been and what happened.

"Slim, I was gettin' a little worried. I had no idea where you went."

"I knew you had left town. I checked and your horse was gone."

"I didn't have time to find you and tell you where I was goin'."

"Sam, the man I killed was the one that shot Pete. His little finger was missin' from his gun hand."

"Well, I guess that part of what happened is the good part."

"I don't know, Sam."

"I know, Slim. You don't like killin' any more than I do. We just have to face it—sometimes there's no other way."

"The only satisfaction is knowin' that people in the future will live because a killer is dead."

Slim gets up and walks to his room at the hotel, lies down, and falls asleep.

The sheriff of Marksville walks into the saloon and talks with Sam.

"Sam, I received a telegram from the sheriff over at Silver City. It seems that one of Colter's men was shot and killed, and another wounded and is bein' held in jail. The telegram asked me to notify Colter, however, there were no details explainin' what happened. Do you know anything about what happened?"

"Sheriff, I've been right here in town sittin' in this saloon. What makes you think I would know anything about it?"

"Well, Sam, your business location burnt down. You have a location in Silver City. There's a new feed company tryin' to start up a business. Your wagon was attacked and your man was shot. Then two were shot by an unknown gunman. To me, that makes me wonder. Then I receive a telegram to notify Colter about his men without any details."

"Sheriff, I can see why you might think that I would know somethin'. Right now all I'm concerned with is rebuildin' my store."

"Sam, I see how you wear your gun—it looks like you know how to use it."

"A little, Sheriff. Just a little."

Sam hesitates tellin' the sheriff about Slim. He does explain that he thinks Colter is behind his problems. The Sheriff tells Sam that some of the ranchers have been pressured by Colter to buy feed from him.

"I don't have any proof of any wrongdoing—nothin' to act on. If anything comes up, let me know, Sam."

"Okay, Sheriff."

When Colter hears about his men, he sends one of his other men to Silver City to talk to the man in jail.

"I don't know who he was, but he was fast with his gun. He outdrew both of us."

"What did he look like?"

"Just a cowboy. Nothin' special about him."

Colter calls his three gunmen into the Office to meet a man he sent for.

"This is Utah. He's deadly fast with his gun. I want you four men to go over to the saloon and take care of that old man, Sam."

"It's not gonna take four of us. I can handle this alone."

"Utah, I want you to have plenty of witnesses tellin' the story the way we want it told."

Slim is just goin' into the hotel when he spots the four men headin' for the saloon. He doesn't like the look of 'em. He follows them to the saloon.

Sam sees them walk in and up to the bar. He slowly gets out of his chair and stands up.

Utah turns around and says, "Hey, old man, you own the Western Feed and General Store Company?"

"Yup. Me and some other old men, the way you put it."

"What's your name?"

"Sam."

"Sam what?"

"Just Sam."

"Well, Just Sam, it looks like you think you know how to use that gun."

"A little. Usually just enough."

"Well, Sam, I think it's time you forget rebuildin' your store in this town—and maybe closin' some stores in nearby towns. I think you're too old to be in business."

Slim is listenin' outside the swingin' doors to the saloon. He walks in and says, "How about me? Think I'm too old?"

Utah turns and asks, "Who are you?"

"They call me Slim."

"Slim who?"

"Just Slim."

"You two think you're funny."

"Hey, Utah, he must be the guy that gunned down our men over in Silver City."

"So you're the fast gun that got those two men?"

"Well, just how fast are you?"

"Just a little. Usually fast enough."

"What is it with you two? You talk the same."

Sam asks Utah the question that Jake taught him to ask: "What's your name? We'd like to put it on your grave marker."

Utah draws—Sam puts a bullet in his chest. He's dead before he hits the floor.

Two of the men draw at the same time as Utah—Slim shoots them both. The fourth man puts his hands up and says, "Don't shoot, I give up."

Just then a gunshot is fired outside. A man falls inside the saloon through the swingin' doors. The Sheriff walks in with his gun in his hand.

One of the witnesses tells them, "That's Colter. The Sheriff told him outside that he was under arrest. He drew on the Sheriff."

"Well, Sam, I guess your company's out of trouble."

"Yes, thank you, Sheriff. Sheriff, meet Slim—he works for the company."

"Say, do you know who that dead guy is over there?"

"Not really."

"That's Utah Smith. He's supposed to be real fast with his gun."

Sam says, "He wasn't fast enough today."

One of the men in the saloon says, "He drew on the old man here— he outdrew him and plugged him right in the chest."

The next day, Slim and Sam are standin' beside their horses. They both take their gun belts off, roll them up, and put them into their saddlebags. The Sheriff, walkin' over to say goodbye, says:

"What on earth are you doin' with your guns?"

"Sheriff, we hardly ever wear a gun. It seems every time one of us buckles up our gun belt, someone dies."

They mount their horses, wave to the Sheriff, and ride out of town.

"Say, Slim, Jake was right. Gunmen don't want their name asked so it can be put on their grave marker."

"Sam, do you ever remember Jake bein' wrong with anything he told us?"

"Guess not, Slim. Let's ride."

SLIM IS REWARDED AND SAM SPINS ANOTHER YARN ABOUT THE BLUE GHOST

Sam returns from Marksville and is sitting with the Old Boys having coffee.

"Sam, you and Slim had some trip."

"Yup, it's one I would like to forget about."

"This much I'll tell you—if it wasn't for Slim, I don't know how it would have turned out."

Sam tells them the complete story anyway, even though he'd rather forget it.

"Sam, did Slim return with you?"

"Yup, I reckon he's sleeping. He's plum tuckered out—it was a rough trip."

"He certainly earned a rest."

"Well boys, I been thinking. We're getting old, this company is becoming too much for us to run, and we're getting older every day."

"I have an idea."

"What's that, Sam?"

"My idea is to turn the running of this company over to Slim and to make him an equal partner."

"Sam, I think it's a good idea. He certainly earned it, both with his work and his gun."

"Speaking of his gun, we know you're still fast. Is he as fast as you?"

"Let me tell you, he is faster than I am. That guy with the missing finger he outdrew had a reputation of being one of the fastest on the draw."

"Come on, Sam. We have heard of Utah Smith, and he was supposed to be lightning fast with his gun. You outdrew him."

"Guess he wasn't fast enough that day."

"What's the difference? Neither of us wear a gun, so that's not important."

Slim walks into the store where the Old Boys are sitting drinking coffee.

"Howdy boys."

"Hi ya, Slim. Sam told us what happened over at Marksville."

"It wasn't a vacation, I'll tell you that."

"Slim, we've been trying to think of a way to thank you. Sam came up with an idea that we all approve of."

"Sam, you tell him."

"Slim, we're getting old. It's time we took on less work. We want you to take over The Western Feed and General Store Company, and we would like to make you a full partner."

"Wow, I don't know what to say."

"Slim, it's all going to be yours someday anyway. There is no one more deserving than you."

"As each of us pass away, you will receive his full share until you are the sole owner."

"I don't want to think of such things, Sam."

"No, no one does, but it's something that has to be talked about and decided on."

"I understand, Sam."

"Maybe I'd better go back to Marksville and see to rebuilding the store."

"Slim, that can wait. It'll take time for all the debris to get cleaned up."

"I want you to take a week or two off and go to my ranch for a little vacation. We can handle things that long."

"While you are there, you can think of someone to replace you. You won't have time to do the work you have been doing—you'll be running the company when you get back."

"Boys, I don't know what to say except thank you!"

"Sam, I was just thinking—Jake lives on through the people he taught to use a gun."

"I guess it goes right along with the memory of dear Sara."

"Wonder where we all would be if it wasn't for Jake and Sara?"

"I don't want to think about that."

"Me neither. I know it wouldn't have been good."

"Well Sam, there's not much going on with the rain today. How about telling the rest of the story about Marshal Jones—the Blue Ghost?"

"I think that would be a good story for such a day. Look how hard it's raining now."

"First, I think we should have some lunch. As soon as the rain lets up a little, I'll go over to Minnie's Restaurant and pick up some sandwiches."

The rain begins to let up. Sam goes out and gets some sandwiches. They have their lunch, and Sam begins to spin his yarn.

"If you remember, the Marshal eventually resigns. However, while he was still a Marshal, he begins to fight for the Indian. The Blue Ghost continued to ride."

"One night, he was ridin' up in the hills when he heard some strange sounds. He could tell it was Indians makin' all the noise. He wondered what was goin' on, so he rode in their direction."

"It was dark—there was no moon out that night."

"When he got to the top of a hill, lookin' down by the light of a large campfire, he could see the Indians dancin' and singin'. From their sound and actions, he could tell they were drunk."

"He could see some of them had already passed out. Eventually, they were all asleep."

"He rode down to see what had been goin' on. There were whiskey bottles scattered all over the ground." He wondered how they got the whiskey. Then he noticed there were lever-action rifles layin' on the ground.

"Someone was supplyin' the Indians with guns and whiskey."

The next morning he rode to the trading post. He went into the trading post and walked around lookin' and listenin'. An Indian woman came into the trading post and wanted a blanket.

The man runnin' the trading post wanted the fur she was carryin' and the jewelry she was wearin' for the blanket. Marshal Jones knew that was a lot more than the blanket was worth.

He walked outside and waited for the Indian woman to come out.

"Does the man in the trading post always want so much for his blankets?"

"Me no talk—afraid, won't get food if trouble."

"Government promise food, no food—people starvin'."

"Where's your village?"

She tells him, then runs off.

He thinks there is somethin' very wrong goin' on here. He gets on his horse and rides off. He rides to a nearby ranch and buys a half dozen head of cattle and takes them to the Indian village. He talks with the Chief and finds out their food is not bein' delivered and everything in the trading post is too expensive for them to buy.

He also finds out that someone is sellin' the Indians whiskey and rifles for silver. There is little silver, and the braves are tradin' it for guns and whiskey. The Chief tells the Marshal his braves were told that white men want to kill Indians, need guns, whiskey make strong.

The next day Pedro walks to the trading post leadin' his donkey. He walks into the trading post and says,

"I need new sombrero."

"I don't have any Mexican hats."

"You have dog."

"No, there's no dog here."

"Sure no dog—I smell dog."

"Look, Mexican, I told you—no dog!"

"Oh, maybe have cup of coffee?"

"Yes, go ahead—help yourself."

He pours a cup of coffee and spills it.

"Oh, sorry. Can I get another cup?"

"Yes, yes, after you clean up the mess you made."

"I clean up very good—maybe you let me clean store for food?"

"That's a good idea. Start cleanin' and leave me alone."

He does a good job cleanin' up. The trader is impressed.

"I come back tomorrow and clean up—help you out."

"Yes, okay."

"You sure no dog here?"

"Look, Mexican, did you see a dog? Well, there is no dog here!"

"Hmm. I think there's a dog."

He keeps askin' about a dog so the agent will think he's a little simple.

Marshal Jones rides to the nearest town and sends a telegram to his contact in Washington, tellin' him what's goin' on. He receives a reply back tellin' him there are people behind a money-makin' scheme, usin' Indian affairs to make money off the Indians.

The Marshal sends another telegram to his government contact resignin' as a U.S. Marshal. I will not be ridin' as a Marshal, however the Blue Ghost will be ridin', makin' war against Indian profiteerin' in the West.

The next day, Pedro is cleanin' the trading post when an Indian brave walks in and asks for food.

"Where's your silver?"

"Have no silver, no money—want food government sent."

"I told you, if you want food, you have to buy it."

"Government sent to Indians."

"No money, no food."

Pedro listens to the conversation as the trader kicks the Indian out.

Later that day, Jones rides to the Indian village. When he gets there, he finds the village had been attacked. Many were dead.

"Chief, what happened?"

"Many white men ride in—start shootin'. Braves with rifles not here—drunk someplace."

"Chief, do you know who any of the men were?"

"Not know. Braves come back, get rifles, put on war paint, take rifles, ride off. Still half drunk on whiskey."

"Braves go crazy—say kill white man."

"Chief, where's the closest ranch?"

"Over hills—follow river."

Jones rides to where he keeps his white horse and Blue Ghost disguise and rides out toward the ranch.

When he gets there, the Indians are attackin' the ranch, ridin' in circles, shoutin' and shootin'. The Blue Ghost rides in, lets out a blood-curdlin' scream, and fires a few gunshots into the air. The Indians, seein' the big white horse and the blue hood, get spooked and ride off.

The rancher comes out of his house.

"Whoever you are, I don't know how to thank you. You sure scared those Injuns off."

"Who are you?"

"I'm the Blue Ghost."

"Well, I'll tell ya—you sure look like a ghost ridin' that big white horse and that blue outfit."

"They won't be back. I'll ride to the village and see the Chief."

"Thanks, Mister!"

The Blue Ghost rides to the Indian village wearin' his blue hood. The Indians get anxious when they see him—they start yellin' and runnin' around. He walks over to the chief and makes a peace sign. He explains to the chief that he's on the Indians' side, that he's a friend. The chief tells him the name of the man sellin' guns and whiskey to his braves.

"His name Big Mike. Man at tradin' post. He sends wagon man to Indians."

Pedro is workin' in the tradin' post when a man comes in with buffalo hides to trade.

"Big Mike says you're a bit east for a buffalo hunter."

"Reckon I am. Things gettin' too hot in buffalo country. The Indians are on the warpath— burnin' and killin'."

Pedro looks at the man. He's a big man, wearin' buckskins and a fur hat. The hunter looks around the tradin' post. Pedro hears him say, "I got somethin' special in my pack." He whispers somethin' to Mike. They walk outside to look at what's inside the pack. Big Mike comes back into the store, gets some money, and returns to the hunter. He pays the hunter, gets a bag, and returns inside.

The Indian agent comes into the tradin' post and tells Mike to hide the food that was sent by the government for the Indians, sayin' another wagon's comin' in today. While they're talkin', Pedro looks inside the bag the buffalo hunter sold Mike. When Pedro looks in the bag, he turns his head away in disgust, closes his eyes for a few seconds, and lets out a sigh. The bag's got six Indian scalps in it. He thinks if Mike paid for the scalps, he must have a customer for 'em.

Pedro tells Big Mike he's gotta go take his siesta.

"Go ahead, Pedro. You been workin' hard. When you come back, a wagon'll be comin' in that I need you to unload."

Pedro goes to the hidin' place where his white horse is hidden. When he rides out, he's ridin' as the Blue Ghost. He's goin' after the buffalo hunter—he plans to kill him. He spots the buffalo hunter on the trail, fires a few shots in the air, and races toward him. He waits 'til the hunter raises his rifle—then he shoots. The buffalo hunter falls. The Blue Ghost ties a piece of blue cloth around his neck and returns to the tradin' post as Pedro.

The wagon of supplies comes in, and Pedro unloads it. He puts it in the back room. Later that day, a rancher comes into the tradin' post and parks a wagon outside, with two men sittin' on horseback.

"Pedro, go with this man and load his wagon with the items he picks out from the back room."

Pedro loads food items into the rancher's wagon and watches him pay for the food—food that was supposed to go to the Indians. The rancher pays less than half the value and drives his wagon off. His two men follow.

Pedro leaves the tradin' post and shows up on the road as the Blue Ghost. He catches up with the wagon and hides behind some boulders. When the wagon gets close, he rides out in front of it, his gun still in its holster.

"Hold it right there—I'll take that wagon."

 "Who are you?"

"I'm the Blue Ghost."

"Now get down off that wagon." His gun's still in the holster—he wants the two men to draw.

The rancher says, "Kill him!"

Both men draw their guns. The Blue Ghost is faster—he kills both.

"Now get down off that wagon and start walkin'."

The Blue Ghost ties a piece of blue cloth around the neck of each man, then takes the wagon to the Indian village.

When he reaches the village, he tells the chief to have his braves unload the wagon and hide the supplies. Then he takes the wagon back toward the tradin' post. He ties a blue cloth to the wagon and turns it loose. The wagon stops at the tradin' post. Big Mike comes out and sees the blue cloth tied to the wagon.

"What's goin' on? This Blue Ghost is everywhere causin' trouble. Seems he knows what's goin' on with everythin' we do."

Pedro overhears what Mike said and realizes he's gotta redirect Mike's suspicions.

The Blue Ghost rides to the Indian village to get help with his plan.

"Chief, I need a brave to ride as the Blue Ghost while I'm inside the tradin' post. I want him to ride up on my white horse, wearin' the Blue Ghost outfit, toss a stone with a blue cloth tied around it through the window, let Big Mike see him, then ride away. I'll be inside the tradin' post and make sure nothin' happens to your brave."

The chief sends for one of his sons and tells him what to do.

The Blue Ghost and the Indian ride to a place where the brave can hide with the white horse. Jones returns to bein' Pedro and walks into the tradin' post.

"Pedro, where you been? I got a wagon out back for you to unload. Clean up the store first, then unload the wagon."

While Pedro's cleanin' the tradin' post, the Indian brave rides in on the white horse, wearin' the Blue Ghost outfit. He throws a stone through the window. Big Mike runs outside. The Indian rears up the white horse, waves to Mike, and rides away. Mike looks at Pedro, shakes his head, and thinks, I didn't think so.

Pedro begins to unload the wagon at the back of the tradin' post— it's loaded with whiskey and lever-action rifles. He wonders where the rifles are comin' from—the soldiers don't even have rifles like that. They still got single-action rifles.

A man named Jess rides to the tradin' post to pick up the wagon. Pedro overhears Jess and Mike talkin'. He finds out Jess owns the saloon in town. Pedro figures even though this man ain't the top dog, he's gotta be stopped.

That night, after the tradin' post closes, the Blue Ghost rides to town under the cover of darkness. All of a sudden, the saloon goes quiet. Everyone's lookin' at a man standin' just inside the swingin' doors. It's the Blue Ghost.

One man starts to go for his gun. The Blue Ghost points at him and says,

"Don't do it."

The man moves his hand away from his gun.

"You—bartender—you're done sellin' liquor and rifles to the Indians."

The bartender comes up with a sawed-off shotgun from behind the bar. The Blue Ghost draws and shoots Jess—the bartender and owner of the saloon.

"Who are you?"

"I'm the Blue Ghost."

He turns and leaves the saloon. On his way out, he hangs a piece of blue cloth on the swingin' doors. Everyone watches the doors swingin' back and forth with the blue cloth hangin' from the top of one.

The place starts buzzin' with talk:

"Who is he?"

"What's he doin'?"

"Why'd he come after Jess?"

The questions echo through the saloon. An old man says,

"I only ever seen one man that fast with a gun. It was back years ago—he was an old man then. His name was Jake."

"Jake who?"

"When asked that, he'd say, 'Just Jake.'"

"Did he ride a big black horse?"

"Why, yes he did."

"I heard about him. He was supposed to be the fastest gunman in the West."

"He must've been fast. He lived to be a very old man—most gunfighters never made it to the age of forty."

Jones realizes there's a bigger problem than he thought. He telegrams his Washington contact. The telegram reads:

"The problem with the Indians and the white men is bigger than I thought. There are powerful people higher up, escalating' the Indian wars for profit. There must be people in Washington behind the problem. Let me know what you find out."

The Blue Ghost realizes that the situation—people profiteering' from the Indian wars—is far bigger than he can stop alone. He thinks, I gotta fight this problem different.

He receives a telegram from Washington. The telegram informs him that there's a high government official behind all the trouble. He goes to Washington and appears in the government official's Office as the Blue Ghost. He makes a lotta noise until the official comes out into his front Office, gun in hand. The Blue Ghost draws and kills him, runs out of the Office, and takes off his Blue Ghost outfit. Underneath, he's wearin' a business suit.

Carryin' a small suitcase, he goes halfway out of the buildin', then turns around and reenters. He mixes in with a group of folks who heard the gunshot and listens to the dead man's secretary give a description of the man who killed her boss.

He identifies himself as a U.S. Marshal and shows the badge he used to wear back when he was a marshal. He takes over the scene until the police arrive—then disappears.

Randell Jones no longer rides as the Blue Ghost. He stays in Washington, fightin' for the rights of the American Indian and exposin' the war profiteering' goin' on in the West. He also exposes that some folks are deliberately escalating' the Indian wars for profit.

The old boys are listenin' to Sam's story when Sam stops and says,

"Right now I need a cup of coffee."

"Say, Sam, whatever happened to that kid Johnny—that Jake got ta walkin' again?"

"He grew up to be a fine young man, and Jake was right—the kid became fast with his gun. Back in those days, the towns were bein' overrun with men that were just plain bad. A Sheriff was needed—one that could clean up those towns and make 'em safe for folks to live in."

"One day, Johnny went to see Old Jake just before he passed. Johnny asked Jake if it'd be alright if he became a Sheriff, knowin' what Jake had made him promise—not to take pay for his gun."

"Jake said, 'Johnny, times are a-changin'. The people livin' in the towns of the West need a good Sheriff. I think it'd be a good idea if you wanna use your gun for good and become a Sheriff.'"

"Well, Johnny became a Sheriff. He rode his horse he named Big Black from town to town and cleaned up many a place. He became the greatest sheriff the West has ever known."

"Is there more to your yarn about the Marshal, Randell Jones?"

"Well, I'll finish the story while I'm drinkin' my coffee."

"Jones stayed in Washington for a few years. He was appointed the first man to head Indian Affairs. He did a lotta good for the Indians. He designed many treaties that benefited both the Indian and the white man."

"Then one day, he left Washington. He gave up bein' a Marshal, Pedro, and the Blue Ghost. Took his white horse and retired with his family on a small ranch and lived out his days peaceably."

"Sam, did you say with his family?"

"Yep. While he was in Washington, he married—and they had a son."

"You know, to this day, that Indian tribe still tells the story of the Blue Ghost that came from Ghost Mountain. They sing and dance to his memory."

SLIM BECOMES A RANCHER

"Sam, we just got a telegram from Slim. The Feed and General Store in Marksville has been rebuilt and is open for business."

"He'll be coming in on Friday's stage," said the Old Boys as they met the stage.

"Howdy, Slim, how ya doin'?"

"Hi boys, good to be home."

"Let's wander over to the store, Slim."

When they get to the store, the Old Boys tell Slim, "We rearranged the store to make room for an Office for ya."

"Well, that's just fine, boys."

"Say boys, I had an idea while I was ridin' on the stagecoach."

"What's that, Slim?"

"I'd like to add a room onto the store and set up a tribute to Sheriff Hank Black, Jake, Appachy Rose, Marshal Jones, and of course, to our Sara."

"Like a sort of museum?"

"Yes. We can include any pictures, guns, saddles, and other memorabilia that we have or find. We can open it to the public to come in and look around. We could also write the stories of each of 'em so folks'll know about 'em."

"That's a fine idea. Let's make the addition attached to the store front and put up the display so people can see it from the street."

"That's a good idea, Sam. I didn't think of that. Where you boys gonna sit and drink coffee?"

"Right here. We can meet and talk to the visitors, maybe spin a yarn or two for 'em."

"Slim, start on havin' the addition built right away."

"Say boys, do ya think we oughta expand our business and open stores in other towns?"

"Well, that's up to you—just don't get so big you lose control of the business."

"Good advice, Sam. Right now I've got enough to take care of."

The door opens and a young man walks into the store. He asks for the boss man.

"He's right over there, son. Slim, someone to see ya."

"How ya doin', young fella?"

"Just fine—and you?"

"I'm doin' just fine. You wanted to see me?"

"Yes, I'd like to open a branch of your store in Jacksonville. The town's growin' fast—there are new ranches and farms openin' every day, and the railroad's comin' into town."

"Son, what's your name?"

"Randell Jones Jr."

"Sam, here's what the young man said. Son, tell me about your father."

"Well, I don't know too much about his life before he went to Washington. He was the first man in charge of the Department of Indian Affairs. After leavin' Washington, we settled in Jacksonville—we had a small ranch there. He passed away a few years ago. Mom died five years ago."

"Son, I know the story about your father before he went to Washington. He was a true hero of the West."

"He was?"

"Yes, son. He was a friend to the white man and the Indians. He went to Washington to fight against the corruption there. There were men profiting off the Indians illegally. First, he fought 'em in the West with his gun, then in Washington."

"Did you say with his guns?"

"You know, his last wish was to be buried wearin' his guns. I didn't even know he owned a gun."

"There was somethin' else he wanted—he wanted to be buried in a blue suit. It had to be a special shade of blue."

"Well, son, come and see me in a day or two when you have a few hours, and I'll tell you the story of Randell Jones."

"Thanks, Sam. I'll be back."

"Son, I want you to come back in the mornin'. I've got an idea I need to think about."

"Okay, Slim, I'll see ya in the mornin'. Sam, I can't wait to hear about my father."

The next mornin', Randell is at the store bright and early to see Slim.

"Randell."

"Please, call me Randy."

"Okay, Randy, do you have the money to open a store on your own?"

"Yes, I have the money from the sale of the ranch."

"Randy, here's my idea. I'll help you open your own store under the name of the Western Feed and General Store. You'll purchase all your inventory for the store from us. That way, you'll be able to take advantage of our buyin' power and the savings we've got on shippin'. We buy at a low price due to our volume of business."

"In order to use us, there'll be an investment on your part of one thousand dollars."

"Next question—do you have a location for your store?"

"There's a buildin' in town that's big enough, and it's for sale."

"Sounds like a great idea, Slim."

"I'll have our lawyer draw up a contract. You understand, you'll have to keep up the reputation we've established, and you must sell at the prices we tell ya to—they'll be the same as ours. We'll add five percent to the cost and pass it on to you. You'll make plenty of profit due to our buyin' power."

"I should have the papers ready tomorrow afternoon. Then I'll go to Jacksonville and help you set up your business."

"Gee, thanks, Slim. See ya tomorrow."

When the Old Boys get to the store, Slim tells them about the arrangement he made with Randy.

"Slim, I never heard of anyone doin' business that way—it sounds like a good idea."

"I have to go see the lawyer and have the papers drawn up."

"See you when you get back."

Sam returns with the copies of the contract. He had three copies printed up—one for Randy, one for him, and a blank copy to keep on hand. Randy comes into the store; Slim and Randy sign the contract.

"Randy, we'll leave on the stagecoach in two days for Jacksonville. That'll give you enough time to have Sam tell you about your father."

Later in the day, Randy comes back to the store to see Sam.

"Hello there, young fella. Sit a spell, have a coffee."

"Want to hear about your father?"

"Yes sir, I sure do."

Sam tells Randy the story of Marshal Randell Jones, Pedro, and the Blue Ghost.

"Now I know why he wanted to be buried in the blue suit."

"I don't know why he wanted to be buried with his guns."

"Well son, with his gun he killed a lotta men. I think he felt that his gun oughta be buried right along with him."

Slim and Randy get on the stage and head out for Jacksonville. After they'd been ridin' for a few hours, gunshots ring out behind the coach. Three men were fixin' to hold up the stage. Slim opens his bag, takes out his gun belt, and straps it on—just then, the stage stops.

"Everyone in there, get out with your hands up!"

"Oh, look here—this one's wearin' a gun."

"Know how to use that shootin' iron?"

Slim answers, "A little."

Slim looks up—the shotgun rider's been shot, bleedin' and dyin'.

"Throw down that strongbox!"

One of the holdup men shoots the lock off the box and opens it. One man's left holdin' his gun on Slim and the others. The other two start lookin' into the strongbox—their guns are in their holsters.

Slim calmly waits and watches the man with his gun on him.

"Look here—this box is full of money!"

When the man says that, the one watchin' Slim looks away. Slim draws and shoots the man in front of him. The other two men draw their guns—Slim shoots. The men are dead.

Slim unstraps his gun. Randy looks at Slim and is about to speak— Slim holds up his hand and shakes his head no.

"Let's get back in the stage."

Slim puts his gun and belt back in his bag and says, "Let's go, driver."

Slim is quiet all the way into town.

When the stage reaches town, the townsfolk see the horses carryin' the bodies of the holdup men. The sheriff walks up to the stage. He says to the stage driver,

"What happened?"

The driver tells the story of how Slim gunned all three bandits.

"What's your name, son?"

"Slim."

"Slim, you're not wearin' a gun."

"Nope. I don't wear my gun."

Slim walks away.

The Sheriff says, "That's the darnedest thing I ever heard."

"Randy, do you know him?"

"Yes, Sheriff. He owns the Western Feed and General Store Company. He's here to help me set up a branch of the store."

"Well, I've heard of him. Now I know who he is—they say he's fast with a gun."

"Sheriff, he's the fastest I've ever seen."

"Well Randy, I don't understand a fast gun that don't wear a gun."

"Sheriff, it was strange—without a thought and in a second he killed three men. Then he wouldn't talk about it. He never said a word all the way to town. After he shot them, he just sat there lookin' out the window."

"Sheriff, I gotta catch up with him."

"See you later, Randy. Still the darnedest thing I ever heard of."

"Hey Slim, wait up."

"Randy, I'm gonna check into the hotel and lie down a while. I'll see you in the mornin'."

"Okay, Slim. See you then."

The next mornin', Slim is up early. He walks outside—it's a beautiful day. Sky's blue without a cloud in it, sun is shinin' bright. Slim takes a deep breath. He's in a better mood. He looks around.

He thinks, This is a big town—a perfect spot for the Western Feed and General Store to be located. Businesses are open, people are out and about. One man's dumpin' a pail of water into the street, another's sweepin' the wooden walk in front of his store. Horsemen are ridin' up and down the street. Ladies are out doin' their mornin' shoppin'.

Slim notices some children runnin' and playin'. The town seems real peaceable.

Then a man sees Slim and says to his friends,

"That's the man that shot the fellas tryin' to hold up the stage—he saved the money comin' in on the stage."

"We oughta go and thank him. Look, he ain't wearin' a gun. You know, that's a strange thing about him—when he got off the stage he wasn't wearin' one then, but the driver said he got out of the stage wearin' his gun."

"After he shot those men, he took his gun off."

"I don't think we oughta say anything to him. The sheriff said he didn't wanna talk about it."

"What's his name?" "Only thing I know is, they call him Slim."

Slim steps down off the wooden sidewalk and walks down the street. When he reaches the men talking, one of them says, "Howdy, Slim."

"Hello boys, it's a nice day."

"Sure is, Slim. We want to thank you for saving the bank's money and bringing the stage in."

"Well, thank you, I appreciate your thanks."

"Slim, could I ask you a question?"

"Sure, go ahead."

"Slim, they say you are fast with your gun. How come you don't wear it?"

"The answer to that question is simple—every time I strap it on, someone dies."

Then he walks away. He goes into a small coffee shop that advertises breakfast on the sign.

There is a young girl working behind the counter. Slim orders breakfast and coffee. When he is finished with breakfast, he orders another cup of coffee. While she is pouring the coffee, Slim asks her, "Is this your shop?"

"No, I just work here—not for long though. The owner is closing it up."

"I wanted to rent it from him, but he wants too much money for the rent."

Slim says, "That's too bad, I'm sorry to hear that."

He pays for his coffee and goes out to find Randy. He spots Randy in the street looking at a building.

"Randy, good morning."

"Morning, Slim. This here is the building I was telling you about."

"It's plenty big enough, Randy."

"Yes, it used to be the livery stable. When the town started to grow, it ended up right in the middle of town. The livery stable moved to the edge of town and left this building empty. It's too big for anyone to buy."

"Randy, the outside looks great. Once bein' a livery stable, it's got the perfect look for a feed and general store."

"All you have to do is remodel the inside to fit your needs. The best thing about it is that it's right in the middle of town, and there's enough room where the corrals are for wagons to pull in and turn around."

"You can store the feed in that part of the store. We can have an opening and a loading dock put onto that side."

"Well, Slim, let's go on down to the livery stable and see old Jeb and buy the building."

"I've already talked to Jeb. He wants to get rid of the property—he doesn't want very much for it."

They buy the store from Jeb and begin to work on the building.

"Say, Randy, a few weeks ago I was in the coffee shop. The girl workin' there told me that the coffee shop is closin', leavin' her without a job."

"What would you think of providin' her a space in part of the front of the store for her to put in a coffee shop and a breakfast counter? I think it would be good for your business."

"The only thing is that I think it would be a good idea to rent her the space for very little. She also could help you in the store on occasion. Your business is gonna be very busy and successful right away—you're gonna need help."

"Slim, I like the idea. Why don't you go and talk to her? Besides, it would be nice to have a good-lookin' girl like her around."

"Randy, do I detect somethin' in your voice?"

"Well, I am fond of her—she doesn't know it."

"I'll go speak to her and tell her about our plans. Randy, what's her name?"

"Her name is Sandy."

"I'll be back after I speak to her."

"Hi, Sandy!"

"Hello, Slim."

"Oh, you know my name?"

"Yes, everyone in town knows your name and what you did at the stagecoach."

He holds up his hand and stops her from talkin', shakin' his head.

"I'm sorry, Slim, I didn't know. You're considered a hero."

"Sandy, a hero doesn't go around shootin' people."

"Sandy, I came to talk to you about somethin'."

He tells her about his and Randy's plan to open her own coffee shop and to work helpin' Randy run the store. She is delighted with the idea.

"I'm sure Randy and I will get along just fine."

He notices her joy when she says that.

Slim says, "Oh, really, I think you will."

"Sandy, when you get off work, come down to the store. You are now part of the Western Feed and General Store Company."

"I'll be there as soon as I close up. I'm so happy, Slim!"

When Sandy closes the coffee shop, she goes right to Randy's store. When she walks in, Slim notices that Randy's eyes light up. Slim smiles.

"Hi, Slim and Randy."

"Hi, Sandy. This is where we planned to locate your coffee and breakfast bar—right here in the front of the store along this side wall."

"That will be perfect, Randy."

"Sandy, we'll have the workers start right away. It'll be ready when the store opens."

"I can't wait to start workin' for you, Randy."

The next day Slim and Randy are standin' on ladders puttin' the Western Feed and General Store sign up on the front of the building. People are gatherin' around and askin',

"When is the store gonna open?"

"Just as soon as the inventory arrives. It's on its way. The store should be open in a couple of days."

Just then they hear gunshots. They start down off the ladder and hear more shots fired. Lookin' down the street, they see a crowd of people yellin' and laughin'. They see the Sheriff standin' in the crowd.

Walkin' up to the spot where the gunshots were fired, they see a woman standin' in the middle of the crowd. She is wearin' a gun belt and just puttin' her gun into her holster. She says,

"Any more takers?"

A man in the crowd says, "I'll give it a try."

He gives her five dollars and stands beside her. There are two beer mugs on the fence rail and a man holdin' a shot glass. When he drops the glass, they draw and fire. She beats him to the draw and breaks the glass mug.

Randy says, "I never saw anything like that before—she's fast with that gun."

"Slim, think you could outdraw her?"

"Oh, I think so."

"Why don't you give it a try? Go get your gun."

"No, Randy, I don't want to put my gun belt on. Remember I told you—I don't wear a gun."

"Oh yeah, Slim, I forgot."

"I wonder who she is."

"Randy, I don't know her name, but I've heard about her. When she was young, she drew against an old man named Jake, shootin' beer mugs."

"Old Jake said she was the fastest with her gun that he did that trick with."

"He then taught her how to draw the right way, and she became very fast."

"Slim, who's Jake?"

"He was the fastest gunman in the West. He's the one that taught me how to use a gun."

"What was his last name?"

"When asked that, he would say, 'Jake—just Jake.'"

She sees Slim standin' in the crowd of people.

"Hey, cowboy, would you like to try?"

"I don't wear a gun."

He steps out of the crowd and says to her,

"Don't make it happen—just let it happen."

He smiles and walks away, leavin' her with a puzzled look on her face.

That evening Slim goes into a restaurant for dinner. It is extremely nice inside, the patrons are all finely dressed. He looks around and sees the girl that was doing the shooting that afternoon. She is dressed in a gown, her hair is done up, and she's not wearing a gun. Slim thinks she sure looks pretty all dressed up.

He walks over to her table and introduces himself. She tells him her name is Sally.

"May I sit and join you?"

"Yes, I would like that."

"Tell me, Slim, where did you hear those words you said to me about just let it happen?"

He tells her his story about being taught to use a gun when he was a young man and Jake was very old.

She looks into Slim's eyes and can tell he admires her. With a flirtin' smile, she looks deep into his eyes and softly says,

"Slim, don't make it happen, just let it happen."

Slim comes out of sort of a trance, a little embarrassed because he was starin' at her, and says,

"Let's order dinner."

They see each other for the next several days—they dine together, take buggy rides, and go on a picnic.

"Sally, I'm going to leave town tomorrow, I have to return to the business Office. Would you come with me?"

"Why Slim, what kind of a girl do you think I am? Do you think I just go travelin' around the countryside with handsome men? Why, that wouldn't be proper."

"It would be proper if you were my wife."

"Slim, are you proposin' to me?"

"I guess I just did. What do you say?"

Smilin', she says, "Oh, a girl has to think about somethin' like that."

Slim says, "I'll give you two seconds."

"Well in that case, the answer is…" she hesitates, "yes."

He kisses her. They are married and head for Slim's home on the stagecoach.

When they reach town, they walk into the store. The Old Boys are sittin' around drinkin' coffee.

"Slim, why didn't ya let us know you were comin'? Say, who's this pretty little thing?"

"This lovely creature is my wife."

Sam chokes on his coffee and says, "Your what?"

"My wife. Her name is Sally."

"Well, I guess this calls for a celebration. Well, little lady, come over here and let me have a look at you."

"Why, you are just a pretty little thing, aren't ya? Slim, you did alright for yourself."

"Sally, you are the first lady of the Western Feed and General Store, and a very lovely one at that."

"Why, thank you, Sam."

"Slim, I've been a-thinkin' a long time about you bein' married someday—you can't live in a hotel room. Sheriff Hank Black started the ranch, and you remember when Jake was a small boy, he went to live with Hank. He left the ranch to Jake. Jake hired Bob and Curly—they built it up to be the finest ranch in the territory. Then I met Jake when I was a dumb kid and called myself Nevada. Jake saved my life and sent me to the ranch to live. When old Jake passed, he left the ranch to me. So you see, the ranch has been passed down from Hank to Jake and to me. Now it's my turn to pass it down."

"Slim, I'm a-goin' to pass the ranch on to you and Sally. Now that you're married, you need a home. I want to do this while I'm still alive. My plan is to have a cabin built on the hilltop over lookin' the ranch. I'll also need a barn to keep my horse in. It's too far for me to walk up and down that hill."

"Sam, I don't know what to say."

"You just said it, and I can see the look on your face."

"Sam, on one condition."

"What's that, Slim?"

"You come down the hill and have your meals with us."

"Reckon I can do that. I don't like to cook anyway."

"Slim, I want to go over to the lawyer's Office right now and sign the deed over to you."

"Sam, are you sure you want to do this right now?"

"Slim, I'm old. My time is short. I want to see you and Sally happy."

"Sam, I don't like to talk about you passin'."

"Nobody does, but it's one of those things that has to be decided on."

"Okay, Sam. I can't wait to tell Sally."

"Right after we leave the lawyer's Office, you can take Sally out to see her new home. I'm going to ride out later and get the hands started on my cabin. I'll tell them what I want them to do."

"Slim, I would like to tell Sally."

"That's a good idea."

When they return from the lawyer's Office, Sam tells Sally.

"Sally, this is yours and Slim's weddin' present. You will be the first lady of the house. There has never been a woman live there."

"Oh, Sam! I don't know what to say… look at me, I'm cryin'." She hugs Sam as tears run down her face.

"Slim, when can we go see the ranch?"

"Right now, let's get the buckboard."

As they ride over a hill, the ranch comes into view.

"Oh Slim, it's beautiful—and it's so big! Look at the black horses!"

"Those horses are all descendants from Jake's Big Black."

"Oh, they're beautiful, Slim."

"Look at the house, Slim. It's beautiful too."

"Oh, let's go inside!"

"Slim, it is a beautiful home."

After they look around the house, Sally wants to go outside.

"Slim, look at the size of that barn. Oh, look in the corral—a baby horse! He's darlin'. Look— he's black with four white stockings."

She goes over to the corral to see him.

"Slim, could I go inside the corral with him?"

"Why sure, be careful, he's full of energy."

The colt comes over to her and rubs his head against her, then turns and runs and jumps around.

"Oh Slim, I love him."

"Sally, he's your weddin' present."

"Oh, I love him—and I love you."

Sam comes ridin' in and calls the hands together and tells them,

"Slim is the boss now, he owns this ranch. Boys, I want you to build me a log cabin up on the hill. Come on up the hill and I'll show ya what I want."

They all ride up the hill. Sally and Slim ride with them.

"Oh Sam, no wonder you want your cabin built up here—the view of the ranch and the river is spectacular."

While Sam and Slim are tellin' the men what they want them to do, Sally is walkin' around. She walks over to Sam and asks,

"That grave over under that tree—is it Jake's?"

"Yes, it is Sally. He wanted to be buried up here on this hilltop. It was his favorite spot on the ranch."

"When my time comes, I'd like to be planted right next to him."

"Sam, what a way to put it."

"Well Sally, that's about what it comes down to."

"Oh Sam, stop it!"

She walks over to the grave and stands silently for a while. Her horse is standin' still beside her, acts as if he knows.

A week or two later, the cabin is all built and the men start on the barn.

"Sam, I'll be sendin' one of the men up the hill to feed your horse and clean the barn every mornin'. You won't have to get up early to take care of your horse."

"Just make sure you're up in time for breakfast."

That evenin', Sally, Slim, and Sam are all havin' dinner together.

"Sam, you have made me the happiest girl in the entire West. I love it here—and I love Slim— and you."

Slim says, "No more shootin' beer mugs in town."

"I promise, Slim. But I think I'll practice here on the ranch once in a while."

"Okay, as long as you don't draw and shoot at me."

"Well… I won't, as long as you behave yourself."

They all have a laugh, and Sam says, "Where's the coffee?"

ROUND UP TIME

Sally rides up the hill to Jake's grave. She gets off the old mare she's ridin' and walks over to the grave. The horse slowly follows her as if the old mare knows it's Jake's grave. Sally sits quietly on the ground, the horse stands beside her with her head down. Sally thinks back to the days when she was a young girl and Jake was a gray-haired old man. Even though he was an old man, he still was handsome wearin' those buckskins and sittin' on that big black horse. She gently smiles and thinks how fast time goes by.

She gets up off the ground, dusts herself off, and begins to clean up the area around his grave. The area had been taken care of, but there were some weeds growin'. She pulls them out and smooths the ground with her hands. The next day, she brings flowers up to Jake's grave and plants them around his grave marker. She thinks this will be the family gravesite—someday Sam, Slim, and I will be here too.

It's round-up time on the ranch. The cowboys are out rounding up the cattle to be driven to the railhead. While they're rounding up the cattle, they notice that there are a lot of young calves that need to be branded. They round up about two hundred head of cattle and drive them to the railhead. The cattle are loaded onto boxcars, and the long train pulls out and heads down the tracks. The cattle can be heard mooing and movin' about. One of the cowhands says, "They'll settle down in a short while." Then the cowhands head back to the ranch.

The hands start the branding. One chases a calf runnin', weavin' in and out. He swings his rope around his head and then lets it fly. The lasso goes around the calf's neck, and then the cowhand brings him over to be branded. The calf is fightin' the rope all the way. Other riders are rounding up the calves and drivin' them in so they can be roped. The calf is branded, and the process begins all over again.

A rider comes racin' into the ranch. He fires a few shots into the air to attract attention. He is yellin', "The train was wrecked and the cattle stolen! Two guards were killed!" One of the ranch hands runs to his horse, jumps on while it's still runnin', and gallops to town to tell Slim.

When Slim hears the news, he gets on his horse and gallops all the way to the ranch. When he rides in, he says, "Get me another horse—I rode this one hard." He goes into the house and tells Sally that he's goin' after the cattle.

"Slim, you'll be killed!"

"Sally, I'll be careful. Don't worry."

"That's easy for you to say."

He kisses her and walks outside. He straps his gun on and heads out to the spot where the train was wrecked. He takes his time—he's got a long way to go and wants to spare his horse from hard ridin'.

Slim reaches the spot where the train was derailed. There are railroad workers cleanin' up. He sees the engine and a few cars piled up, and a few dead cattle on the ground. He rides up to one of the workers and asks, "How did they stop the train?"

"The tracks were dynamited right at the bend where the train was goin' slow. The engine went right off the tracks, and a few cars piled up stoppin' the train. It's a good thing the train was goin' so slow, or the entire train would have derailed."

Slim rides in a wide circle around the wreck to see which way the cattle were driven off. He slowly follows the trail—it's not difficult to follow two hundred head of cattle. He rides for two days and spots a canyon up ahead. He's smart enough not to ride into the canyon—there would be guards watchin' the entrance. He'd ride right into a trap. He turns his horse off the main trail and heads for the rim of the canyon. From there, he can look down into the canyon.

He sees the cattle bunched up in the back of the canyon. A few riders are keepin' the cattle herded together. A few more men are sittin' around a campfire eatin'.

Slim hides in the rocks and wonders how he's gonna get the cattle back. He's outnumbered, and he don't want to stampede the herd—they'd scatter all over the county.

When Sam found out that Slim rode out alone to try to get the cattle back, he strapped on his gun and followed him. He's followin' the same tracks that Slim followed. He sees the canyon and thinks Slim must've turned off, headed for high country. Then he sees where a horse turned off the trail—he follows the tracks up to the rim of the canyon.

Slim spots him comin' and calls to him. Sam rides over to the spot where Slim tied his horse. He joins Slim in the rocks.

Slim says, "Look down there."

"Slim, nighttime is comin' on. We better sit the night out and figure what we're gonna do in the mornin'."

The risin' sun awakens them in the morning. They look down, and there's only a few men awake.

"Slim, this is the best chance we'll have—most of 'em are asleep."

"Sam, look—what's that dust in the distance?"

"Looks like a group of riders comin' this way."

"We better sit tight and see who they are. They could be part of the outlaw gang comin' to get the cattle."

The cloud of dust comes closer and closer. When they get near the canyon, they stop. "We can't ride into the canyon—we don't know what's in there. Could be a trap."

"Hey, look over here—two riders turned off and headed up to the top of the canyon. Stay here till I get back."

Slim and Sam see him comin' and recognize him as their ranch foreman. They wave him up, and they go down to meet him. They tell him what's goin' on.

"We're not gonna ride in shootin'. We'd lose men. Go back down and have your men scatter in the rocks. Tell 'em when I shoot to start shootin'. Don't shoot at anyone—just let 'em know we're all up here in the rocks. Have one man at the mouth of the canyon. When we start shootin', the sounds'll echo throughout the canyon."

They start shootin' and yellin'—the echoes make it sound like they're everywhere.

Slim yells down, "Drop your guns—you're surrounded!"

The outlaws have no cover, standin' in the middle of the canyon. They surrender.

"Drop your guns, get mounted, and slowly drive the herd out of the canyon."

They do—and drive the herd all the way back to the ranch.

Slim, Sam, and the ranch hands bring the rustlers into town and turn them over to the Sheriff.

"You brought in the whole gang! We've been after them for months."

"All we knew is that they rustled the cattle, changed the brands, and sold them."

"We don't know who buys the cattle from them. Whoever they are, they must drive the cattle to market and sell them undetected."

"Sam, there is a big reward for the capture—dead or alive—of this gang."

"Sheriff, we don't make money with our guns. Give the reward money to the new school fund."

"Ya sure, Sam?"

"Yup, that's the way Slim and I want it done."

"This money will pay for the entire school!"

"Wait till the townspeople hear about this. The kids will be happy to have a new school."

"Sam, how did you capture them without firing a shot?"

"Well, Sheriff, I gave out an Indian war whoop. When it echoed throughout the canyon, they thought they were surrounded by Indians—so they gave up."

Slim smiles and says, "Let's get outta here, Sam."

Slim and Sam decide as long as they're in town, they might as well take the hands over ta the saloon for a drink or two.

In the mornin', Sam, havin' coffee with the Old Boys, is tellin' them the story of how he single- handedly captured the whole gang.

One of the Old Boys says, "Oh, like the time you were a-fightin' a dozen wild Indians? Ya surrounded 'em and captured 'em all!"

"Hey, that's a true story. I ran around 'em so fast they were surrounded and gave up!"

Slim looks at Sally, "He'll never change."

They all sit laughin'.

"Ah boys, you know I'm justa joshin' ya."

"Why Sam, we thought you really did those things."

"Hey Sam, how's that new cabin a-workin' out?"

"Oh, just fine. Say, why don't ya boys come on out in the morning ta see it? I'll send a wagon to pick ya up."

"That sounds like a good idea. What time you goin' ta send the wagon?"

"How about ten?"

"We'll be ready."

"When ya get there, I'll tell you a story about Jake."

"Don't tell us he single-handedly surrounded a dozen Indians!"

They all have a good laugh, includin' Sam.

"No boys, when I spin a yarn, it's the truth."

"Ah, we know that, Sam. See you in the mornin'."

In the mornin', Sam sends a wagon to pick up the Old Boys. When the wagon rolls through the gates of the ranch, one of them says, "Look up there on the top of that there hill—there's Sam's cabin."

Slim greets them and tells them, "You'll have to walk up the hill. Think you can make it?"

"Why you young whippersnapper, what do you think?"

"Just 'cause we're old, you don't think we can climb a little hill?"

"Lookin' up there, I guess it is quite a ways."

"We don't expect you to walk. Bring over the horses."

The Old Boys ride up the hill.

"Hey Sam."

"Howdy boys, git down off them nags and come on in."

"Say, Sam, this is a fine-lookin' cabin."

"Oh, look out the window, Sam! You can see the whole ranch and the river from up here. No wonder you wanted the cabin built here."

"Say, look—you have your own barn too!"

"Yup, this is my favorite spot on the ranch."

"Hey, the coffee's hot—let's get a cup and sit out on the porch."

"Hey Sam, look down there! That big black horse is rearin' up—he's a beautiful animal."

"Yup, he's sired many of the young horses you see. He has to be kept separate from some of the other horses so we don't get any mixed breedin'. The mares in the field with him are not related to him. There are a few stallions down there—we have to keep close track of which one they breed. They're all descendants one way or other of Jake's Big Black."

The youngest horse on the ranch is Sally's colt—the one in the corral near the barn.

"Oh look, he has four white stockings. He sure is a cute little feller."

"Boys, it's time for lunch. The cook made up some vittles for us and brought them up just before ya boys got here."

"Well Sam, there's only one thing I like better than drinkin' coffee, and that's havin' grub."

"Well what are ya waitin' for?"

They go into the cabin and have lunch.

Slim comes home and he finds Sally sittin' on the bed cryin'.

"Sally, what's wrong?"

"Slim, I was cleanin' up the closet—look what I found in this old trunk." She holds up Jake's old worn buckskins.

"Look—his black boots, hat, and his gun belt and gun."

"Why are you cryin', dear?"

"Oh, I was just rememberin' Jake. He was such a wonderful man. I could see him in these buckskins, sittin' up on that big black horse of his. Then I just got all choked up, thinkin' that all we have—the business and this ranch, our life together—is all because of him. I couldn't hold back the tears."

"Come over here." He holds her in his arms. He says, "I know how you feel. It's mixed feelings of sadness and happiness all at the same time."

"Slim, I'm so thankful for everything we have, and I love you."

"Sally, these things of Jake's are just what we need in our little museum, payin' tribute to Jake and the people that helped form the West."

He gives her a tighter squeeze and says, "Sally, I love you too."

Sittin' on the front porch of Sam's cabin, one of the Old Boys asks Sam,

"When ya gonna tell us another yarn about Jake?"

"Keep ya shirt on—let me drink my coffee."

Sam finishes his coffee, sits back, and lights his pipe. He begins to spin his yarn.

Jake was about forty years old. He'd been carryin' the deputy marshal's badge for ten years. By now, his reputation had spread throughout the West. The Marshal would contact him about an assignment in whatever area Jake happened to be.

Jake received a telegram from the Marshal that two men were holdin' up banks, and he thinks they were headed Jake's way. Jake rides out toward the town where the last bank was held up. He says to Big Black,

"I think we picked up their trail—looks like they're headed for Spring Creek."

The riders are way ahead of Jake. Before he gets to town, they rob the bank and ride out. When Jake rides into town, he sees a group of men gathered together with the local Sheriff. Jake rides up to the men and identifies himself as a Deputy U.S. Marshal. They tell him the bank was just robbed and they're goin' after the holdup men. Jake asks the sheriff if they'd let him handle the bank robbery. The Sheriff agrees.

"Sheriff, let's go over to the bank and talk to the people that were held up."

They walk into the bank. When the manager sees them, he says,

"Sheriff, why aren't you out after the bank robbers?"

Jake says,

"There's no reason to go chasin' shadows around. These men've been robbin' banks and alludin' possess all over the West. Tell me what happened."

"Well—who are you?"

"I'm a U.S. Deputy Marshal."

"Oh, Marshal, I didn't know! It was awful—he put the gun right in my face and made me open the safe. They took all the money. Oh, I'm so upset—I'm afraid what the townspeople will do. Look—I'm still shakin' just thinkin' about it."

"What'd they look like?"

"Oh, I don't know. I was so scared."

"Marshal, I can help you!"

"Oh good. What's your name, son?"

"Jim—I'm the teller here."

Jake tells the manager to go home and get some rest.

He was no help. Jake thinks he's afraid of his own shadow.

"Jim, what do you remember about the holdup men?"

"One had a large scar down the side of his face. The other wore a bandanna—he had a half- moon shaped scar over his right eye."

"You say only one wore a bandanna, and they both had large scars on their face?"

"Yes, that's right, Marshal."

Jake thinks about the identity of the two men. Something doesn't sound right—he's not sure what.

Jake rides to the edge of town. It had rained the night before, and the ground was firm. He could see the tracks in the dirt—they were real distinct. He gets off his horse and looks at the tracks closely. When he was a boy, Two Arrows taught him not only to follow tracks, but to look at 'em.

Jake notices that, at the edge of town, the tracks of one of the horses changes—they ain't as deep as they were. There was less weight all of a sudden on one of the horses—the rider got off. Lookin' around, he sees two or three wagon tracks. From the direction the horses were goin', one set of tracks heads into town.

Lookin' around, he realizes that if the rider dismounted, he would've been wide open to view from the townspeople. Someone would've seen him.

Jake gets on his horse and rides a short way out of town, followin' the two horses. As he rides, he's thinkin'. Then it hits him—one of the holdup men returned to town. But how'd he do it without bein' seen?

Jake rides back into town and up to the Sheriff's Office. He tells him what he's discovered. Then he walks over to the saloon and sits down, lookin' for a man with a scar on his face. The Sheriff joins him.

"Jake, it oughta be easy to spot a man with a scar on his face."

"Well, that's another thing that has me a-thinkin'. Why would one man wear a bandanna and not the other two? And why wouldn't they cover their faces to hide the scars? It's as though they wanted the scars to show. That don't make no sense either."

"Well, we'll look for a man with a scar."

A man comes rushin' through the saloon doors, leavin' them swingin' back and forth. He talks real fancy:

"Gentlemen! I am the Great Marco—magician and actor extraordinaire! Come one, come all to see our performance tonight at the meeting hall!"

"Not only will you see me perform, but you'll see and hear Rosily sing and dance! Gentlemen, she wears very little clothes. She's beautiful, with a lovely body."

"Then you try to sell snake oil—a remedy for every possible ailment!"

"No, no, my good man, the only thing you may purchase is a photo of Rosily—wearin' less clothes than she performs in!"

"Give me one of them tickets!"

"Me too!"

"Me too!"

"And me!"

Every man in the saloon buys a ticket—'cept Jake and the Sheriff.

"My good Sheriff, I'd like to present you with a free ticket. You don't wanna miss our performance."

"Why, thank you."

"How about you, my good man?"

Jake says, "No thank you."

"Well, suit yourself."

He leaves the saloon.

The Sheriff says, "He's a strange one. His outfit was just as strange."

"Sheriff, that's the way those actors are—full of themselves, loud, and arrogant."

"Sheriff, didn't he say they just arrived in town this mornin'?"

"Yes, I saw that big red wagon comin' into town seconds after the bank was robbed."

The saloon is empty—everyone's at the show the troupe is puttin' on. The only people in the saloon are Jake and a couple of old men.

The show ends, and there's a rush of men comin' in. They're hootin' and hollerin' about Rosily.

"Look at this picture! I've never seen a woman like that before!"

"I know! We all got the same picture—just look at those legs!"

The Sheriff walks in and sits down with Jake.

"How was the show, Sheriff?"

"I was surprised. Not that bad. Rosily is all that the Great Marco said she was. But Marco— he's a big ham."

"Jake, see that guy that just came in? He's the set-up man. He arranges the props. He's also a comedian—real funny while settin' up the stage."

"I noticed he's wearin' a gun. The way he wears it, looks like he knows how to use it."

Jim, the bank teller, comes in and walks over to Jake and the Sheriff.

"Say, I remembered something—one of the men was wearin' a silver belt buckle."

"It had some sort of Indian design on it. Looked like crossin' spears with feathers hangin' from 'em, carved into the buckle."

"Jim, that's important information—I'm glad you remembered."

"Guess it slipped my mind, Jake."

"Jake, we have plenty to look for—men with scars. One of them is in town, and maybe he's wearin' a silver belt buckle."

"It seems so, Sheriff. Actually, it's too much information."

"What do you mean, Jake?"

"Well, think about it for a while—scars that ain't covered, one man wearin' a bandanna but not coverin' his scar, and a belt buckle that no one could forget."

"Yeah, I see what you mean, Jake."

The prop man is standin' at the bar.

One man says to him, "Your act is very funny."

"Thank you."

"You been workin' towns in the territory?"

"Yes, we started west of here and worked our way east until we got to this town."

"Jake, that Marco is talented—now that I think about it. He does his magic act, then he comes back on stage later and does a theatrical performance. After he puts his makeup on, you'd never know it was him."

"Did you say makeup?"

"Yeah, I guess it's actor's makeup."

"Well, Sheriff, I think I'll call it a night."

Jake walks to the hotel and up to his room. He takes off his gun belt and his buckskins. He lies down and thinks most of the night.

In the mornin', when he awakes, he cleans up, puts on his buckskins, and straps on his gun belt. While he's strappin' on his gun belt, it all comes to him. He rushes to the Sheriff's Office. The Sheriff is just wakin' up.

"Good mornin', Jake."

"Hello, Sheriff. Sheriff, I've got it all figured out. I know how they did it."

"Sit down, Jake. I was just gonna have some coffee—join me."

"I sure will."

"Now, what was you sayin'? I wasn't quite awake when you came in."

"Sheriff, once we had all the information, I was able to piece it all together. The bank robbers are a well-organized group. They had things figured out right down to the smallest detail. Actually, they had it all figured out too good. That's what made it easy to figure out."

"The bank robbers didn't have scars—it was theatrical makeup. The theater wagon would wait outside of town until the bank was robbed. Then they'd drive the wagon toward town. The two men would race out of town on horseback. When they reached the wagon, one man would get off his horse and jump into the back of the wagon, ridin' right back into town with the bank money hidden in the show wagon. He'd remove the makeup, takin' off the scar. He could then walk around town unsuspected with the theater group."

"The man that rode off leadin' the extra horse most likely let the horse go. If he ran into a posse, he wouldn't have to run—they'd be lookin' for a man with a scar on his face carryin' bank money. Most likely he's gone on to the next town to scout out the area."

"Well, now we know how they did it and who they are. We need the proof. Questionin' won't work—they'll never confess. They're all actors."

"Jake, the troupe has another show tonight. I'll search their wagon while they're on stage. If the evidence is there, I'll find it."

"Good idea, Sheriff. I'll be in my room when you're finished."

The sheriff searches the wagon. He don't find anything at first. Then he looks for a hidden compartment. He finds one under the floorboards—a false bottom. When he opens it, he finds the bank's money and money from other banks, still in the bags marked by each bank. He takes the money to his Office and locks it in his safe, then goes to Jake's room.

Tellin' Jake what he found, they decide to arrest the entire troupe after the performance.

When the entertainers return to their wagon, they're arrested.

Rusty, the prop man, ain't with them.

Jake says, "He probably went over to the saloon—I'll bring him in, Sheriff."

Jake walks to the saloon and up to the swingin' doors. He checks his gun and looks in over the doors. He sees Rusty standin' at the bar. He walks in and says,

"Rusty, you're under arrest for bank robbery."

Rusty looks in the mirror and sees Jake standin' behind him. He stares for a few seconds.

Jake says, "I know what you're thinkin'—don't do it."

Rusty turns and draws.

One gunshot is heard.

Rusty falls.

Jake turns and walks out of the saloon.

One of the spectators says,

"He didn't even look at him after he shot him."

Another man says,

"Look, he didn't have to. He's been shot right in the heart. He was dead before he hit the floor."

The next mornin', Jake is up early and packed to travel. He saddles Big Black and walks, leadin' his horse to the Sheriff's Office. He ties Big Black to the hitchin' rail and walks in.

"Leavin' town, Jake?"

"Yup. It's time to move along."

"Sheriff, get someone to dress in Marco's clothes and drive the wagon to the next town. When the other bank robber rides up to greet the wagon, arrest him. I'll be seein' you."

Jake turns and walks out, unties his horse, gets on Big Black, tips his hat to the Sheriff, and rides out.

A few men walk over to where the Sheriff is standin'.

The Sheriff says, "He's the darnedest guy I ever saw. He solved the crime without even leavin' town. Anyone else'd be wanderin' around, ridin' all over the place lookin' for the bank robbers."

"Sheriff, you didn't see him draw. He drew, shot, and holstered his gun before Rusty's body even hit the floor."

"Then he just turned around and walked out—leavin' the doors swingin' behind him."

ANOTHER OLD MAN JOINS THE OLD BOYS

It's early in the morning, there are white fluffy clouds in a light blue sky, the sun is out and it's a bright day. Sam is riding to town enjoying the day and the ride. When he reaches town, he rides to the town corral, unsaddles his big black horse, and turns him loose in the corral. Then he walks up the street to the store. As he walks, he looks around thinking how much the town has grown. He stops and looks at the sign hanging over the front of the store that reads, Western Feed and General Store. He stands looking at the sign for a minute or two, then he smiles. As he looks at the store, he sees in his mind the small store that Sara owned. He sees her standing out front sweeping the wooden sidewalk. He whispers to himself, "Days gone by."

When he walks into the store, the Old Boys are already there drinking coffee. Slim is busy at work in the back of the store.

"Sam, come on in, the coffee's hot. Someone pour Sam a cup."

They sit and chew the fat awhile.

"Hey Sam, I wanta ask ya a question."

"Sure, what's that?"

"Remember when ya told us the story about the Blue Ghost? Often you said his horse didn't leave any tracks—how did that happen?"

"Well, I thought you boys would have figured that out. One thing is that he never put shoes on that big white horse of his, and whenever he didn't want his horse to leave tracks, he tied skins over the horse's hoof."

"That was an old Indian trick. You would have to look close and know what you were looking for to see the tracks."

"The other thing is whenever he took action or stood on a hill where he could be seen, he always picked hard ground."

"An old Indian trick, Sam?"

"Yup, those Indians came up with some unusual tricks, and they usually worked."

"Hey boys, the stage just pulled in down the street."

"Anyone get off?"

"A woman and an old man."

"Looks like he's headed this way."

A few minutes later, he walks into the store and asks for Slim.

"Hey Slim, someone out here to see ya."

"Be right out."

Slim comes out of the back of the store and says, "Hello, what can I do for you?"

"Slim, my name is Walter. For years I owned a saloon and had these things in this box on display for many years. The room you have of memorabilia of western legends on display is known about all over the territory. What I have in the box is not so much, however, the story behind it makes it unusual. I want to give it to ya for your display room."

He opens the box and takes out two beer mugs—one is broken. He also takes out a shot glass.

"I know where they came from. It looks like a mug Jake broke drawing against someone."

"Yes, Sam, but the importance of this set of mugs is that it was the first time he did it."

Sam says, "Ya don't say."

"It was in my father's saloon many years ago. I was just a young kid sweeping the floor. There was a young man that thought he was a gunslinger, lookin' for Jake. He wanted to draw against him—he thought he was faster than Jake."

"Jake told the young man to come outside. They set these two beer mugs on a fence rail. One of the men dropped this shot glass. They drew when the shot glass was dropped."

"I should say Jake drew, broke the mug, and put his gun back into his holster before the young man cleared his holster. The young man never fired his gun. I don't know what his name is. He called himself Nevada."

Sam says, "It's a good thing that dumb kid never drew down on Jake."

"Sam, it sure was. Jake convinced the kid he wasn't a fast gun. That young man disappeared—no one knows what happened to Nevada. I ran out and picked up the mugs and shot glass and have had them all these years."

Sam says, "That's some story."

Slim says to Walter,

"Sam can tell ya where that young man went and what happened to him."

"I'd like to know, Sam."

Slim says, "Before he tells you that story, would you like to meet the guy that called himself Nevada?"

"You mean he's here in town?"

"Yes, he's sittin' right there."

"Sam, it was you?"

"Yup, I was that dumb kid. I learned fast that day that I wasn't a gunfighter."

"Sam, I've heard both you and Slim are real fast with your guns. The stories of ya both being fast spread throughout the territory."

"Jake taught us both how to draw fast and shoot straight."

"Neither of you wear a gun?"

"No, we don't wear our guns—however, we've had to strap 'em on from time to time."

The Old Boys and Walter sit talkin' the rest of the day.

Slim asks Walter where he's stayin'.

"I'm goin' to stay over at the hotel. I sure would like to find a place to live in this area. I like it here."

"I have an idea, Walter. Why don't you come and stay at the ranch? We have a big bunkhouse with plenty of room—you can live there as long as you want."

"That sounds great, Slim—on one condition: you give me some work to do around the ranch."

"Oh, I guess we can do that alright."

"Walter, I'll send a wagon in the mornin' to pick ya up."

In the mornin', the wagon picks Walter up and takes him to the ranch. As the wagon comes over a hill, Walter says,

"Wow, look at this spread. How far does it go?"

"As far as you can see."

"Look at all those black horses."

"They've been breedin' them ever since Jake owned the ranch. They're all descendants of Jake's big black horse, given to him when he was young by an Indian."

"Is that Sam's cabin up on the hill?"

"Yup, that's where he lives."

The wagon driver takes Walter to the bunkhouse. When he walks in, he's greeted by the ranch hands—they all introduce themselves.

"There's more hands out workin'. We have a day crew and a night crew—we rotate shifts so there are always riders watchin' the cattle. We have a few men, all they do is ride watchin' the horses."

Sam saw the wagon come in, so he gets on his horse and rides down the hill. Walter sees him comin',

"Look at that old boy ride—and what a beautiful horse!"

Sam rides up to the bunkhouse.

"Walter, you still ride?"

"Sam, I may be old, but I ain't dead yet—yup, I can ride."

Sam tells one of the hands to go out and get that gray gelding.

"He'll be a good horse for Walter."

The cowboy rides out to bring in the horse. He doesn't want to be caught—he's bein' playful, runnin' and bouncin' around. The cowboy is ridin' a good horse that can run the gelding down. He tosses his loop—it goes right around the horse's neck. The horse comes under control as soon as the loop goes over his head and around his neck. He brings the horse in and saddles him up.

Walter and Sam ride off up the hill to Sam's cabin. Inside the cabin, they're havin' coffee.

"Walter, let's go out on the front porch—there's a couple of rockin' chairs to sit in, and we'll drink our coffee."

"Let me fill your cup up."

Sittin' in the rockin' chairs, Walter is lookin' around at the ranch below.

"I see why you wanted your cabin built up here. The view of the ranch and the river is spectacular."

"Look in the corral near the barn— that colt is havin' a good time for himself."

"He sure is pretty with those four white stockings and that white blaze on his nose."

"That's Sally's colt—she'll be ridin' him when he gets bigger."

"She sure will look good sittin' on his back."

"Sam, could we take a ride around the ranch? I sure would like to see those black horses up close."

"Just as soon as I finish my coffee. We'll take a ride down near the river too."

They finish their coffee, get mounted, and ride down the hill and out onto the range. One of the ranch hands says,

"Look at those old bucks—they look twenty years old ridin' across the pasture."

A couple of the hands have a laugh.

"Sam, why so many corrals out here?"

"The horses have to be kept separated due to breedin' control. We don't want interbreedin'. We keep black mares for breedin', and from time to time we bring in new mares for the black stallions to breed."

"Any males born other colors 'cept black are gelded and used by ranch hands or sold."

"We only sell geldings so no one can use 'em for breedin' stock."

They ride back to Sam's cabin and sit on the front porch enjoyin' the view.

"Sam, where did Slim meet Sally?"

"Now there's a story for ya. Slim was in a town and he heard gunshots. When he checked to see what was goin' on, there was Sally shootin' against men at beer mugs. She was outdrawin' them all. She drew against Jake when she was young—he said that she was the fastest that ever drew against him. He worked with her and she became faster and faster. She would go around from town to town drawin' against anyone that wanted to challenge her. She would charge 'em five dollars to draw against her."

"Most of the men just wanted to see her draw."

"Walter, she was a sharpshooter. She could perform other tricks as well."

"Sam, it's a small world—here we are together, and it's over a broken beer mug."

"Sam, what are those boys doin' down there?"

"They're gettin' ready for the barbecue. Once a year we have a big barbecue and invite the whole town. They come on ridin' horses, draft horses, and ridin' in all sorts of wagons. That in itself is a sight."

"Everyone has a great time. There's singin', dancin', all sorts of music, and games for the adults and the children."

"Slim is real big on havin' the kids play games and be in all the events. He loves the kids."

"Sam, see that big black horse over there?"

"That one?"

"No, the one over by the big rock."

"Ya."

"He looks powerful. Look at the muscles and that wide chest."

"The last couple of years, one of the cowboys has tried to ride him. He ain't broke—I don't think he can be. Anyway, no one has stayed on him for more than a few seconds."

"Is he mean?"

"Oh no, he just don't like to be ridden. After he throws the rider, he goes over and nudges him with his nose and whines like he's laughin'."

"Do you think anyone'll try to ride him this year?"

"I don't know, but as they say, there's always one in every crowd."

The next day, Sam and Walter ride into town and up to the store. Inside, Sam explains, "This group is called the Old Boys. Sit down, join us, and become one of the Old Boys."

"Is the coffee hot?"

"It is. I'll get the pot and pour."

"Hey Walter?"

"Ya Slim?"

"I put the beer mugs on display. Say, you ain't seen the display yet—come on in and look around."

"Is that the buckskins Old Jake wore?"

"Yes. Sally found 'em in the back of a closet in an old trunk, along with his boots, hat, and his gun belt."

"We don't have anything that belonged to the Yellow Rose of Texas—we only got this write-up on her that Sally wrote from one of Sam's stories."

"Would you look at the story Sally wrote about the mugs and Jake, see if she got it accurate?"

"Guess I can do that for you one of these days."

"Sam, did you tell Walter the story about the Yellow Rose of Texas?"

"Ya, I sure did one night sittin' around the cabin."

"Sam, whatever happened to her?"

"She went on workin' for the Texas Rangers for several years. She met a man who'd retired from the Rangers and got married."

"There's one story I remember about her I didn't tell ya. It was one of the most unusual gunfights of the old wild west."

"What was so unusual about it?"

"Well, I'd have to tell ya the whole story."

"Sam, we'd like to hear it, wouldn't we boys?"

"Yes, we're always ready to hear ya spin a yarn."

"Well sit back, boys, and I'll spin you a yarn about the Yellow Rose of Texas."

"The Rangers booked her into a town to sing in the saloon. There was a gang of outlaws workin' outta that town. The Rangers had no idea who they were or where their hideout was located. They knew Rose would be able to find out.

The saloon she was booked into was run by a good-lookin' woman named Katy. She was tough and so mean she could bed down with a rattlesnake. Katy won the saloon in a card game. The man she won it from accused her of cheatin' him—she shot and killed him. Witnesses said it was self-defense.

When Rose came out on stage to sing, the men went crazy—yellin' and applaudin'. Katy was walkin' around the saloon; nobody noticed her while Rose was on stage Katy didn't like that— she was used to bein' the center of attention. After a few nights, Katy began to hate Rose.

While Rose was singin', she noticed two men walk into the saloon and go into Katy's Office. She followed 'em. A short while later, four more men came in, went to the bar, and had a beer. Rose had an eye for spotin' bad guys. She watched as the two men came out of the Office and joined the others at the bar.

'What did Katy say?'

'She's in such a bad mood 'cause of this songbird, we just left her in there a-hollerin' and a-cursin'.'

A few nights later, the two men are back and go straight into the Office. Katy follows 'em.

'Katy, we need to set up our next job.'

'I got it all planned. In a couple of days, the miners are sendin' a wagonload of gold down from the mines. I want you to git that gold.'

'Katy, everyone knows us around here. The men a-ridin' guard and the driver will recognize us.'

'Then kill 'em all.'

'The wagon's scheduled to leave Thursday mornin'. I don't trust 'em. I want you out there overnight until the wagon comes down the road.'

'They might bring it at a different time to trick us.'

'I woulda never thought of that.'

'Ya wouldn't. That's why I'm the brains of this outfit and you do the work. Today's Tuesday— get out there and keep an eye out.'"

Katy was right. The next morning, a wagon comes down the trail with four guards and a driver bringin' it to town. They attack the wagon, kill all five men, and take the wagon to their hideout in the mountains.

That afternoon, a man comes drivin' a wagon into town yellin', "The miners' wagon was held up! Those dirty skunks killed 'em all! I got their bodies in the back of the wagon."

Rose walks to the livery stable and rents a horse. She's carryin' saddlebags. When she rides outta sight of the townsfolk, she takes her gun belt out of the saddlebags and straps it on. When she reaches the spot where the holdup took place, she sees the ground stained with blood where the guards and driver laid dyin'. She follows the wagon tracks up into the mountains until she loses the trail. Now she knows the hideout is somewhere up in the mountains.

She rides back to town, stops just before enterin', and puts her gun belt back into her saddlebag. Back in town, she sits in the hotel window watchin' the street. She sees the four men ride into town—they'd been a-ridin' hard. Their horses were all lathered up. A short while later, the four men ride out.

The next mornin', one of the outlaws rides into town. Rose sees him. She puts on her ridin' clothes, goes to the livery stable ta git a horse. She rides outta town and finds a place where she can hide and watch the trail. When the man rides by, headed for the hideout, she follows him. Hidin' in the boulders on the mountain, she can look down and see the hideout—the six men and the wagon marked Minin' Company. She rides back to town and gets ready for that evenin's show.

Texas Ranger Bob was due to come into town that evenin' to see how Rose was doin'. While she's singin', Bob walks into the saloon, up to the bar, and orders a beer. When Rose finishes her performance, she tells the crowd, "I'm tired and goin' to bed. I'll see you boys tomorrow night." She walks to her hotel room. Bob, understandin' her message, walks over to the hotel and checks into a room.

Later that evenin', Rose comes down the stairs and walks up to the desk. She tells the desk clerk she couldn't sleep and is goin' out for a walk. The clerk tells her it's kinda late for a woman to be out alone. She agrees and goes back upstairs. While she was talkin' to the clerk, she was readin' the register book upside down to get

Bob's room number. It was easy ta do— his was the last name in the book.

Rose knocks on Bob's door. He opens it, and she goes into his room. She tells Bob what she's found out.

The next mornin', Bob goes and gets some Texas Rangers that were nearby. Rose meets them on the trail. She leads them to the outlaws' hideout. The outlaws ain't there. The Rangers ride down to the cabin. They search the place—no gold, no money. Bob says, "The wagon's here. The gold has to be here someplace."

"Hey Bob, this wall sounds strange. Listen when I tap on it."

"Let's open the wall."

"Look! A hidden room full of gold and bags of money!"

"Load it into the wagon. We're takin' it to town."

Rose had left for town as soon as she showed Bob where the hideout was. Bob wanted her to keep watch. They didn't know where the gang of outlaws was.

While they're bringin' the wagon into town, one of the outlaws is headin' for the hideout. He sees the wagon comin' along with the Rangers. He turns his horse around and races back to town. In town, he goes into Katy's Office and tells her.

"I want that gold. Find the boys and get that wagon."

"It's almost in town."

"I don't care. Wait till they git to town. Git me that gold. We'll all leave town together—with the gold and the money."

Katy goes up to her room and changes into her ridin' clothes. She straps on her gun belt and goes back downstairs.

Rose sees the men gettin' ready for the wagon to come into town. She gits on a horse and rides to warn the Rangers.

"When we get to town, let the horses bring the wagon in. We'll ride into town behind the buildin's and come in from the other end. When the outlaws come out to stop the wagon, we'll arrest 'em. There's gonna be shootin'."

Two of the outlaws come out of the saloon to stop the wagon. The Rangers ride into view. Bob says, "Hold it right there. You're under arrest. Drop your guns."

The outlaws draw and start shootin', hidin' behind the wagon. The Rangers take cover and return fire. One outlaw is shot tryin' to run into the saloon. Gunshots come from inside the saloon. One of the Rangers sneaks down the side of the street, runnin' from cover to cover. He gets into position and has a clear shot at the outlaw hidin' behind the wagon. He shoots— the outlaw is wounded and falls.

All the Rangers fire at the saloon at the same time. One of the bullets hits and kills one of the outlaws. Bob yells to the ones in the saloon:

"Give up and come out! You got no place to go."

One outlaw says, "I'm givin' up."

But the leader says, "You're not goin' anywhere. Now start shootin'."

Bob tells the Rangers, "Stop shootin'. We'll wait 'em out."

One of the Rangers climbs onto a roof. He's at the right angle to get a shot at the outlaw near the door. He signals to Bob. Bob yells again:

"Give up and come out or we'll start shootin' again!"

The men inside answer by firin' back. The one on the roof takes aim and fires. The outlaw falls. He waves to Bob lettin' him know he got him.

Bob yells again, "There's only one of you left! Give up or we're comin' in!"

Katy's been hidin' in her Office. She's wearin' her gun. She's fast on the draw. The last outlaw decides to come out shootin'. He figures gettin' shot is better than bein' strung up.

Now there's only one more to get—Katy.

Rose says, "I'll go in and bring her out."

When she walks into the saloon, Katy comes out of her Office.

She asks Rose, "Who are you?"

Rose replies, "I'm the Yellow Rose of Texas—a Texas Ranger."

Katy says, "Why, you dirty rat!" She draws her gun. Rose outdraws her.

Bob comes runnin' in when he hears the gunshot. "Rose, are you all right?" Then he sees Katy layin' on the floor with her gun in her hand. He goes over to check on her.

Bob says softly, "She's dead."

Rose puts her gun back in her holster and softly says, "She's better off. Hangin' is a rough way to go." She turns and walks out of the saloon.

The Yellow Rose of Texas continued to be a Texas Ranger workin' undercover. It's a shame her identity was never known as a Texas Ranger—she played a big part in the success of the Rangers.

"Sam, that was some story. I guess there were a lotta women that helped settle the Wild West."

"Yup, reckon there was."

"Let's have another cup of that coffee."

THE BIG BARBECUE

"Walter, the barbecue is tomorrow. Ride up and have breakfast with me, then we'll ride down together."

The next mornin' the townsfolk begin to arrive for the barbecue. It looks like a parade of wagons and horses comin' through the gates of the ranch.

One wagon is carryin' the band members and their instruments. They unload the wagon, set up their instruments, and start playin'. There's a guitar player, a drummer, a trumpet player, and a fiddle player. The daughter of the fiddle player also plays guitar and sings.

Sam and Walter ride down the hill. The people attendin' the barbecue all look up the hill.

"Look, here comes Sam and Walter ridin' down that hill."

"Sam looks pretty sharp ridin' on that big black horse."

"I think that gray is a good-lookin' horse."

"Yes, he is good-lookin'. He's a pretty shade of gray."

"Howdy folks!"

"Hey ya, Sam."

"Say, you folks all know Walter, don't ya?"

"Sure we do. How are you, Walter?"

"Just fine, and you folks?"

"Say Sam, that band sounds good."

"Wait 'til you hear that fiddle player turn loose and hear his daughter sing."

Everyone is havin' a great time. The fiddle player begins to call a square dance, and you could smell the barbecue pit burnin'. The children are runnin' around, laughin' and playin' games. After the square dance, three of the ladies from town go up on the stage and sing. They have fine voices and sound good singin' together.

A couple of men ride out on the range to look at the black horses. Slim and Sally are right in the mix of those havin' a good time. Time passes quickly. The ranch cook rings his triangle and yells out, "Come and get it!" Everyone sits down at a very long table, and the ranch hands serve the food.

After everyone has eaten, the hands bring large coffee pots and start servin' coffee. There's fresh cold milk for the kids. The owner of the saloon has brought kegs of beer, and he starts servin' the beer. The men yell out, "That's what we been waitin' for!"

Everyone is full and just sittin' around. The band starts playin' a slow song, and the dance area fills up with couples. They dance to a few slow songs, then the fiddle player starts playin'. Everyone stops dancin' and stops to listen. He's playin' fast — everyone is clappin' their hands in time with the music.

A few cowboys start dancin', bangin' the heels of their boots. The ladies watch and shake their heads. When the fiddle player finishes his song, his daughter sings again.

In the middle of her song, a rifle shot rings out. Sam falls to the ground.

"He's been shot in the back — look, right in the shoulder!"

Slim rushes over to Sam along with Walter. They bring Sam into the house and lay him on the couch. The doctor, who is attendin' the barbecue, follows Slim and Walter into the house.

"Doc, what do you think?"

"If I can get the bullet out before he loses too much blood, he should be alright — unless his age is against him."

Slim tells one of the hands, "Saddle my horse." He takes his gun out of his saddlebag, straps it on, and rides toward the rocks across the pasture. When his horse reaches the corral fence, he jumps it. Then Slim slows his horse down, rememberin' that Jake told him not to rush into trouble.

He rides into the rocks, gets off his horse, and starts to look around. He sees hoofprints. He kneels down and looks at the tracks — the horse had a rear shoe missin'. While he's kneelin' down, he puts his finger into the track without a shoe, then he looks up in the direction the rider rode off.

He gets up and says to his horse, "Let's go git him, boy."

Slim follows the horse into town. The horse is tied up to the hitchin' rail — it has a rear shoe missin'. Slim ties his horse up beside the other horse. He checks his gun — it's loaded. He puts it into his holster and then moves it a little to make sure it's free in the holster.

He walks into the saloon.

There are four men standin' at the bar. Slim asks, "Which one of you rode that bay tied up out front?"

A cowboy turns around and says, "I do. What of it?"

"You just ride in from the JJ Ranch?"

"I ain't been near no ranch."

"That's funny — I just trailed your horse from the ranch."

"I said I ain't been near no ranch. You callin' me a liar?"

"Guess I just did. Now drop your gun belt and come with me. I'm takin' you to the Sheriff for attempted murder."

"You ain't takin' me anywhere."

When he says that, he draws. Slim outdraws and shoots him. He falls back against the bar, blood comin' out of his chest. Slim puts his gun back in his holster, turns, and begins to walk away. He hears the man's body fall.

Slim rides back to the ranch and goes in to see Sam.

"Doctor, is he gonna be alright?"

"Yes — he's too mean to die."

"Hey, I heard that!"

"Now just lie there and rest. I gave you somethin' to make you sleep — you'll be asleep in a few minutes."

Several weeks pass, and Sam is almost fully recovered. He rides to town.

"Sam, how ya doin'?"

"Not too bad, boys. My shoulder's a little stiff."

Sam tells the story to the Old Boys — how Slim shot the man in the saloon.

"Did Slim tell you that story?"

"Yup. He didn't want to talk about it, but I asked him what happened after he rode out after the gunman that shot me."

Three strangers ride into town and go into the saloon. One of them is lookin' for his brother. He asks the bartender if he's seen him.

He describes his brother to the bartender.

"There was a young man in here a few weeks ago. I'm sorry to tell you — if that was your brother — he drew on a man, and he was gunned down right where you're standin'."

"Where's his horse?"

"Down at the livery stable."

"Let's go see if it's my brother's horse."

The three men walk into the livery stable and look at the horse. The brother to the man shot asks the man runnin' the livery stable, "Who shot my brother?"

"It was a local businessman."

"I said, who shot him?"

"His name's Slim. He runs the Western Feed and General Store up the street."

"He's gonna pay with his life. Then we'll get the old man that shot our father."

"Well, he ain't in town right now."

"We'll go back to the saloon and wait for this Slim to come back in town."

The livery stable man sneaks to the store and tells Slim about the three men.

Sam says, "I know who they are, Slim. I shot and killed their father a few years back. You shot the brother — now they're after both of us."

Slim doesn't say a thing. He walks outside to his horse, takes his gun belt out of his saddlebag. He straps his gun on, checks his gun, and walks down the street. People out on the street see him wearin' his gun — they know somethin' is goin' on.

Slim walks to the saloon and stands in the street. He calls the three men out. He thinks it's better to face them now than be dry-gulched by 'em.

Sam jumps up, goes to his horse, and does the same thing Slim did. He straps his gun on. He walks down the street and stands beside Slim just as two of the men come out.

Sam sees the third man standin' inside the saloon behind the swingin' doors. One of the men in the street says, "You killed my brother — I'm gonna kill you."

The two men draw. Slim outdraws them and shoots them down in the street.

At the same time they draw, the man in the saloon standin' behind the swingin' doors is about to shoot Slim. Sam draws at the same time as Slim.

The man falls out through the doors and falls — the swingin' doors still swingin' as he lays on the wooden sidewalk.

Neither Slim nor Sam say a word. They turn and walk to their horses, take their gun belts off, and put 'em into their saddlebags.

Sam gets on his horse.

Slim says, "Thanks, Sam."

Sam just nods his head and rides off.

Slim goes back into the store. A short while later he leaves, slowly walks to his horse. Mountin' his horse, he says, "Let's go home, boy."

SLIM FIGHTS CORRUPTION WITHOUT HIS GUN

Sam stays in his cabin for a couple of days, then he walks to Jake's grave. He stands there a few minutes, then says, "Jake, I had to kill another man, thought you would like to know. I don't like it."

Slim also stays in the house for a couple of days, then he decides to ride up the hill and see how Sam is doing. Sam sees him coming and walks over to where Slim is tying up his horse.

"Sam, how you doing?"

"Okay, Slim. How about you?"

"I doing alright."

"Sam, I was about to have lunch, thought you might like to ride down and join me."

"Slim, that sounds like a good idea."

They ride down the hill together, neither one says a word.

While eating lunch Slim asks, "Sam, does the fear ever leave—that comes just before the calm when I draw?"

"Slim, if it does, hang your gun up and never put it on again. The fear you feel is not of being shot, it's knowin' that you have to shoot someone. The feelin' of killin' someone, takin' a life, is the most unpleasant feelin' I ever have."

"Jake would be glad to hear that. Remember he said, never begin to like killin'."

"Slim, the men we have killed were all killers of innocent people. The only good thing that comes from usin' our guns is that they won't go on killin' again. We saved a lot of lives."

"Sam, I'm goin' to see Randy and see how he's doin' with his store, and make sure things are alright. Will you take care of things in town?"

"I sure will, Slim. Let's head for town."

Slim tells Sally of his plans, kisses her, and tells her he'll spend a few days with Randy.

Slim and Sam ride to town. They go into the store and have coffee with the Old Boys. When it's time for the stage to leave, Slim is on the stage. The ride is hot and the road is bumpy. Finally, the stage makes a stop in a town on the way to Jacksonville. When the stage pulls out, there's a new passenger on board.

"Hello, my name is John, I'm pleased to meet you."

Slim introduces himself and sits quietly.

John asks Slim, "What sort of work do you do? I'm part owner in the Western Feed and General Store."

"Say, that's a big outfit."

"You're just the man I want to talk to. I'm a hat salesman."

Slim says, "When we get to town, talk to Randy at the Jacksonville store. If he likes your product, we'll make an appointment to talk."

"Say, Slim, are you a cowboy?"

"Well, you could say that. I live on and run a ranch."

"I see you don't wear a gun. I thought all cowboys wore guns?"

"I don't wear mine."

"Oh, I see."

When the stage pulls into Jacksonville, there's a commotion goin' on in front of the Western Feed and General Store. Slim looks down the street and sees Randy standin' out front with three other men. He walks down to the store to see what's goin' on. He hears one of the men say, "You have until noontime tomorrow." Then they walk away.

"Randy, what's goin' on?"

"Slim! Where did you come from?"

"I just came in on the stage."

"Slim, that man bought my mortgage from the bank. Now he's demandin' full payment by noon tomorrow or he's gonna foreclose. I understand he's done that with other properties as well."

"Randy, I'm goin' to talk with the bank manager."

Slim walks to the bank and talks to the bank manager. He tells Slim that the man came in and paid off several mortgages.

Slim asks the bank manager, "What's he doin' with the mortgages, demandin' full payment?"

"There is no law against that."

Slim asks, "How much was the mortgage that was paid off on Randy's store?"

"It was three thousand dollars, without any interest due, because it was paid off in advance."

Slim has the bank manager loan him three thousand dollars. He walks up the street askin' people if they've seen the three men. He's told they're in the saloon. He goes into the saloon to see the men— he sees them standin' at the bar. He realizes the two men standin' with the one in a business suit are gunmen.

He walks up to the one in the suit and tells him he's there to pay off Randy's mortgage. He takes out the three thousand dollars and says, "Now give me the contract marked 'Paid in Full.'"

The man objects. Slim tells him he has no choice. One of the gunslingers says, "I don't think you heard the man."

Slim says, "Mind your own business."

The gunman reaches for his gun. Slim pushes his hand away from the gun with one hand and punches the man with his other hand. The man falls down unconscious. As he's fallin', Slim takes his gun from his holster. He points it at the other gunman and says, "Pick up your friend and get outta town."

He then turns to the man in the suit and says, "Now what were we doin'?"

"Here's the contract. I'll mark it paid."

Slim hands him the three thousand dollars and says, "Thank you," then turns and walks out of the saloon.

Slim walks to Randy's store and tells him he paid off the man holdin' the mortgage and makes arrangements for Randy to pay him back—without interest. Slim sends a wire to Sam and has him pay the bank loan in full.

"Randy, these eastern gangsters can't be fought with a gun. I'm goin' to the state capitol and see what can be done."

Slim arrives at the state capitol and makes an appointment with a member of the legislature. He explains the situation about the mortgage deals. The member of the state legislature agrees with Slim and is concerned.

"I'm going to draw up a bill and submit it to the votin' body. The bill will contain laws preventin' the purchase of mortgages and then demandin' full payment. It'll also set standards for a maximum amount of interest that may be charged for loans—governin' banks and individuals loanin' money.

"Slim, it's gonna take a couple of days for me to draw this bill up. When I present it for a vote, I'd like you to appear and tell your story."

"I'd be pleased to."

Slim is notified that the bill is goin' in for a vote. He reports as requested. Followin' the readin' of the bill, Slim tells the story of his experience. He's asked to leave the room while a vote is taken. A short while later, the man that drew up and introduced the bill comes out to see Slim—he's smilin'.

"Slim, we did it and more. A state bank examiner position will be appointed to oversee the bankin' laws."

They shake hands, and Slim returns to Jacksonville and to Randy's store.

"Slim, a hat salesman came in to see me—his name is John. I liked his hats. I told him you'd talk to him when you get back. He's comin' in today."

"Tell him to meet me at the Golden Lady Restaurant at seven tonight. I'm goin' over to the saloon. I think the sheriff is there— I want to tell him what happened at the capitol. He knew I was goin'."

While Slim is talkin' to the Sheriff, there are gunshots heard from outside the saloon. The Sheriff runs out to see what's goin' on. A few minutes later, Slim hears more gunshots. A man comes runnin' into the saloon.

"That easterner is dead! The Sheriff went after the two men that killed him!"

"The Sheriff was wounded!"

"It was the two gunmen you ran outta town, Slim."

Slim says, "Here we go again."

The bartender says, "What did you say?"

"Oh, nothin'," Slim replies, then walks out.

He goes to his room and takes out his gun. He straps it on, checks it to be sure it's loaded, and walks out of the hotel. He walks to the doctor's Office to see how the sheriff is doin'.

"He's gonna be alright," the doctor says. "I wounded one of them."

"Slim, you're wearin' a gun. Do you know how to use it?"

"A little, Sheriff."

Slim walks out and onto the street.

"Doc, I've seen Slim in town a few times in the past—never saw him wearin' a gun."

"Sheriff, haven't you heard of him?"

"All I know is he's got somethin' to do with Randy's store."

"Sheriff, he owns the Western Feed and General Store business. You never heard of two cowboys named Sam and Slim?"

"Well, I'll be… That's Slim the fast gun."

"That's right, Sheriff. He never wears his gun unless he plans to use it. He says every time he puts it on, someone dies. I don't think I'd want to be those two—not if Slim's goin' after 'em."

Slim walks down the side of the street, tryin' to stay under cover—usin' doorways, rain barrels, and anything else he can find. Walkin' along the wooden sidewalk, his foot slips a little. He looks down—it's blood. The sheriff said he wounded one of them. He follows the blood trail to the livery stable. The trail leads inside the barn.

He stops, rememberin' Jake's words: Don't rush into trouble.

He looks around and thinks for a minute. He looks for the livery stable man—he don't see him anywhere. He's worried for his safety. He looks into the barn through a crack in the wall. He sees the livery stable man lyin' on the ground. He knows where he is, so he don't have to worry about him for the time bein'. He wants to check on the man to see if he's alive and needs help. He takes a chance and goes into the barn to the man. He's unconscious—looks like he was hit on the head.

Just then, he hears a noise comin' from one of the empty horse stalls. He very quietly sneaks over to take a look—it's the wounded man. He's not in very good shape. His partner left him there alone to die.

Slim wonders where the other one is. A horse is makin' a sound behind the barn. Slim walks out the back door. He sees the gunman goin' to get on his horse.

"Hold it right there."

The man turns—he's got his gun out. He's about to shoot. Slim fires his gun first. The gunman falls at his horse's feet.

Then he goes in to check on the livery stable man. He has come to and is tryin' to get up. Slim rushes to him and helps him up.

"Did you get him?"

Slim softly says, "Yeah, I got him."

"Come on, I'll take you to the doctor's Office."

"Oh, I'm alright."

"No one gets hit in the head, knocked out, and is alright."

They go to the doctor's Office, and the doctor looks at the man.

"You have a concussion. Go home and stay in bed—I'll be by to see you later on."

"Slim, did you git 'em?"

"Sheriff, you got one. I got the other."

"Dead?"

"Yes, Sheriff, they're both dead."

Slim walks to the hotel, takes his gun belt off, and puts it away in his bag. He then goes to meet the hat salesman.

Slim says, "I don't want a sales pitch—tell me about your hats, the company you work for, and how much a hundred hats will cost wholesale."

"A hundred?"

"Yes, I have a few stores."

The salesman works out the figures and tells Slim the price.

Slim says, "Ship them to our main store. Only include western hat styles—I don't want any of them eastern-style hats."

Slim puts his gun away and fights corruption in the West by visitin' the capitol and gettin' new laws passed—and stronger penalties for crimes committed. He decides this is the best way to fight the bad men of the West—by gettin' legislature passed instead of usin' his gun.

He was often offered government positions and even asked to run for Office. He always declined any offers. He went on fightin' corruption. Every time the eastern gangsters tried to operate one of their schemes in his state, he'd get a law passed that made it illegal—with strict punishment.

He visited the legislating body so often they all knew him by his first name. He became very popular with the people livin' in his state.

Even though he was fightin' corruption in the West without a gun, he knew there'd be times in the future he'd have to strap his gun belt on again.

SLIM MEETS A YOUNG DEPUTY U.S. MARSHAL

Slim continues to fight for the citizens of his state by gettin' legislature passed. He keeps makin' it difficult for the outlaws—more Marshals are appointed, and punishment for crimes is gettin' more fierce. The outlaws are havin' rewards put on their heads, and more bounty hunters are ridin' out lookin' for 'em.

A U.S. Marshal infiltrated an outlaw gang and became one of the gang members to find out what their plans are. The leader of the gang tells his members, "He's gonna put a bounty of five hundred dollars on Slim's head to anyone that kills him."

"Tomorrow we're headed for town to kill him and burn down his store. We'll kill anyone that gets in our way, includin' the Sheriff, and burn the town down if we have to."

That night the young deputy has to make a decision—he decides to sneak outta the outlaws' camp and ride to warn Slim and the town Sheriff.

The next day he rides into town and warns Slim. He tells Slim, "I'm stayin' in town."

"Slim, word is you're fast with your gun. I'd recommend you strap it on—I'm only a few hours ahead of 'em."

Sally tells Slim to put his gun on and stay in the store. Sam puts his on too. The deputy marshal tells Slim, "I'm headin' to the hotel to watch for 'em ridin' into town. When I spot 'em, I'll come to your back door—I don't want 'em to see me."

"What's your name, son?"

"Jim Roberts."

"How old are you?"

"I'm twenty-two years old."

"You're twenty-two and you're a deputy marshal? That's a little young, ain't it?"

"Yes sir, I'm the youngest deputy marshal."

"Well, you better get over to the hotel."

A few hours later there's a knock on the store's back door.

"Slim, I just saw two of the gang members ride into town."

Sam sits on the front porch of the store, watchin' any strangers in town. He sent the old boys walkin' around town keepin' an eye on folks.

Slim had to go outta the store to the bank. While he's in the bank, Sam sees a man head down an alley between stores carryin' a rifle. Sam follows him and watches him climb up on a roof. Sam positions himself so he has a clear view of the man.

When Slim comes outta the bank, he's stopped by two men in the street. They make small talk, then a gunshot is heard—they're confused, 'cause Slim didn't get shot. The man falls from the roof, and Sam walks to the saloon and watches the men inside.

Slim goes to the hotel to let the deputy marshal know what just happened.

"Now there's only five left, Slim. We ain't gettin' outta this without a fight."

"It's two against five—watch the little short guy, he's the fastest with a gun."

"Jim, are you fast with your gun?"

"Yeah, I'm pretty fast."

"Let's go get 'em. They're in the saloon."

Headin' for the saloon, the sheriff joins 'em. After they walk in, Sam comes in—now it's four against five.

Slim says, "I'll take the small guy." When the five outlaws see the Sheriff, they draw their guns and the shootin' starts.

When the smoke clears, the five outlaws lie dead on the floor. The sheriff was slightly wounded.

The next day Jim walks into the store.

"Howdy, Marshal."

"How ya doin', boys?"

"Join us for a coffee."

"Don't mind if I do, thank you."

"Take a seat."

"I came to see if Slim is here."

"No, not yet, he's on the way. Should be here in about a half hour."

"Sam, where did you and Slim learn to draw? I never saw anyone as fast as you two."

"Well, son, that's a long story. The short of it is that a man named Jake taught us. He taught Sally too—she's almost as fast on the draw as Slim and me."

"I don't understand. You're all fast with a gun, and none of you wear a gun."

"The way Slim would answer that is—every time we strap on our guns, somebody dies. We don't like killin'."

"All right if I go look around the display room while I'm waitin' for Slim?"

"Sure, go right ahead."

When Jim comes out of the display room, he says, "No wonder y'all are fast on the draw if Jake taught you."

"My father used to tell me about Jake and his big black horse."

"What was his last name?"

"Nobody knows. When Jake was asked, he'd say, 'Just Jake.'"
Slim walks into the store.

"Good mornin', boys. How 'bout pourin' me a cup of that coffee?"

"Jim, how ya doin' this mornin'?"

"Not too bad, and you?"

"Oh, I'm alright. It'll take a few days to get over yesterday's shootout."

"I know what you mean, Slim. I'm not happy about havin' to shoot someone."

"Slim, I was wonderin' if you have a job around here for me. I don't think I'm cut out to be a Marshal."

"Jim, I got this store and a ranch to run. Some of my men are retirin', I sure could use help both here and on the ranch."

"That would be great, Slim. I was brought up on a ranch."

"When I head for home today, come with me. We'll put you up in the bunkhouse and get you settled in. Tomorrow mornin' you can start work."

"I'll be back when you're ready to leave."

Jim joins Slim on the ride home. When he sees the ranch, he can't believe his eyes.

"Look at the size of this ranch—and those black horses!"

"Look at that stallion, he's a beauty."

"That horse can't be broken. He wants no part of it."

"Slim, watch him move—he's got a strong spirit. He won't do anything if he thinks he's bein' made to. He's gotta be trained so he wants to respond."

"Say, you know a bit about horses?"

"My father trained horses all his life—he taught me."

"See Slim, a horse with a strong spirit ain't a mean horse—he's just very independent."

"Jim, when anyone tries to ride him, he throws 'em, then goes to the man he just threw and nudges him with his nose a couple of times."

"Slim, can I work with him?"

"Sure, as long as you think it's safe."

In the morning, Jim is up early. He brings in the black stallion and notices he's got a white star on his forehead.

"I'm gonna call you White Star. You like that, don't ya?"

Jim always talks in a soft voice and moves slow when he's near the horse. While trainin' the horse, he doesn't try to make the horse do anything he don't want to. Trainin' a horse like this is a slow process.

Jim brings the horse into the corral and turns him loose, then he goes into the barn and comes out with feed. If he feeds the horse in the corral, the horse'll want to go into the corral. Then Jim brings him water. He pats the horse on the neck and rubs the white star on his forehead. Jim does the same thing with the horse for a few mornin's before goin' to town to work in the store.

Slim notices right away that Jim is a hard worker and learns fast. Jim was put to work loadin' and unloadin' wagons in the beginnin'. Each day, he's given additional duties.

In the mornin', Jim is workin' with the horse. At this point, all Jim has to do is whistle, lettin' him know he's in the corral. The horse races in and into the corral. White Star wants to be in the corral in the mornin'. Jim cuts half his feed back, hooks a lunge line onto him, and gets him to walk around, lettin' him stop when he wants to—then gently starts him walkin' again. Jim can tell when the horse has had enough. He stops and gives him the second half of his feed. Jim does the same thing every mornin' for a week. At the end of the week, the horse wants to be worked on the line for a while. When he's had enough, Jim stops and feeds him.

Jim takes the saddle out and puts it in the middle of the corral on the ground while he works the horse on the line. White Star is more interested in the saddle than walkin' around. The horse knows that the saddle had been put on him when he didn't want it, and someone would try to get on his back. Jim lets him go over to the saddle and check it out. Then he works White Star on the line. When he's finished, he feeds him and leaves him in the corral with the saddle.

The next mornin', Jim brushes White Star, then puts the saddle on his back—the horse shakes it off. Jim puts the saddle on him while he feeds him. A few days pass, and the horse lets him put the saddle on. Jim puts the saddle on the horse and tightens the cinch. The horse tries to buck it off. Jim catches the horse, calms him, and gives him an apple. Each time he saddles the horse, he gives him an apple. The horse is slowly bein' conditioned to want to do what Jim wants him to.

Soon the horse'll do anything for Jim because he wants to—not because he's made to. The day comes when Jim attempts to ride him. The horse tries to throw him off—he don't try as hard as he did with others. Each time Jim rides him, the horse bucks less. Then one day, he lets Jim ride him. Jim walks the horse around the corral until the horse understands what Jim wants, then Jim rides him out of the corral.

Jim never broke White Star's spirit—he trained the horse to want to do what Jim wanted. The only thing is, Jim's the only one White Star would let ride him. As time went on, Jim trained the horse to do all sorts of tricks.

Jim trained Sally's colt and many other horses on the ranch. The ranch hands all like and respect Jim, both as a person and a ranch hand—especially for his skill with horses. Jim and the horses seem to understand each other.

Jim is to Slim and Sally the son they never had.

"Sally, someday Jim will inherit all we have."

She agrees with Slim.

A HALF BREED DISCOVERS HIS WHITE SIDE

A covered wagon traveling through Indian country is attacked by a band of renegade Indians. The Indians kill the man and woman in the wagon, then they set the wagon on fire. The horses run away and the wagon tips over; a small child is thrown clear of the burning wagon. She walks, wanderin' around. Silver Feather is an Indian brave from a peaceful tribe out huntin'. He sees the smoke billowin' up off in the distance, rides to the smoke and sees the wagon burnin'. Then he sees the child wanderin' around in a daze—she's holdin' a toy doll. He rides to the child, picks her up, puts her on his horse, and rides to his village. Not knowin' who she was or where she came from, the Indians kept her and raised her.

She grew up to be a beautiful woman. She falls in love with the Chief's son—they're married Indian style. A year later, she gives birth to a boy. The boy is named Sky Hawk. By the time he reaches his eighteenth birthday, he's a great hunter, skilled with his bow and arrow, tomahawk, and knife. His arrows go long and straight. When Sky Hawk was young, he found a gun belt and gun in the things his father left him. He would secretly practice drawin' the gun without ammunition—he became very fast on the draw.

One day, an old white hunter drifts into the Indian village. He becomes friends with Sky Hawk. He stays in the village for a few years. During this time, he teaches the half-breed the ways of the white man. They hunt and fish together every day and become close, like father and son. Sky Hawk's father was killed when he was just a boy—his grandfather, the Chief, taught him the Indian ways. One day, the White Hunter sees him practicin' his draw. He tells Sky Hawk that he has to leave for a few days. When he returns, he brings ammunition for Sky Hawk. Soon, Sky Hawk becomes fast on the draw and accurate with his revolver.

White Hunter—the name given to him by the Indians—and Sky Hawk leave one mornin' to go huntin'. While they're huntin', they hear gunshots off in the distance, soundin' like they're comin' from the village. They get on their horses and gallop to the camp. Ridin' to the village, they see it's been attacked. There are teepees on fire, women yellin' and screamin', and wounded lyin' on the ground. Sky Hawk runs over to the Chief of the village and asks what happened. The Chief tells him that three white men rode in and started shootin' and burnin', then they drove off with the horses. Small Bear runs up to Sky Hawk and tells him his mother's been wounded. He runs to her—she's critically wounded. He holds her in his arms; she tells him not to forget that he is both Indian and white.

She reaches up and touches his cheek. Her hand is soft, then her body goes limp and her hand drops. Sky Hawk holds her in his arms and looks up at the sky for a long while. He lays her down and his blood rages. He gets on his horse, a black and white pinto, and rides until he catches up with the men that attacked the village. He knows these are the men—they're drivin' the small herd of horses they took from the village. He gets off his horse and climbs into the boulders ahead of the men. When they come into view, he lets out an Indian war cry and lets his arrow fly. The arrow strikes one of the men in the chest. When he falls off his horse, the other two men dismount and run for cover. They hide behind some rocks, lookin' up at the boulders, and see an Indian standin' on top of a boulder. The Indian holds his bow up in the air, moves it up and down while he lets out a war cry, then disappears from their view.

The two men stay under cover with their guns ready as they keep lookin' for the Indian. A long time passes—there's no sight of the Indian. Standin', lookin' up at the boulders, they hear a voice behind them.

"You lookin' for me? Don't move. Put your guns in your holsters and turn around."

They see the Indian standin' with his gun in his holster. They go for their guns—Sky Hawk outdraws them. They lie dyin', bleedin' in the sand. Sky Hawk says, "I leave your bodies for my animal brothers. They will feast on you."

Sky Hawk returns to his village. The fires are out, the wounded have been cared for. He drives the horses into the corral and returns to his mother's side. He can hear the mournful Indian song bein' sung for the dead and the drums slowly beatin'.

Sky Hawk walks a short ways from the village, sits on a rock with his legs crossed and his eyes closed, as he mourns the loss of his mother while listenin' to the death song.

White Hunter walks over to Sky Hawk and sits beside him.

"Son, you've learned the ways of the white man. It's time you went among 'em to see what they're like. I think that's what your mother meant with her last words. I'm gonna take you into town."

"I can't go to town lookin' like an Indian."

"No, we'll stop outside of town. You wait while I go in and buy you some clothes. I'll pick up a horse for you too, so no one'll see you ridin' that Indian pony."

They ride for town and find a place for Sky Hawk to hide. White Hunter tells him, "We'll just use your first name—Sky. You'll call me by my real name—it's Clem."

Clem takes out a piece of string. Sky Hawk knows he's about to measure somethin'; he'd shown Sky before how to use a string to take measurements. He asks Clem what he's gonna measure.

Clem tells him, "I gotta have an idea of what size clothes to buy you."

He measures Sky's arm length and ties a knot in the string. Then he measures the length of his leg and ties another knot. He does the same with his foot, then rides for town. Clem buys the clothes, boots, horse, and saddle.

He returns to where Sky's waitin'. Sky dresses in white man's clothes. Clem tells him, "You don't look like an Indian—I never noticed, but you look more like your white mother than your Indian father."

"Well, I am a half-breed."

They put the saddle on the horse, then the bridle and bit. Sky asks, "What are these?" Clem tells him, "They're spurs, Sky. This is a ranch horse—they respond to the spurs."

Sky says, "A horse ain't supposed to be subject to these things. I'll never use these things on my pinto. I tie a piece of rawhide around his nose with two reins tied to it—no bridle, saddle, bit, or spurs."

Clem says, "I know that. But the white man's ways with a horse are different than the Indian ways."

They ride to town. As they ride through, Clem explains what they're seein'. They ride up to the saloon and tie up their horses.

Sky asks Clem, "What's that noise?"

Clem tells him, "That's a piano—someone's playin' white man's music."

They walk into the saloon. Sky stops and looks around—men drinkin' at the bar and sittin' at tables. At one table, men are playin' cards. Then a young girl walks up to Sky.

She says, "Hello, handsome. Want to buy me a drink?"

Sky just looks at her. Clem says, "He don't have time—we just stopped in for a drink."

She says, "Have it your way," and walks off.

They walk up to the bar. Clem orders two beers. When Sky tastes the beer, he makes an awful face.

Clem says, "Don't like it?"

He says, "No—tastes terrible."

While they're standin' at the bar, they hear gunshots from the other end of town. They go out and stand on the wooden sidewalk in front of the saloon. They see two men racin' toward the saloon on their horses. They're shootin' people as they gallop through town. When they reach the saloon, they shoot at Sky.

He draws his gun—in a split second, the two men fly off their horses.

The sheriff walks up to Sky and Clem. He's wounded—a flesh wound on his shoulder.

"That was some shootin', cowboy. I saw you draw. You're fast with that gun. Those two hombres just robbed the bank and killed the teller. Son, come over to my Office. There's a thousand-dollar reward on each of 'em. You just made yourself two thousand dollars and saved the bank a lot more than that."

After the sheriff walks away, Clem explains the reward money to Sky. They follow the Sheriff to his Office. Sky collects the reward.

While they're in the Sheriff's Office, they see a wanted poster on the wall. It reads:

"WANTED – $500 REWARD FOR SELLING LIQUOR TO THE INDIANS."

Sky says, "This man sells whiskey to the renegade Indians."

"Yup," says Clem. "Then the Indians get drunk—then raid white men."

Clem asks the sheriff if he knows anything about him.

The sheriff says, "All we know is that he drives a team of horses— one horse is brown, the other's black. Nobody wants to go after him—he's got those renegades protectin' him."

"Well, we'll be seein' you, Sheriff."

"Okay, I'll see you around town."

"Clem, we need a place to live."

"I know just the spot. When I was a kid, I was chasin' a deer. The deer disappeared into a huge pile of boulders. When I looked for him, I found a hidden passageway through the rocks. The passage opened up into a small canyon surrounded by a big pile of boulders. Inside the canyon, there's a small waterfall and a stream runnin' through."

They ride to the canyon. Clem says, "This is a perfect place to live and hide out. We need a house and a barn."

Clem goes to town, rents a wagon and a team of horses, and buys lumber. He makes a few trips to town for supplies. They build a cabin and a barn for the horses.

Sky tells Clem, "Take the wagon to town and pick up supplies and horse feed."

Clem goes to town, buys the supplies. Returnin' to their canyon, he sees a wagon pulled up under some trees. One horse is black, the other brown. When he gets to the canyon, he tells Sky.

Sky says, "It's time for Sky Hawk to ride."

He goes into the house and comes out dressed like an Indian. He rides out on his pinto, heads to where Clem saw the wagon. He rides up to the wagon. The whiskey salesman sees him.

"Want some whiskey, Injun?"

"No. Come to destroy whiskey. You sell no more to Indians. I burn wagon."

The man picks up his rifle. "You crazy Indian—I'll kill you."

Sky Hawk draws and shoots the man.

Sky Hawk rides back to the cabin and changes into white man's clothes. Then he takes the wagon full of whiskey—and the dead man—into town, to the Sheriff's Office. He collects the reward and rides out of town.

He rides into the canyon and puts his horse up.

"Clem, I picked up these posters of men that are wanted for murder. When we need money, I'll hunt down one of these men for the reward."

While Sky Hawk is visitin' the village, he hears about a small band of Indians attackin' ranches. He rides out and hunts for the murderin' Indians. He finds them camped out—there are too many for him to attack, so he watches 'em until some of 'em leave. Three leave the camp. He follows them—they go down to the river. He appears in front of them and tells 'em, "It's time to die."

He shoots one with an arrow, throws his tomahawk and kills the second one. The last one attacks Sky Hawk with his knife—but he's no match for Sky Hawk, who's an expert with a blade. He leaves the three dead Indians and goes back to the camp.

There are three more Indians sittin' around the campfire. Sky Hawk walks out into the light of the fire.

He says, "You die tonight."

The Indians go for their rifles—Sky Hawk draws and fires three shots. He puts his gun back in his holster.

"I don't like Indians that kill white men, women, and children," he says.

He returns to his cabin.

As time went on, his reputation as an Indian protectin' white men— and the Indians against killers, red or white—spread around the territory. However, no one knew who he was as an Indian except the members of his village. His reputation as a white man, bein' a bounty hunter and only goin' after murderers, also spread across the territory. Two reputations. Two different men. All one man—a half-breed.

There was a man ridin' through the territory killin' Indians and white folks. He was a ruthless outlaw. He robbed banks and stagecoaches. He was wanted all over the territory. He killed one sheriff durin' a bank robbery and shot a woman holdin' up a stagecoach.

Sky Hawk, dressed as an Indian, went after him. He finally picked up his trail. The killer, knowin' someone was followin' him, figured that if he got on a stagecoach and tied his horse behind it, his tracks would be mixed in with the other horses. He stopped a stage, tied his horse behind, tossed his saddle on top of the stage, and got in.

Sky could read the tracks where the stage stopped and the outlaw got on. He rides around and up in front of the stage. He climbs into a tree and hides. When the stage goes under the tree, Sky Hawk silently drops onto the roof. He unties the outlaw's horse, and grabbin' the rails on the top of the stage, he swings into the window feet first, kickin' the outlaw with both feet. Inside the stage, Sky

Hawk opens the door, throws the man out, then jumps out himself. The driver and the shotgun rider never knew it happened.

Sky Hawk runs to the man and finds him dead—his neck's broken. Sky Hawk had carried his white man's clothes with him. He changes into 'em from the bag he'd been carryin'. He catches the outlaw's horse and rides his own, with the outlaw's body tied to the horse behind him. He didn't want anyone seein' him ridin' his pinto.

He takes the outlaw's body to town and collects the reward.

Jim, tellin' the story, says:

"I knew Sky Hawk personally. He met a woman, got married, and had two children. He was no longer two people—he lived with his family as a white man. A few years ago, I contacted him. He's down the hill, livin' in the ranch house with his family. He's my ranch foreman—and the next one to own the JJ Ranch."

JAKE MEETS A REAL STRANGE CHARACTER

"Sam, when ya gonna tell us the story about Apache Rose?"

"Ah, I'll get around to it one of these days."

"We sure wanna hear that story."

Sam tells the old boys that he would eventually tell them the story. "First, I have a story about Jake meetin' a strange character."

Jake was ridin' towards the town of Little River when he spots someone further up the trail. He sees a man standin' by a broken wagon — there ain't no horses in sight. When Jake rides up to the man, he don't look at him. He stands there lookin' off and talkin'.

"Sky blue, horse black, wagon broke… sky blue… can't go… must stay… sky blue… horse black… must stay… no Indians. Nope, no Indians."

Jake says, "Are you alright? Can I help you?"

The man keeps lookin' away, sayin', "Sky blue… no Indians."

Jake asks if he wants a ride into town.

"Can't go, wagon broke."

Jake leaves the man and rides into town. He rides up to the Sheriff's Office. Gettin' off Big Black, he walks into the Office.

"Sheriff, I met a man on the way into town standin' by an old broken-down wagon—"

The sheriff cuts him off.

"That was Crazy Joe. He's out there by that broken wagon every day. He comes into town once in a while to buy food. He walks into the store, looks at the wall and says, 'Joe likes beans, Joe likes bacon, sky blue, Joe likes coffee.' The storekeeper knows that's how Joe places his order. Joe'll get his stuff, put money on a barrel, and say, 'Sky blue, wagon broke, can't go.' He always walks out into the middle of the street, stops, looks at the saloon, and says, 'No, don't drink, sky blue, no Indians.' Then he disappears outta town. Some of the boys followed him one day. Must've known he was bein' followed 'cause he just kept walkin' 'round and 'round in a big circle. Finally, the men gave up and came back to town sayin' he's as crazy as a loon."

Jake leaves the Sheriff's Office, walks down the dusty street leadin' Big Black to the hotel. He gets a room, washes off the trail dust, and puts on his buckskins. He takes Big Black to the livery stable, then walks up the street to the saloon.

As usual, there's a wise guy in the saloon.

"Well, lookie here, a cowboy all dressed in buckskins."

Jake thinks, Oh no, there's always one.

The man says, "Hey cowboy, how come you wear buckskins? Are you an Indian or somethin'?"

Jake don't say a word. He walks up to the bar and orders a beer.

"Hey buckskins, I'm talkin' to ya!"

Jake walks over to the man and says, "I'm tired of punks like you in every saloon."

"What are you gonna do about it?"

Jake sees the man put his hand on his gun. Jake draws fast and hits the man over the head with his gun, knockin' him out. Everyone gets quiet. Jake turns to the bar and drinks his beer. He turns without sayin' a word and walks out of the saloon.

The men in the saloon are talkin'. They can't believe how fast Jake drew his gun when the man reached for his.

When the man wakes up, the fellas help him up and tell him he's lucky to be alive. He says, "He was fast as a rattler, I didn't even see what happened."

Jake spots Crazy Joe leavin' town. He decides to follow him. Joe knows Jake's followin' him, so he starts walkin' in a big circle. Jake stops followin' and hides. He keeps Joe in sight 'til he goes through an openin' in the rocks. Jake follows him. Joe leads him deep into the big rocks to the place where he lives. He's got a shelter that protects him from the sun and the rain.

Jake stays outta sight watchin' him. Joe lays down in his shelter and falls asleep. Jake quietly goes up to Joe and looks around. He can tell Joe's been livin' there for some time.

Jake goes back to his horse, takes a blanket from his saddlebag, and returns to Joe's camp. He waits for Joe to wake up. Joe's scared. He trembles at the sight of Jake. Jake holds out the blanket. Eventually, Joe takes it and jumps back, away from Jake. Jake tells him he's a friend and not to be scared. Joe calms down and sits, holdin' the blanket, rockin' back and forth. It seems like he no longer knows Jake is there. Jake leaves.

Jake visits Joe every day for a week. Each time, he brings him somethin'. Joe lets Jake enter his camp and sit with him. Each time, Joe keeps repeatin', "Sky's blue, wagon broke, can't go."

Jake reaches out to touch Joe. He says, "It's alright… it's alright, Joe."

Joe looks at Jake and says, "Who are you?"

Jake says, "My name's Jake. I'm a friend."

"A friend…" Then he goes right back to sayin', "Sky blue, wagon broke, can't go."

Jake thinks he's makin' progress with Joe. He leaves. This time, Joe says, "Goodbye."

Jake smiles and says, "Goodbye, Joe."

The next day Jake visits Joe. Much to his surprise, Joe recognizes him.

"Hello, Jake. The sky blue, wagon broke, can't go."

"Jake, I brought some food for you."

Joe just sits, lookin' off into space.

"Look Joe, I brought you some candy."

Joe says, "No candy. Boy dead." He then looks away and repeats, "Sky blue, wagon broke, can't go."

"Jake: What are you talkin' about? What boy?"

"Boy dead."

"Yes Joe, I know. What boy?"

"My son."

"Joe, ya had a son? What happened to him?"

Joe says, "Blue sky, wagon broke, can't go."

"Joe, did somethin' happen to your wagon?"

"Blue sky… wagon broke… can't go."

"Joe, the sky is blue. What happened? Did your wagon break?"

"Wagon break… boy dead."

Jake figures that's enough for today. He could hear the tremblin' in Joe's voice.

Jake stops in to see the Sheriff. He tells him about Joe and the little progress he's makin'.

"Well I'll be… nobody ever took the time with him like you. Everyone thinks he's completely crazy. Even when he comes into town, folks stay away from him. The women take their children inside 'til he leaves. What are you gonna do next, Jake?"

"I think I'll just keep visitin' and talkin' to him."

"You headed out to see Joe today?"

"Yes, after lunch."

"I'd like to go with ya, Jake."

"Sheriff, I don't think that's a good idea. He ain't ready to see other people yet — for that matter, he may never be."

"Well, Jake, I'll have another cup of your coffee and have lunch. Join me?"

"Sure thing."

Followin' lunch, Jake heads out to see Joe.

Jake visits Joe each day. Another week passes. Joe knows Jake and waits for his visit. Jake decides to question him more—seems the more Joe talks, the better he gits.

"Joe, tell me about the blue sky."

"Jake, the sky blue."

"Yes Joe, tell me about the blue sky."

"My wife said the sky is blue, then it happened."

"What happened, Joe?"

"She's dead. My wife, my boy—dead."

"Joe, this happened when your wife said the sky is blue?"

"Yes. Wife and boy dead because of blue sky."

"Joe, did your wagon break?"

"Wagon broke, couldn't get help. Boy dead, wife dying—both dead."

"Joe, tell me what happened."

"We were in a wagon. My wife said, 'Look how blue the sky is,' then there were gunshots behind us. Some men from town were drunk, riddin' out on the trail shootin' their guns. The team ran away. Before I could get control, the wheel hit a rock and the wagon flipped over. It landed on my son—he was dead. My wife was hurt very bad. The wagon was all broken up. The horses ran away. I couldn't take her for help, I couldn't go. I stayed with my wife. She died in my arms."

Joe begins to cry. Jake lets him cry; he thinks it will help. When he stops crying, Jake gives him a drink of water. Joe falls asleep. Jake leaves for town.

The next day, Jake visits the Sheriff.

"Sheriff, I'm gonna bring Joe inta town today. In a couple of hours, head out—we'll meet you on the trail. I want to see how he'll be with another person."

The Sheriff agrees. Jake picks up another horse and some clothes, then heads for Joe's camp.

When Jake reaches Joe's camp, he's not there. Jake looks around, then sees smoke. He rides to see what is burnin'. Jake stops Big Black and looks—down the trail, Joe is standing by the broken-down wagon where Jake and Joe first met. Jake rides up to Joe.

"Joe, what are ya doin'?"

"This old wagon reminds me of my wagon, so I burnt it."

Jake says, "I understand, Joe. Joe, I have a surprise for you. I'm taking you to town today."

"Let's go over to the river and take a bath. After that, ya can shave. Look, Joe—I brought you some new clothes." Joe bathes, shaves, and puts on his new clothes, then they head out for town.

"Look ahead, Joe—a rider comin' this away." Jake and Joe meet the sheriff on the trail.

The Sheriff says, "How ya doin', Joe?"

"My name ain't Joe—it's Randy Stark."

The Sheriff says, "Randy Stark! The sheriff from the town of Double Pass?"

"I was."

"We thought you were dead after they found your wagon and the graves. We figured you wandered off and died."

Jake is surprised—as is the Sheriff.

"Joe—I mean Randy—no one in town will recognize you as Joe, so you ride into town as Randy Stark."

Riddin' inta town, Randy stops in front of the saloon. He thinks about the drunken men that spooked his team of horses, then he rides on with Jake and the sheriff to the Sheriff's Office. They dismount and walk inside.

The Sheriff says, "Sit down, we'll have a cup of coffee. Randy, you're gonna have to do somethin' with yourself. My deputy is quittin'; he's gettin' married and is gonna start workin' at the bank. You're a lawman—how about bein' my deputy?"

"I'd like that just fine. Guess I'll have to buy a gun."

Jake says he'll work with him on his draw. Jake teaches Randy to draw his gun—he becomes very fast.

One day Jake says he's amovin' on. He gets on Big Black, says goodbye to the Sheriff and Randy. Then he says,

"Randy, don't make it happen—let it happen."

He turns Big Black and slowly rides out of town.

The time Jake spent with Joe—and Joe tellin' his story—snapped him back to normal. Burnin' the wagon put it all behind him. He remembered who he was. Following the retirement of the Sheriff, Randy Stark became the sheriff of the town named Little River.

JOHNNY VISITS JAKE

"Hay Sam, it's time to close up the store. Let's walk over to the saloon for a beer."

The saloon doors open and the old boys walk in. Everyone greets them. They walk up to the bar. One of the old men jokingly says,

"Ya bunch of scoundrels, move over — make room for the good old boys."

One man says, "Boys, y'all are older than dirt!" They all have a good laugh. They order beer and then go sit at a table.

While they're sittin' at the table, a man named Jed walks over and sits down with them.

"Howdy Jed."

"Hello boys, mind if I sit a spell?"

Sam says, "Pull up a seat and rest those old bones."

"Say Sam, remember Johnny? The boy that got shot and couldn't walk? Jake, Bob, and Curly got him ta walken agin."

"I sure do remember that boy."

"The last time I heard about Johnny, he was about fifteen years old, a-ridden Big Black Jr. to Jake's ranch. When he was a-getten close ta the ranch, a cowboy rode out from behind the rocks and up to Johnny — he had his gun out. He said, 'Get off that horse, I'm takin' him.'

Johnny was wearin' his gun. When the man reached for Big Black Jr.'s reins, Big Black bolted. The man took his eyes off Johnny for a

"

second. Johnny drew his gun and shot the man in the shoulder — he fell to the ground unconscious.

Johnny ran to the man — he was bleedin' quite a bit. Johnny tried to lift the man and put him on his horse, but the man was too heavy. Johnny takes his shirt off, rolls it up, puts it on the wound, and presses. The bleedin' slows down. Johnny thinks that he'd betta git the cowboy help or he'll die. If he leaves him with no pressure on the man's shoulder, he'll bleed to death.

Johnny gets an idea. He takes a heavy stone and places it on the man's shoulder, applyin' pressure to the shirt rolled on the wound. The flow of blood slows down.

Knowin' time is important, Johnny mounts Big Black Jr. and races as fast as Big Black Jr. could run to Jake's ranch. Bob and Curly sees Johnny comin' — they know somethin's wrong seein' him ridden his horse so fast. Curly runs to meet Johnny. Bob runs inside to get Jake. Johnny tells them what happened.

Jake says to Bob, "Get Johnny another horse. Ride out with him, see what you can do. Curly, get a wagon hitched up and head out to help Johnny and Bob." Jake sits on the porch waitin' for them to get back.

When Bob and Johnny get to the wounded man, they give him some water, apply pressure to the wound, and wait for Curly and the wagon. When Curly gits there, they place the man in the wagon and head for the ranch.

When they arrive, Jake tells them to put the wounded man in the bunkhouse to bed. Curly removes the bullet from the man's shoulder — he passes out.

Later in the day, Jake goes to the bunkhouse ta see how the man is doin'. Johnny is in the barn brushin' down Big Black Jr. Jake walks up to the bunk.

The man says to Jake,

"Who is that kid? He is some fast on the draw. He shoots straight too."

"He's a boy I taught how to use a gun."

"Ya taught him? Who are you?"

"Jake. Just Jake."

Jake calls Johnny, Bob, and Curly into the bunkhouse.

"Do you know who this hombre is?"

"No Jake, we never saw him before."

"He calls himself Laredo. He's a wanted outlaw — there's a price on his head. Johnny, you will collect a large reward for his capture."

Johnny says, "Wow!"

"What did the kid do after that?"

"He used the reward money to go to school back East to be a doctor. Afta shootin' Laredo, he hung up his gun. He didn't want to hurt people — he wanted to be a doctor and help people."

JAKE RIDES TO MEXICO

"Hay Sam, I was over ta the saloon and there was an old cowboy talkin' about Jake travelin' to Mexico after some bandits."

"You never told us that story."

"Let's sit a spell with a cup of coffee. I'll tell ya boys about the time Jake chased a bunch of banditos across the border into Mexico."

Jake and the townsmen were in the saloon havin' a cold beer. It was a hot summer day in Laredo, Texas, when the stage came racin' into town. The driver was a-shoutin', "We were held up a few miles outta town! Those dirty sidewinders took a young woman right outta the coach and rode off with her!"

Hearin' the commotion outside, the men run to see what's goin' on. Jake walks out behind 'em over to the coach where the sheriff is standin'. The stage driver is tellin' the sheriff what happened. Jake listens before he says anything.

"Sheriff, after they took the strongbox, they looked inside the coach and saw the young woman. The leader excitedly says, 'Ah chihuahua, a señorita! She is very beautiful, she will make us mucho pesos.' Then they took her and rode off."

"Sheriff, get a posse together. I'm headed out to see if I can pick up their trail. Meet up where they held up the stage."

"Okay, Jake."

Jake goes to the livery stable, saddles up Big Black, and rides out.

The posse catches up with Jake. He tells the Sheriff, "The trail's easy to follow. They're ridin' hard—they'll have to slow down to rest their horses soon."

"Jake, I'm worried about the girl. No tellin' what those Mexican bandits'll do to her."

"Sheriff, they said she would bring a lotta money. Sounds like they plan to sell her."

"They can't sell damaged goods."

"I see what ya mean. At least she has that much in her favor."

"I'm still worried. No tellin' what those Mexicans'll do when they get all drunkened up."

Thinkin' they're safe, the bandits stop to rest and eat. One of 'em starts drinkin' tequila, a few of the others join him. Eventually they're all drunk, lyin' around sleepin'. One of the bandits wakes up—he's starin' at the girl. Gettin' up, he heads in her direction. When he gets close, she yells, "Go away!"

The leader wakes up and tells the bandit to leave her alone. He's so drunk he argues with the leader.

The leader says, "You dare to talk to me like that?" He draws his gun and shoots the bandit.

The sound of the gunshot wakes 'em all up.

The leader says, "Anyone else have any ideas about this girl, you'll end up just like him. Get on your horses, we're ridin'."

"Say, Jake, ya think we better rest awhile?"

"Good idea, Sheriff. Let's stop here."

They rest awhile, then head out after the bandits. They ride at a steady pace the rest of the day and into the evenin'. The sky glows orange and red as the sun is settin'.

"Sheriff, let's camp out here."

"Good idea, Jake. Set up camp, boys. One of you set up a picket line for the horses. The rest of you get a fire goin'. I sure could use some viddles."

Finishing up their beans, Jake and the Sheriff sit around the fire drinkin' coffee as the darkness of night rolls in.

"I don't know if we can catch up to the bandits before they reach the border."

"Well, we'll ride hard early in the mornin'. We'll leave before sun-up."

The posse rides for two days, reachin' the border.

"Jake, they've crossed the border. Our jurisdiction ends here."

Jake takes his deputy marshal's badge and hands it to the Sheriff.

"Officially, this badge has no jurisdiction in Mexico. But my gun ain't got any restrictions on it. Sheriff, I'm headed out after that girl. I'll be bringin' her back."

Jake crosses the Rio Grande River and rides into Nuevo Laredo, Mexico. He stops in the Mexican village to rest his horse and get somethin' to eat. Jake enters a cantina, slowly looks around, then sits down at a table.

Outside the cantina, word has already spread around that a Gringo just rode into town. The Mexicans didn't like Gringos—people were gatherin' out in the streets. One Mexican named Gonzales says, "I hate Gringos. What does he want? I'm goin' into the cantina and see what this dog of a Gringo wants."

Hey Gringo, looks like you are far from home. What are you doin' here in my fine ciudad?

Jake says, "Just passin' through. You're right, this is a fine city."

"What's your name, Gringo?"

"Jake."

"What's your other name?"

"Just Jake."

"Just Jake, el perro of a Gringo."

Jake sits quietly, not sayin' a word after bein' called a dog. He no longer speaks, just quietly lookin' straight ahead. He knows this Mexican is lookin' for a fight.

"What's a matter, Gringo? Lost your tongue? Hey, I'm talkin' to you!"

Jake slowly gets up, adjusts his gun so the Mexican sees it—and how he wears it. He stares directly into the Mexican's eye and slowly shakes his head no, then slowly walks out. The Mexican is humiliated in front of his friends, left standin' alone.

Jake finds a place to take a bath. He's been wearin' his travelin' clothes. After his bath and shave, he puts on his buckskins. He looks totally different after cleanin' up and wearin' his buckskins.

He returns to the Cantina to get somethin' to eat. When he walks in, everyone looks up and the place grows quiet. The Mexicans don't know what to think seein' Jake standin' tall in his buckskins. They see how he wears his gun—they begin to whisper.

Gonzalez is still in the Cantina, standin' at the bar drinkin' tequila. He is drunk. When he sees Jake, he says,

"Are you that fast gun from over the border?"

"You don't look so fast."

"I am fast enough. But right now, I'm hungry and want somethin' to eat."

He sits down and ignores the Mexican and eats his dinner. Jake quietly asks the waitress if the bandits with a girl passed through town. She tells him they passed through two days ago. He thanks her and gets up to leave.

"Hey Gringo, where you goin'? You made a fool outta Gonzalez" (referrin' to himself). "I can't let you get away now!"

Movin' away from the bar, he prepares to draw on Jake.

Jake says, "Don't do it." He draws his gun and puts it back in his holster so fast Gonzalez didn't have a chance to draw.

"Wow, you are fast, Señor. I make a big mistake. Why are you here in México?"

"I'm lookin' for a gang of bandidos that kidnapped a woman off a stage."

"What is this word kidnapped mean?"

"It means they took— they stole the girl."

"Oh Señor, they may be goin' to sell her. Many rich men buy young girls."

"Gonzalez, where do these men buy the girls?"

"Mexico City."

"Thank you, Gonzalez. I'm headed to Mexico City. Adios, amigo."

"Adios, Gonzalez."

Jake heads out for Mexico City. After ridin' a few days, he reaches the Sierra Madre range. Jake, ridin' Big Black, travels between 50 and 100 miles each day. Soon, he is out of the mountains.

Jake rides all day and into the night, day after day. One mornin', Jake spots a young Indian boy racin' his horse near the desert. The horse falls, and the Indian boy is injured. Jake gallops Big Black to where the boy is lyin', not movin'. Gettin' off his horse, Jake notices the boy is a Mescalero Apache. Jake gives the boy some water. He comes to.

Jake doesn't speak the Mescalero dialect. Usin' sign language, he finds out the boy's name is Odle Paw, meanin' Buffalo Bird. The boy passes out again. Jake knows he has to get the boy to the Indian camp or he'll die.

Takin' his rifle from his saddle, he fires three shots into the air. He knows the Indians will hear the gunshots and come to investigate.

Soon, the Indians appear and surround Jake with their weapons pointed at him. Jake makes the sign of peace. Two Indians are already attendin' the boy.

One Indian speaks a little Spanish and tells Jake the boy is the son of Chief Santana. He then motions for Jake to get on his horse.

The Indians lead Jake to their camp. The Chief comes out to greet them. He tells the Indians to take his boy into the wickiup.

Santana thanks Jake by sayin', "Ahehe'e." He then says, "ash," meanin' friend. Santana raises his hand and says, "tian nide," meanin' buckskin man. He then gestures toward Jake's horse.

Jake nods, mounts Big Black, and rides out.

Jake rides for days and through another mountain range. On the other side of the mountains lies Mexico City.

Jake stops Big Black, lookin' at the city, thinkin', "This city dates all the way back to the Aztec Indians."

He rides into Mexico City, inhabited by wealthy people from Spain and local Mexicanos.

Jake rides up to a canteen, dismounts, ties up Big Black, and walks inside. All eyes are upon him.

He asks for a glass of water and sits down. He sits watchin' a boy sweepin' the floor. He asks if anyone saw banditos bringin' a young American girl into the city.

No one knows anything.

Jake has some food and then walks outside. When he goes to git on his horse, he feels a tug on his clothes. It's the boy that was sweepin' the floor.

"Señor, do you have money? I know what you ask."

Jake says, "What can you tell me?"

"How much money yah have?"

"I have a few American dollars."

"If you give me some, I tell you about girl."

"Here is a few dollars. What do you know about the girl?"

"She was sold to Señor Dlonso. For a few more dollars, I can show you where his hacienda is."

"What about the bandits that brought her to Mexico?"

"I know who they are."

"Who are they?"

The boy stands silent.

"Okay, here is a few more dollars."

"They have a shack outside of the city. I can show where."

Jake mounts Big Black and puts the boy up behind him. They ride to the shack.

"Hey kid, what's your name?"

"Carlos."

"How do you know so much, Carlos?"

"I listen in the cantina, I watch in the street, and I ask questions."

"Señor, the cabin is just ahead, behind the trees."

"Okay Carlos, we'll walk from here."

They walk through the trees and underbrush until they spot the shack. Jake slowly moves closer, thinkin' about what he's gonna do. The bandits must be inside—their horses are tied in front of the cabin. He thinks if he can get to their horses and turn 'em loose, the bandits wouldn't have any way of escape.

Jake tells Carlos to stay where he is. Then he works his way under cover to the horses. He quietly unties the horses and leads 'em away out of sight.

Returnin' to cover where he can see the front door, he gently tosses a small rock against the cabin to get them to come outta the cabin into the open. When they hear the noise, one of the bandits opens the door and looks out.

He yells, "The horses are gone!"

Three men come a-runnin' out of the cabin.

"How did the horses get loose?"

Just then Jake steps out and says, "I let 'em loose."

The Mexicans draw their guns—Jake outdraws them and shoots two of 'em. The third drops his gun.

"Don't shoot, Señor! I give up!"

The two Mexicans lay dead in the dirt. Jake takes the third man into the cabin.

"Where's the money you stole from the stage back in Texas?"

"What money? There's no money!"

Jake draws his gun, points it right in the Mexican's face.

"Ya wanna die like the men outside? If you don't tell me where the money is, I'll shoot you right here."

"No, no, Señor! Don't shoot! I'll tell you! It's right here."

He takes the bag of money out from under the floorboards.

Jake tells the Mexican to get out and run. There was no sense bringin' him in to the Federalizes—they would do nothin'. Besides, Jake didn't want too many people to know about him and what he was doin', especially now he was carryin' all the money.

"Sam, what about the kidnapped girl?"

"I need a cup of coffee and a chew of tobaccy before I continue."

"Sam, it's darn near eatin' time—you better tell us the rest of the story. We wanna hear about the girl."

"Well, sit back boys." He spits his chew tobaccy and begins finishin' his story.

Jake rides back to the city with Carlos. Carlos is ridin' one of the bandits' horses. When they get to the city, Jake asks Carlos where Dlonso's hacienda is located. Carlos tells Jake how to get there. Jake gives the three horses that belonged to the bandits to Carlos.

"Mucha gracias, Señor Jake."

They say goodbye, then Jake heads for Dlonso's hacienda.

The hacienda is a large estate with walls all around. As always, Jake takes his time thinkin'. He then rides up to the front gate. A Mexican opens the gate. Jake rides into the plaza. There are many peons, men and women workin'. They all look at Jake sittin' on that big black horse wearin' his buckskins. His black hat, boots, and especially his gun belt show brightly against his tan buckskins. All the peons stop workin' and look at Jake. One runs into the house, another walks up to Jake.

"¿Cómo puedo servirle, Señor?" (How can I serve you?)

Jake says, "¿Me traes agua, por favor?" (will you bring me water please?)

"Sí, sí, Señor."

The peon brings Jake some water. He gives Big Black a drink, then he takes a drink. Jake looks around slowly, then he sees a man standin' with a young woman on the porch of the house, lookin' at him. The girl is an American, dressed in a beautiful Spanish gown. The man is dressed in a black Spanish suit with white decorations. He motions Jake to ride closer.

Jake leads Big Black up to the hitchin' rail in front of the porch, thinkin' the young woman is the one he's lookin' for. If I speak to her alone, I can find out what's goin' on.

The man on the porch introduces himself.

"I am Dlonso. This is my hacienda. You are welcome, Señor. Please come in."

Jake thinks, The Mexican speaks good English.

"Thank you, Señor."

Walkin' in, Jake introduces himself as Jake.

"You are a long way from your home, Jake."

"Yes, I'm visitin' your great city today. I'm ridin' around lookin' at your beautiful country. When I saw this great hacienda, it was so hot I thought I could get water here."

"You are most welcome, Señor Jake. Come in and sit. You must stay for dinner."

Jake thinks he is too hospitable—this puts him on his guard.

"Señor, my servidora (female servant) will show you where to clean up."

Returnin' to the great hall, Jake is offered wine and a cigar. Dlonso offers to show Jake around outside while awaitin' dinner. Jake accepts the offer.

"Ah, Señor! I had one of my workers water and feed your horse. He is brushin' him down now."

"Muchas gracias."

Followin' their walk around, Jake notices certain areas he was not shown. This arises suspicion.

Returnin' to the porch, they sit makin' small talk. The dinner bell chimes—they all sit down at a large table. Wine is served, and then dinner. Jake notices the young woman hardly speaks, even when he addresses her.

Followin' dinner, Dlonso is called outside—there is some kind of commotion.

Jake and the young woman are not left alone—an old woman stays by her side. The girl says she doesn't speak English. She gets up to get more wine for Jake, and he joins her.

"What is your name?"

"Janet."

"Were you taken off the stage in Texas?"

"Yes."

"Are you a prisoner here?"

"Yes."

"Want to go home?"

"Yes."

"I'll get you outta here."

Just then Dlonso reappears.

"Have you two been gettin' along?"

Jake says, "A little. She doesn't say very much."

"Sí, she talks very little."

As the evenin turned to darkness, Jake decides to take action. When Dlonso was showin' Jake around the estate, he looked around very carefully. One thing he noticed—it would be easy to git to the roof from the second story windows.

When Jake was shown to his room, he asked the servant where Dlonso and Janette's rooms were. The servant said, on the other side of the house—they have separate rooms.

Jake opens his window and climbs to the rooftop. He crosses the roof to the other side of the house. Lowerin' himself down, he looks into the rooms. Findin' Janet's, he enters through the window.

"Oh Jake, it's you!"

"I've got to get you outta here. I'm surprised you have individual rooms."

"Dlonso has strange ideas—thank goodness. He believes the women of the hacienda must be pure. He never touched me. Some of the other girls weren't so lucky."

"What other girls?"

"Outside in that small building, he has two or three girls waitin' ta be sent to Spain."

"He sells them to men in Spain?"

"Like slaves."

"Yes Jake, he makes a lot of money. The women are all beautiful."

"How many men does he have guardin' them?"

"There are three Mexicans—all professional gunmen. They're killers."

"So Janet, this Dlonso ain't such a good character."

"No, Jake! He also has other illegal things goin' on."

"Janet, this changes everythin'. Which room is Dlonso's?"

She opens the door and points it out.

"Wait here till I come back to get ya. Change into some ridin' clothes."

Jake enters Dlonso's room. He wakes him up, ties and gags him, leavin' him on his bed. He then goes outside to free the other girls.

There's one guard at the door.

Jake says, "Drop that gun."

The Mexican turns to fire. Jake shoots him, wakin' up the other two gunmen. They come outside a-shootin'—Jake shoots them both.

Janet is comin' out the front door and runs to Jake.

"Are you all right?"

"Yes, I'm fine. Let's git outta here. Janet, get those girls out. I'll get a carriage."

By the time the girls change outta their dressin' gowns and come outside, Jake has the carriage ready. They ride to Mexico City.

In the mornin', they tell the Federalizes what's goin' on at the Dlonso Hacienda and about the auction where girls are sold as slaves. The Federalizes raid the hacienda, arrestin' Dlonso. They discover others involved and arrest them too.

"Janet, you have to buy some trail clothes. We have a hard trip ahead of us. I'll trade this carriage and horse for a good trail horse and a mule, then pick up supplies."

Jake realizes it'd be different travelin' with a woman.

"Okay, Jake. I won't be long."

Meetin' Jake outside, she says, "How's this?"

Jake says, "Ya look better in those clothes and with your hair down than you did back at the hacienda."

Smilin', she says, "Why thank you, Jake."

"Let's head for Texas, Janet."

"I can't wait ta git there, Jake."

They traveled for a few months through mountains and desert. Approached by Indians, they recognized Jake as the one who saved the Chief's son. The Indians escort them until they were outta Indian country.

One day Jake says, "There it is—the Rio Grady—and over there is Texas."

They ride until they reach the first stage depot, catchin' the stage to the town of Laredo.

When the stage pulls into town, one of the men recognizes Big Black tied to the back of the stage.

He yells, "It's Jake's horse!"

The townspeople run to the stage. They cheer when Jake and the young woman step down off the stage. They're all congratulatin' Jake, shakin' his hand, pattin' his back.

Janet says to Jake, "Wonder how they'd react if they knew the whole story."

The Sheriff comes up and hugs Jake.

"Thought you were dead."

Laughin', Jake says, "Not yet, Sheriff."

"This must be the girl."

"Yes Sheriff, this is Janet."

"Did you get the bandits, Jake?"

"Yes Sheriff, I also got the money back. It's in the back of the stage."

A few days pass. Jake and Janet have dinner at the hotel together.

"Jake, I'm leavin' tomorrow mornin' on the stage. Will you come and see me off?"

"Of course, Janet."

Jake doesn't sleep much that night. He's up early to see Janet off. She gets on the stage, reaches down, kisses Jake, and says, "Thank you, Jake. I'll never forget you."

The stage pulls out. Jake goes into the saloon.

"Give me a beer."

"It's a little early for drinkin', Jake."

One of the men waves his hand. "Never mind."

The bartender shakes his head and serves Jake a beer. Jake sits quietly, sippin' his beer for a while, gets up, and leaves. He goes out, gets on Big Black, and rides off.

Jake was never seen in Laredo again.

"Sam, it sounds like Jake was upset with Janet leavin'."

"Jake never forgot Janet. That's why he never married."

JAKE AND THE INDIANS

"Hay Sam, are ya done with that customer?"

"Yup, he needed a few bags of horse feed."

"Well, come sit down. Y'ave been a-workin' too hard."

"It feels good ta sit a spell."

"Say, Sam, I wanted to ask ya—how'd Jake become friendly with the Indians?"

"Well, it's like this. Remember, Jake spent a lot of time with Two Arrows when he was young. In his later years, he would spend time in Indian camps. Jake learned many Indian skills and customs. Durin' his trip deep into Mexico, he saved the Chief's son, and he aided with peace talks from time to time. The word of Jake— buckskin man to the Indians—bein' a friend to the Indians spread amongst the Indian nations. They knew he was a man the Indians could trust, a man of his word. Jake, as a U.S. Deputy Marshal, would not allow any injustice done to the Indians."

"One time Jake came across a small raidin' party a-wearin' war paint. They stopped when they saw Jake. Jake asked what they were up to. The Indians told Jake they were after two white men that murdered two Indian braves and beat an Indian girl. Jake asked what these men looked like, and the Indians gave a good description."

"Jake didn't want the Indians a-riddin' after the white men— 'specially wearin' war paint. People seein' them may get the wrong idea. 'Return home,' he said, 'I'll bring these men back to your village.'"

"Jake picked up the trail the Indians were followin'. It led him into some high country. Jake spots a campfire. If it's the men he's after, apparently they didn't know the Indians were after 'em. If they did, they wouldn't have stopped and lit a fire."

"Jake slowly sneaks up on the campsite. Lookin' the men over—it's not the men he's after. He walks into the camp. One of the men reaches for his gun. Jake says, 'Hold it right there,' as he points his gun at them. 'Relax boys, I could smell that coffee and thought I might git a cup.' He puts his gun away."

"He tells the men he's on the trail of two murderers. These men saw the ones Jake is after earlier that mornin'. They explain just where they saw 'em. Jake says, 'Thanks. You might as well bed down here for the night.' Jake thanks them and spends the night."

"In the mornin' Jake is up early, a-cookin' breakfast. As one of the men wakes up, he says, 'That coffee sure smells good.' The other man says, 'Forget the coffee, smell that bacon cookin'.'"

"'Get up boys, breakfast is ready.'"

"Lookin' off in the distance, Jake is watchin' the sun rise. The mountains look purple, with an orange and red sky behind 'em. The mornin' breeze is cool and gentle, the early mornin' birds are a-singin' their song. Jake says, 'It's goin' be a nice day.'"

"They sit awhile, drinken' coffee and talkin'. 'We don't know your name.'"

"'They call me Jake.'"

"'My name is Red, and this guy we call Hang On.'"

"'I can see why they call you Red with that hair. But Hang On—what kind of name is that?'"

"'His real name is John. We call him Hang On because of the way he hangs on to a horse while breakin' 'em.'"

"'You boys break horses?'"

"'That's how we make money. We're headed towards ranch country ta see if'en we can get work.'"

"Jake says, 'I have a few horses that need breakin' at my ranch. I'll tell ya how to get there. See the foreman and tell him I sent ya.'"

"Red and John work at Jake's ranch breakin' horses. They work there until all the horses are broke and trained, then they move along."

"Jake rides to the place where Red told him they saw the men he's after. He trails 'em into the town of Rollin' Rock. He sees their horses tied up ta the hitchin' rail in front of the hotel."

"Jake walks into the hotel, gets a room. He asks the clerk if the men ridin' the horses out front just checked in. Jake gives a reason for askin', sayin' the horses look like they been a-ridden hard—it's strange they've been left standin'. The clerk tells Jake they said they wanted to get rooms and then take their horses to the livery stable."

"'Oh, I see.' While Jake signs the book gettin' his room, he looks at the two names of the men. The names are Joe and Jim."

"Knowin' the two men are comin' out to attend to their horses, he sits on the porch to git a good look at 'em. The two men come out of the hotel and lead their horses down the street to the stable. Jake goes into the hotel and up to his room. He puts his things in his room, then takes his horse to the livery stable."

"'Wow! Young fella, that's some horse you got there. My name is Claud, I'll take good care of your horse.'"

"Jake pays the old man and is about to leave."

"'Say there, what's your name?'"

"'They call me Jake. Just Jake.'"

"The old man watches Jake walk away, rubbin' his chin, and says, 'Well, I'll be.'"

"That night, Claud is in the saloon tellin' everyone that Jake—the fastest gun alive—is in town. They wonder what he's doin' in town. Claud tells everyone Jake is a U.S. Deputy Marshal— maybe he's after someone."

"Jake, havin' changed into his buckskins, walks into the saloon."

"'Howdy, Jake,' Claud says."

"Jake nods his head."

"'Step right up here, Jake, I'll buy ya a beer.'"

"'Thanks, Claud.'"

"'Claud, let's take our beer over and sit at a table.'"

"'Right behind ya, Jake.'"

"'Claud, I'm in town to arrest Jim and Joe.'"

"'Ya mean the Strong brothers?'"

"'If that's their name, that's the ones I'm affta.'"

"'What'd they do, Jake?'"

"'They murdered two Indians and attacked an Indian girl.'"

"'Why, them dirty snakes! Did the Indian girl die?'"

"'No, she'll be fine.'"

"'Jake, those two Strong brothers are a nasty bunch of sidewinders. They'd just as soon kill somebody as look at 'em.'"

"'Claud, I want you to keep quiet about this and find out all ya can about 'em.'"

"'Ain't you in a hurry to arrest 'em?'"

"'No. I know where they are.'"

"The next day, Jake walks into the saloon. The Strong brothers are standin' at the bar. Jake hears the end of their conversation—'Shot that redskin right between the eyes.' One of the men at the bar says, 'Just what those redskins deserve.'"

"Jake thinks the people in this town must be Indian haters. He orders a beer, slowly drinks it, a-watchin' everyone in the saloon. It seems there's only a few men in the bar that hate Indians. He thinks, I hope I don't have to fight them all when I arrest the Strong brothers."

The next mornin' Jake visits the Sheriff's Office.

"Good mornin', Sheriff."

"Good mornin', Jake."

"You know my name?"

"Everyone in town knows your name."

"Like a cup of coffee?"

"Sure would."

Jake takes a sip and says, "Ya call this coffee?!"

"I guess it's been around too long. Maybe I should make a fresh pot."

Jake coughs a few times and says, "Good idea."

"Jake, what brings you to my town?"

"Sheriff, I'm here to arrest the Strong brothers for murderin' two Indian braves and beatin' up a young Indian girl."

"Indians? A few men in town ain't gonna like you arrestin' those brothers for killin' Indians."

"How do you feel about it, Sheriff?"

"Jake, to me, people are all the same—and murder is murder. I'll help any way I can."

"Sheriff, I'm gonna arrest 'em outta town, in case there's any shootin'. We won't shoot up your town. I think you better stay out of it, so you don't anger the Indian haters in town."

Every mornin', Jake walks to the livery stable, saddles Big Black, leads him to the hotel, ties him to the hitchin' rail, then sits on the porch of the hotel waitin' for the Strong brothers to ride outta town.

Jake's patience pays off.

One mornin' the Strong brothers ride outta town together. Jake gets on Big Black and rides out followin' the two brothers.

Two men in town are watchin' Jake leave. One says, "I think that deputy marshal is after the Strong brothers—somethin' to do with the Indians they killed."

They decide to follow Jake.

Jake is slowly ridin' behind the brothers when Big Black starts to act up.

"Easy boy, what's wrong?"

Jake realizes Big Black is warnin' him that someone is behind them. Jake leads Big Black behind some big boulders. When the two men ride by, Jake rides out.

"You boys followin' me?"

"No, Jake, we were just out for a ride."

"Well, I think you better return to town."

"Okay, Jake. We weren't headed anyplace special."

They ride out, headed for town. Jake doesn't trust 'em.

He speaks to his horse, "We better keep an eye out, big boy. They're up ta somethin'."

Jake rides on after the Strong brothers.

Further down the trail, a gunshot rings out. The rifle bullet just misses Jake. He turns his horse and rides to cover.

He says to his horse, "They're up there in those rocks. Stay here, boy. I'm goin' after 'em."

Jake walks through the boulders and slowly works his way around behind the men. He steps out and says, "Ya boys shootin' at me?"

It's the men from town.

One of the men, startled, turns to shoot at Jake.

Jake draws and fires. The man is dead.

The second man puts up his hands.

Jake tells him, "If ya don't want to end up like your friend, pick up his body and get outta here."

"Okay, I will—just don't shoot."

He picks up the body, puts it on a horse, and heads out for town.

Jake knows the Strong brothers heard the gunshots—no tellin' what they'll do next. He decides to return to town.

The sheriff sees Jake ridin' in and goes out to meet him.

"Jake, I just got a wanted poster—the Strong brothers are wanted for bank robbery. I wondered where they'd go when they leave town. Now I know."

"Jake, we gotta get 'em."

"Sheriff, there's no hurry. If they don't know about the wanted poster, they'll be back."

A few days later, the Strong brothers ride inta town. They ride up to the saloon, dismount, and walk inside. When they get in, they're loud and obnoxious as usual. They walk up to the bar and order a beer.

Jake walks in behind them.

He says, "You boys are under arrest for murder and bank robbery."

They don't look to see who it is—they think it's the Sheriff.

They turn and draw their guns.

Jake fires two shots. The Strong brothers are dead before they hit the floor.

The Sheriff hears the gunshots and rushes into the saloon. Jake is slowly puttin' his gun back in his holster, shakin' his head.

"Jake, what happened?"

Some of the men in the saloon tell the sheriff what happened. Jake tells some men to take the bodies out and tie them onto their horses.

"Jake—the reward?"

"Give it to the poorest family in town."

Jake walks out of the saloon. He looks up at the clear blue sky, gets on Big Black, and leaves town, leadin' the two horses carryin' the dead bodies.

Jake rides for a few days. He sees smoke risin' in the distance.

It's the Indian village.

Jake rides in and up to the Chief's tent. A tall Indian steps out.

Jake doesn't get off his horse. He drops the reins to the two horses he was leadin' and says, "I told you I would bring them back."

The Indian Chief thanks Jake and asks him to stay to celebrate.

Jake says, "I don't celebrate the death of men."

He turns Big Black and rides out of town.

DEPUTY MARSHAL JAKE

One mornin' the old boys are sittin' around waitin' for Sam. When he comes in, they have his coffee ready for him. They all sit talkin' awhile.

"Hay Sam, tell us about Jake bein' a deputy Marshal."

"Well, I'll tell ya boys—if you were a ruthless character, you didn't want Jake after ya. Jake only went after the worst men, most were murderers. If he was after you, he was relentless. He had skills he'd learned from the Indians that other Marshals didn't have. These skills and his fast gun made it impossible to get away from him."

"Sam, did Jake go after cattle rustlers or bank robbers?"

"Not unless there had been a needless killin'."

"Boys, this reminds me of a story about Jake goin' after an entire gang of outlaws—there were six men in the gang. They would rob banks, stagecoaches, and rustle cattle. It seemed they had to kill someone every time they committed a crime. Lawmen all over the county were after 'em."

Jake was in a small town, sleepin' in his hotel room when a bunch of no-good cutthroats robbed the bank. For no reason, they shot and killed the bank teller and the bank manager. Jake looked out the window and saw the men ridin' out of town. There was total confusion in the street. The bandits were too far away for Jake to see what they looked like.

Jake looks at the horses the gang members are ridin'. He notices that one horse is brown with a white rear quarter and one is white spotted black. Most people would be confused, lookin' at the riders and not noticin' anything about them.

The Sheriff was roundin' up a posse—they rode outta town at a full gallop after the outlaws. Jake stayed in his room for a while, then came down and went to have breakfast.

"Hay Sam, why didn't Jake ride with the posse?"

"Jake very seldom rode with posses. He thought they'd run their horses thinkin' they could catch up with outlaws that had a head start—with their horses kickin' up a lotta dust the outlaws could see from far off. The outlaws could see how close the posse was gittin'. It would be easy for the outlaws to ambush 'em or shoot a member of the posse from a long distance.

"Jake didn't like the fact that members of the posse had different ideas, and they often didn't work as one group."

Jake knew he was goin' after the outlaws. As usual, he took his time. However, he knew that the posse would destroy the tracks left by the outlaws ridin' over 'em. Jake decided, as he had done in the past, he would slowly follow the trail of the posse until they gave up. He'd then pick up the trail of the outlaws.

Jake buys a mule, loads it up with supplies and ammunition, saddles Big Black, and heads out followin' the posse.

Soon he met the posse returnin' on the trail. The sheriff asked Jake where he was goin'.

Jake replied, "I have some travelin' to do."

Jake asked the Sheriff what happened.

"We lost the trail up in the high country. The ground was too hard for us to follow."

Jake rode on, followin' the posse's trail to where they lost the trail of the outlaws and had to give up.

Jake got off Big Black and looked around. He could see things others couldn't. Two Arrows had taught Jake how to read signs when trailin' someone. Jake spots a small stone that had been moved—he could tell it had been moved by the small impression it left in the ground.

Further ahead he sees a small branch that was bent. He knew what direction they headed. Eventually he picked up their trail again and followed them to the town of Red Rock.

Jake camped out in the hills overlookin' the town for a couple of days. He didn't want to go into town too soon after the bandits.

In the mornin' he breaks camp and rides inta town. Ridin' slowly, still wearin' his trail clothes, everyone notices Big Black. They pay little attention to Jake.

Spottin' the brown horse with the white hind quarter in front of the saloon, Jake rides up and ties his horse to the same hitchin' rail. He walks slowly into the saloon, up to the bar, and orders a cold beer.

Movin' slowly and wearin' his trail clothes, he's unnoticed. He sits at a table in the corner so he can see everyone in the room.

Sittin' at a table are six men playin' poker. He thinks these men are the ones he's after. He has to be sure. He also knows his fast gun is no match for six men.

The saloon doors swing open. A little timid man walks in by the table where the men are playin' cards. One of the cowboys trips the little man—he falls down and says, "Oh! My, my." The cowboys laugh.

Jake sees a possible opportunity to challenge one of the outlaws.

He says, "You tripped that man on purpose—it's not funny."

The man stands up and says, "Mind your own business, cowboy, or you'll be the next one on the floor."

The cowboy is about to reach for his gun when one of the men at the table grabs his hand.

"We don't want any trouble in this town. Sit down and let it go."

The man sits down. Jake now knows which one of the men is the leader—he would be the most dangerous member of the gang.

Sam, was Jake challengin' the whole gang?

"No, I think he just challenged the one man. I think Jake wanted him to draw on him. He would've been able to eliminate one of the outlaws if he had drawn."

Jake knew, even though the outlaw didn't draw, that he had made an enemy. He would use this to his advantage.

The little man says to Jake, "I'm glad he didn't draw—he's a killer, you know. I don't want anyone hurt because of me. They were just havin' fun. I'm used to it."

Jake says, "I don't consider it fun."

"Well thank you, cowboy. Will you have a beer with me?"

"Yes, I will."

They sit at a table drinkin' beer together.

"I usually drink alone. No one will drink with me."

Jake says, "I'm proud to drink with you. Say, what's your name?"

"Jake. Just Jake."

"My name is Leo—Leo Frans. Pleased to meet you."

Jake gets up from the table and says goodbye to Leo. He thinks that Leo may be able to give him more information in the future about the gang. For now, he doesn't ask any questions— he don't want anyone to know he's interested in the gang of outlaws.

Jake returns to his hotel room, takes a bath, and shaves. He puts on his buckskins and goes out to get somethin' to eat. He enters a small restaurant, sits down, and orders some food. He asks the waitress about the gang of outlaws.

She didn't know much about them, other than the fact she didn't like 'em.

The owner of the restaurant comes out to talk to Jake.

"I understand you were askin' my waitress about Curly's gang."

"That's what they call themselves?"

"Yes. Curly's the leader—he's the meanest of the bunch."

"What is it that you wanted ta know about 'em?"

"Anything you can tell me. By the way, my name's Jake."

"They call me Cookie."

"Well Jake, that gang of outlaws operates outta this town. Every so often they leave town for a while, but they always return. The Sheriff watches 'em, but they never do anythin' in town the Sheriff can arrest 'em for. Besides, there's six of 'em—the sheriff only has one deputy. They'd be no match for the gang.

A few of the townspeople think there's someone in town behind the gang, providin' 'em with information."

"Who could that be?"

"We're not sure. There's the Sheriff, the mayor, and the board of directors—they all know what's goin' on in other towns with gold and money shipments. It could be any one of 'em."

Jake thanks 'em for the information and walks out of the restaurant.

Outside the restaurant, Jake stands thinkin' for a moment. On the street corner, there are three old men standin' around talkin'. One of 'em says,

"Look, that's Jake—the fastest man on the draw in the West. Wonder what he's doin' in our town."

"Isn't he the one that lets people draw agin him shootin' at beer mugs?"

"Yeah, that's him. I'd like to try."

"Well, ask him."

"Okay, I will."

"Hello Jake, I heard ya let men draw against ya shootin' beer mugs. I'd like to try it, if you'd let me."

"Not now—maybe later."

"Well, let me know."

"Okay, I will."

Jake walks into the saloon. Everyone looks up at him—standin' tall in his buckskins, wearin' his black hat, boots, and gun belt. Everyone notices how he wears his gun, with his holster tied down. He walks up to the bar and orders a beer.

Standin' at the bar is the cowboy that tripped the little man. He recognizes Jake as the one who questioned his actions.

"Well, lookie here—a smelly buffalo hunter."

Jake just smiles.

"Hey, buffalo hunter, what are ya doin' in these parts?"

"I ain't a buffalo hunter, I just wear buckskins."

"Ya look like a buffalo hunter to me."

Just then Curly rushes to the bar.

"Pete, do you know who ya talkin' to?"

"Yeah, a smelly buffalo hunter."

"Pete, that ain't no buffalo hunter—that's Jake, the fastest gun alive!"

"He don't look so fast to me."

"Well, believe me, he is fast."

Curly takes Pete away from the bar.

Outside, a group of men are gatherin'. They heard Jake was in town and might let 'em draw against him, shootin' at beer mugs. When Jake walks outside, the men gather around him.

"Jake, let us shoot against ya!"

Jake says, "Okay boys, get yourselves some beer mugs, bring 'em on out here."

Pete, hearin' the commotion, comes outside.

Jake says, "It'll cost each of ya boys five dollars."

They pay Jake and line up the beer mugs on the fence rail.

Jake notices Pete watchin' and slows down his draw. Well, of course Jake outdraws 'em all. Pete, watchin', doesn't think Jake is so fast—he don't know Jake deliberately slowed down his draw.

"Hey, buffalo hunter—beer mugs don't shoot back."

"Pete, would you like to draw agin' me?"

"What, shootin' beer mugs?"

Then he draws on Jake.

Pete lies bleedin' in the dirt. He's dead. Curly and the gang come out of the saloon. Jake is standin' over Pete with his gun still in his hand. He turns toward Curly, pointin' his gun at him.

One of the men standin' 'round tells Curly, "Pete drew first."

Curly says, "I told him not to draw on Jake."

He shakes his head and says, "Let's go back inside."

Jake thinks, Now there's five left. Jake has patience—he can wait until one of the outlaws makes a move. He was taught by Two Arrows: the best weapon when huntin' is patience. Jake was huntin' these outlaws.

A few weeks later, two of the outlaws ride outta town. Jake follows 'em. Sittin' atop a hill, he watches 'em. They hide behind some big boulders, waitin' for somethin'—or someone.

Off in the distance, Jake sees what they're awaitin' for—a stagecoach is comin'. Jake rides down the hill. He has to let the outlaws stop the stage and attempt to rob it, in order to arrest 'em for holdin' up the stage.

When the stage comes 'round a bend, the outlaws stop it at gunpoint and tell the driver to throw down the strongbox.

Jake rides out and says, "Drop your guns."

They do. Jake arrests 'em and follows the stage into town.

He turns the outlaws over to the sheriff and leaves town, headin' back ta Red Rock.

He says to Big Black, "Only three left, big boy."

He waits for nightfall to ride back inta town, puts his horse in the stable, then returns to his hotel room for a much-needed sleep.

Jake sleeps till noontime. When he gets up and leaves the hotel, the sun is overhead and it's hot. Jake has lunch and heads for the saloon for a cold beer.

Sittin' at a table are the three outlaws. Jake thinks they're waitin' for the two he put in jail to return with money from the stagecoach holdup.

Hours pass. The outlaws become more restless. Night rolls in, and the town closes up for the night.

The next mornin', Jake is up early, lookin' out his window to see what Curly and his men do.

Jake sees Curly walkin' alone in the street. He goes into the general store. He's in the store for half an hour. He leaves the store and walks to the saloon.

Jake thinks, He was in the store a long time—'specially when he ain't the sociable type.

Jake decides to visit the Sheriff's Office. He talks to the Sheriff, revealin' that he's a U.S. Deputy Marshal and he's after Curly and his men for the murder of a bank teller and bank manager.

He tells the Sheriff, "I put two of the men in jail for a stagecoach robbery. Sheriff, I don't wanta confront 'em until I find out who's supplyin' them with information. It has to be someone right here in town."

"Sheriff, who's on this board of directors I heard about?"

"The board's made up of a few of our most prominent members of our town," says the Sheriff. "Jake, the board has a meetin' tonight. Why don't you attend and see what you think?"

"Good idea, Sheriff. I think I will."

Jake attends the meetin' with the Sheriff. He sits quietly, watchin' the members come in one at a time. The last one to arrive is the storekeeper—the timid little man.

Jake thinks a moment, then leaves the meetin' before it begins. He walks down the street to the livery stable where he keeps Big Black. He spends time brushin' his horse and a-thinkin'. He has to come up with a plan. He could arrest the three outlaws at any time, but he wants the one behind the gang.

Jake returns to the Sheriff's Office.

"Sheriff, I have a plan. I want you to tell the storekeeper there's a secret shipment goin' out, and you want to use his store to ship it from so no one knows. Let's talk to the bank manager— we need five thousand dollars to ship."

The sheriff and Jake talk to the bank manager and explain Jake's plan. The bank manager agrees and gives five thousand dollars to the Sheriff.

"What's the best way to work your plan, Jake?"

"We'll have your deputy pick up the money at the general store and ride outta town with it. To protect his life when the bandits come after him, he'll throw the bag of money on the ground and ride off. I'll be on the trail to be sure your deputy remains safe. Now, we'll mark some of the money and put it in the bottom of the bag. I'll follow the outlaws to see where they go with that money. Sheriff, tell the storekeeper to have the money ready at sunup. Have your deputy pick it up right after the sun rises."

In the mornin', the deputy picks up the money and rides outta town. He rides for a half hour, then two outlaws begin shootin' at him. He drops the bag of money and gallops away.

Jake is hidin', watchin' the outlaws. He follows them back to town. Once back in town, they go into the hotel and stay there for a few hours. When they come out, Curly ain't with 'em— and they ain't carryin' the bag of money. Curly is nowhere to be seen.

Jake figures Curly has the money and is goin' to deliver it to their contact in town.

The sheriff watches the storekeeper. He opens the safe and is about to put somethin' in it when the sheriff rushes in and says, "Hold it right there!"

The sheriff says, "Where did this here money come from?"

"It's my money—money I use to run this store," says the storekeeper.

The sheriff says, "Let's have a look." He finds the marked bills and arrests the little timid storekeeper. He then returns the money to the bank.

Jake decides it's time to arrest Curly and the other two outlaws. He walks into the saloon. Two are sittin' at a table, one's at the bar. Jake patiently waits until all three are together before he makes his move.

"Curly, you and ya boys are under arrest for bank robbery and murder."

"You're not gonna hang us!"

They stand and reach for their guns. Jake gets two of 'em. The Sheriff, standin' behind Curly, hits him over the head. Jake holds his fire, then puts his gun into his holster.

"Thanks, Sheriff. We took Curly alive—he'll stand trial, along with the two outlaws I put in jail."

Two days later, Jake saddles Big Black. He says to his horse, "Another job done in the name of justice. Let's go, boy."

Jake rides outta town.

APACHE ROSE

Sam sits down with the Old Boys and says, "Well, I think it's about time. Now for the story of Jake and Apache Rose—sit back, boys, I'm gonna spin a yarn like no other."

Jake was gettin' along in years. He was ridin' Big Black along a trail when he saw smoke a- comin' from a distance. He turned off the trail and rode up a nearby hill. Gettin' to the top of the hill, he could see a cabin on fire down in the valley. He kicks up Big Black and races down the hill. Big Black was gettin' older too, but he could still run like the wind.

On the way to the burnin' cabin, Jake could see five men come runnin' out of the cabin—he recognizes them as the Dancen brothers. Jake pulls Big Black up to a slidin' stop. He's off the horse and headed for the cabin door before the horse even comes to a full stop.

He rushes into the burnin' cabin, now filled with smoke. The rafters are on fire and startin' to fall. Jake sees a man on the floor with a bullet hole in his forehead. On the bed is a beaten, naked woman. Jake grabs a blanket and covers her body. As he wraps her in the blanket, he notices a silver dollar layin' on her naked belly. He picks it up and carries her to safety.

He lays her on the ground and gives her a drink of water. The woman is in shock—followin' her husband's murder, bein' beaten and assaulted. She just lays on the ground, speechless, starin' straight at the sky. Jake doesn't know what to do, but he knows he has to get her help. The town is too many miles away to take her there, so he takes her to the nearby Indian village where he knows the members of the tribe—the same village that Two Arrows brought Jake to when he was a young child.

Jake rides in, leadin' a horse with the woman gently tied on. A few Indians see them comin' and run out to help. Gray Hawk, a young Indian brave, carries the woman into the old woman's teepee. The old woman asks Jake what's happened. He explains. The old woman tells Jake that physically she'll be fine—it's mentally she's worried about.

The old woman takes care of the young woman for two weeks. Her physical injuries are almost healed. Mentally, she remains the same. The old Indian woman says, "Her spirit hasn't come back."

Jake camps out near the Indian camp, sleepin' under the stars. One mornin', the risin' sun awakens him. The mountains look like they're wearin' a veil of purple haze. He starts a campfire and heats up coffee. Lookin' toward the river, he sees the young girl sittin' on a rock just starin' at the rushin' water. The sound of the river rapidly flowin' by soothes her. She sits on the rock listenin' to the river rush by every day for days.

One mornin', Gray Hawk walks over close to where she's sittin'. He picks up a stone and tosses it into the river.

"I sit with you?"

She doesn't answer him.

"What ya name?"

Again, she doesn't respond.

"I call you Rose."

Gray Hawk is very concerned. He talks to the old Indian woman.

"What we do? Rose not right in head."

"Gray Hawk, we must bring spirit back."

"Maybe make her angry and get her to want to get even for what they did."

"Talk to her. Tell about what happened to husband and house—may help her recover."

Gray Hawk realizes this could be dangerous, but considerin' her mental state, it couldn't make things any worse.

In the mornin', Gray Hawk sees Rose sittin' on the rock starin' at the river. He walks over to where she's sittin' and sits down beside her.

"Rose, you know what happened to your husband, your house, and what they did to you."

"Rose, git mad—they took everything from you."

"You must get even—they need to be punished."

She does not speak, but Gray Hawk sees the change in her eyes. For several days, he speaks to her and tells her the same thing. Each time, her eyes brighten a little more.

One mornin', Jake is up early, starts his coffee. He sees Rose sittin' on the rock. Jake decides to take a little shootin' practice while his coffee's a-brewin'. He sets up a few targets and practices drawin' and shootin', never missin' a target. He returns to his campfire and starts to pour a cup of coffee.

Jake hears a voice behind him.

"Could I have a cup of that coffee?"

Turnin' around, he's surprised to see Rose standin' behind him.

"You sure can, honey. Sit down here."

She sits and silently drinks her coffee. Then she speaks.

"It was you that brought me out of the fire."

"Yes, it was. I'm sorry about your husband. After I brought you here, I went back and gave your husband a proper burial."

"I don't know how to thank you."

"You already did this mornin' by speakin' to me."

"What is your name?"

"They call me Jake. Just Jake. What's your name, honey?"

"I don't remember—I seem to've forgot."

"That's okay. Gray Hawk named you Rose. You'll remember in time."

"Jake, can you teach me to shoot like you do?"

"Why sure I can. When do you want to start?"

"Today—I want to start today."

"Okay. We'll start after we have breakfast."

Jake thinks givin' her somethin' to do will help her recovery.

The Old Indian woman hears Rose talkin'. She calls Gray Hawk, and they all sit at Jake's campfire talkin'.

Jake and Rose finish their coffee, and Jake says, "Let's get started with your lesson."

He goes over to his saddlebag and takes out a spare gun belt and gun. He unloads the revolver and adjusts the gun belt to fit Rose's small waist. He straps the belt on her and tells her to get used ta wearin' the belt and gun.

"Jake, this is heavy."

"You'll get used to it in time."

"When can I learn to draw?"

Jake, rememberin' how Sheriff Hank Black taught him, says, "After you get used to wearin' and handlin' the gun safely, then you can begin to practice drawin' an empty gun."

Rose wears the gun belt for a few days. Then Jake starts teachin' her to draw. When the gun feels natural in her hands, he loads it.

"Take practice for a few days. Rose, we're gettin' low on ammunition. I'm goin' to the closest town to pick up some. The town's two days ride—I'm goin' ta leave first thing in the mornin'. Keep practicin' while I'm gone. I'll be back in four or five days."

Jake rides out for town at sunup. After two days' ride, he reaches town. He rides Big Black up to the front of the saloon, gives his horse a drink of water, and then walks into the saloon. His throat is dry from breathin' in trail dust.

"What can I do for you, old man?" "A cold beer, barkeep."

"Been ridin' long?"

"Yup, a couple of days. This beer sure tastes good. Think I'll go sit down and rest my legs awhile."

Jake walks over to a table and sits down where he can keep his back against the wall. He knows too many gunfighters been shot in the back.

The saloon doors swing open and a fancy-dressed cowboy walks in. Jake looks up and thinks, This ain't no ranch hand. He looks like another fast gun out to make a name for himself.

He walks up to the bar and says, "Hey, barman, give me a beer," hittin' his hand on the bar. The man is loud and arrogant.

He looks around the room and sees Jake sittin' at the table.

"Hey, barkeep, what's a smelly old buffalo hunter doin' in here?"

He doesn't see the way Jake is wearin' his gun.

The bartender says to the man, "He's no buffalo hunter. He's just an old man that wears buckskins."

While the gunman is lookin' at the barkeep talkin', Jake gets up outta his chair. When he turns around to look at Jake, he sees a man standin' straight and tall. His buckskins are worn, his gray hair long under an old-lookin' black hat—then he notices the way Jake wears his old, worn gun belt and holster.

"Hey, old man, you wear that gun like you know how to use it."

"Just a little, son."

"What's your name, old man?"

"They call me Jake. Just Jake."

The bartender tells the man, "Don't rile him. He's faster than he looks."

"Hey, old man, the bartender says you're fast. How fast are you?"

Jake draws and shoots the beer mug right beside him off the bar.

"Wowee! I never saw anyone that fast! Good thing I didn't draw on ya!"

"Instead of tellin' you to draw, I just thought I'd show you first and let you make up your mind just how far you want to push me. Besides, I don't feel like killin' anyone today."

"Son, you better change your attitude. You're too arrogant. Some old man may put a bullet right through your heart."

Jake gets up and walks out of the saloon and across the street into the gun shop.

An old man walks up to the gunslinger in the saloon and says, "It's a good thing you didn't draw against Jake. He's the fastest gun there ever was. If you drew, you'd be dead on the floor with a bullet through your heart."

"Is he the fast gun that would let you draw against him shootin' beer mugs?"

"That's him. They call him Jake."

In the gunshop—

"Hey, Jake, ain't nobody plugged you yet? You have to be the only gunfighter that lived to a good old age."

"Nope, Stan, I'm still ridin' around the range. Plannin' to head for my ranch soon and put up my gun and saddle."

"Still ridin' that big black horse o' yours?"

"Yup. He's been a good animal all these years. He's carried me all over the West. He needs ta get home and rest too."

"Stan, I need some ammunition. Say, let me see that small gun belt and holster hangin' up there."

"The black one?"

"Ya, the smooth black one."

"This is just right. Do you have a small gun to fit this holster?"

"I have a small pearl-handled one just the right size."

"That'll be just fine. Stan, is there a leather shop in town?"

"Yup, just down the street on the right."

"Say, Jake, are ya teachin' a kid how to use a gun?"

"You might say that—a young person anyway."

"Thanks, Stan. Be a seein' ya."

"Ride safe, Jake."

Jake walks down the street to the leather shop.

"Hello there, what can I do for ya?"

"I'd like ya to carve a rose on this here holster."

"I can do that for ya right now."

"Thanks!"

Jake is lookin' around the shop while the shopkeeper is carvin' the rose on the holster. He sees a small black saddle just the right size for Rose.

"I'll take this saddle if you will carve a rose on each side up near the horn."

"Sure thing."

While Jake is in town, Gray Hawk spots a black and white pinto standin' off in the distance on a rise. Each day the horse comes closer to the Indian camp. Gray Hawk moves closer ta the horse until they're a few yards apart. When he reaches out toward the horse, he balks, jumps, and bounces away.

Even though the horse gets a glare in his eyes, Gray Hawk can tell it's not a mean look. He tries to approach the horse for several days. Finally, he decides to ignore the horse and sit in the grass. He knew the horse was inquisitive, or it wouldn't have been comin' close ta the Indian camp The horse, wonderin' what Gray Hawk is doin', comes closer to him each day.

Finally, the horse walks up close ta Gray Hawk and lets him touch him before he jumps away. Gray Hawk takes a rope with him and sits down in the grass. The horse walks up to Gray Hawk. He slowly stands and touches the horse. Gray Hawk slowly slips the loop of the rope over the horse's head.

Feelin' the rope on his neck, the horse jumps and rears up. Gray Hawk gently talks to the horse and moves with him as he pulls on the rope, causin' as little resistance as possible. Finally, the horse calms down and stops resistin' the rope. Gray Hawk leads the horse in circles and then toward the corral.

The big pinto horse runs around the corral, throwin' his head and snortin'. Every muscle in his body can be seen, revealin' his power. Gray Hawk works with the horse, gentlin' him. He doesn't want to break the horse's spirit—just bring him under control. The horse must want to be ridden and like his rider.

Gray Hawk begins to ride the horse without a saddle inside the corral. It's time to try a bridle and a bit. It takes a while ta git him to take the bit. In a few days, Gray Hawk is able to ride the big black and white horse outside the fenced corral.

In the meantime, Jake has returned. Rose has continued practicin with the big old gun. He gives her the new gun, holster, and saddle. Rose has taken to the big black and white stallion, and the horse likes her. When he sees Rose, he whinnies and jumps around on his front legs throwin his head.

Gray Hawk walks over to the corral where the horse and Rose are standin'.

"Rose, you like horse?"

"Yes! I love him."

"You take your horse. I catch and train him for you."

"You did this for me?"

"Uh! Not broke to saddle. Get new saddle Jake bring you—I train."

She goes and gets her new saddle and brings it to Gray Hawk. In a short time, Rose is ridin' her horse. Gray Hawk tells Jake," they belong together."

One mornin', Rose goes to the corral to see her horse—he's not there. Gray Hawk tells her, horse jump fence run off.

"No horse ever jump fence before—too high."

Rose mopes around for a few days, then hears horse hoofs poundin' the ground.

"Rose, horses comin'. Your horse runnin' in front—open gate!"

The big pinto stallion leads four mares and three colts into the corral.

"Close gate quick!"

"He bring family to us."

"He does alright, Gray Hawk—four mares and three children."

Gray Hawk understands her and laughs.

"We have plenty horses now."

Jake is awakened one mornin' by the sound of gunshots. He looks, and it's Rose practicin'. He walks over to her and says,

"That's good shootin'. You hit all six targets, but you did somethin' wrong."

"What did I do, Jake?"

"How many shots did you fire?"

"Six."

"How many bullets in your gun?"

"It's empty. It only holds six."

"That's right. Always reload before you empty your gun. You never want to be caught with an empty gun."

"Oh, I'll remember that, Jake. Sounds like good advice."

Gray Hawk says,

"She fast with gun—almost fast as you. She good with bow and arrow too."

"I know, I've watched you teachin' her. She's a natural."

"Well, we'll see what she has on her mind now she knows how to use her gun."

Jake says,

"Honey, come over here and stand beside me. Gray Hawk, when I tell you, drop a stone. When he drops the stone, draw and fire. We'll use that cactus for a target."

"Anytime you're ready, Gray Hawk."

He drops the stone. They both draw and fire.

"Well, Rose, whatever you trained with a gun for, you're ready."

"I'm going to hunt those men down that attacked me and killed my husband, and I'm going to kill them."

"Rose, I never told you, but I know who they were. They were the Densen brothers. I heard they split up and are in different towns."

"Rose, another thing—when I went into the burnin' cabin, I found this silver dollar on your belly."

"I remember." "The one that tossed it there after he assaulted me—he has a scar over his right eye."

"That would be Zeke."

"I'll get him last."

"Rose, you have to think about this for a while. You need a plan."

Jake calls Rose and Gray Hawk over to his campfire to join him for coffee.

"I've come up with a plan. It's gonna take all three of us, if you'll help, Gray Hawk."

"Me help."

"Good. I'll tell you my plan. Our plan has to be foolproof. You have to get them one at a time, and you can't let them know who you are."

"The first part of my plan—I got the idea from Gray Hawk, when he called you Apache Rose. We have to disguise you as an Indian princess." "Me get old woman." "Okay Two Arrows."

The old Indian woman takes Rose into her teepee. About an hour later, they come out. Rose is wearin' a white buckskin Indian dress with a red rose painted on the front. She's wearin' a black wig that covers her blond hair. Around her wig is a red headband. She straps on her black gun belt and holster, walks over to her big pinto stallion, and gets on him.

"How do I look?"

"Look like real Indian princess."

"She sure does, Gray Hawk."

The old Indian woman comes out of her teepee and puts two red marks on Rose's face—one under each eye.

"You go to war, must have war paint. Her skin dark from sun, war paint distract from color of body. You must sit in sun—legs too white."

Rose does what the old Indian woman says until her legs are as dark as the rest of her.

"Here's how my plan will work. I'll scout out the town. If I see one of the Densen brothers, I'll come back and let you know. Gray Hawk, you'll ride to a predetermined meetin' place with her Indian disguise and her pinto horse. Rose, you'll drive a wagon to meet Gray Hawk. When you meet him, you'll change clothes, mount your horse, and ride into town, leavin' the wagon with Gray Hawk. When ya finishe in town, you'll gallop back to Gray Hawk, change clothes, and drive the wagon away. Gray Hawk, you'll bring her clothes and horse back to the village. You must remain unseen."

"I'm headed for Rock River, a town just south of here. I heard one of the Densen brothers was holed up there."

Jake rides to town and sees one of the Densen brothers. He rides back to the Indian village to tell Gray Hawk and Apache Rose. They follow the plan. Jake rides back into town so he'll be there when Apache Rose rides in.

Gray Hawk and Rose meet as planned. She mounts her horse and rides for town.

She rides right down the main street of town. Her horse prances down the street. She rides right up to the saloon and sees Jake's horse tied up in front—the signal that Densen is inside. She ties her horse next to Jake's. Everyone in the street is lookin' at her. Some folks call others out of stores and shops to see her.

She walks into the saloon and sees Jake sittin' at a table. He looks at Densen.

"Densen, turn around."

He turns around and can't believe his eyes.

"You talkin' to me?"

"I kill you. Draw."

"Wait a minute, Injun, what you want to kill me for?"

"No talk. Just shoot. You, mister, drop glass. When he drop glass, draw."

"Wait a minute—you serious?"

"Drop glass anytime."

The man holdin' the glass finishes his shot of whiskey, holds out the glass, and drops it. Densen goes for his gun. He never gets it all the way out of his holster before Apache Rose fires. The man looks at her, then falls to the floor dead.

"Hey Injun, what's your name?"

"Apache Rose."

She takes a silver dollar out of her gun belt and flips it on his belly, turns, walks out, mounts her horse, and races to meet Gray Hawk.

From where Gray Hawk is hidin', he can see no one is followin' her. Everyone in the saloon is dumbfounded—they never saw anythin' like that before.

One man says,

"Wonder why she wanted to kill Densen?"

Another man says,

"That silver dollar must mean somethin'."

Word spreads around town about what happened in the saloon. One old boy says,

"I hope she never comes lookin' fa me."

Jake walks out of the saloon, not sayin' a word to anyone, gets on his horse, and rides to a nearby town where he heard one of the Densens was.

Seein' Densen, he rides to the Indian village to tell Apache Rose. They wait a few days, then head for town, followin' the same plan. Apache Rose rides into town. Jake is standin' outside by Big Black. As she rides by, he says,

"The one on the front porch wearin' the blue shirt."

By now, the news of his brother bein' shot by an Indian woman has reached town. Densen sees her comin' down the street on that big pinto, all dressed in the white Indian dress. He steps out into the street. He knows he's a faster draw than his brother was. He thinks he can outdraw her.

She pulls her horse up and gets off.

"Hey squaw, you killed my brother!"

"Yes. Now kill you."

When she says that, he reaches for his gun. She draws and fires. His bullet goes straight into the dirt at his feet. He grabs his chest—blood runs out through his fingers. He falls on the ground, dead.

She reaches in her gun belt, takes out a silver dollar, flips it onto his belly.

"Apache Rose kill all Densens."

She gets on her horse and races out of town. When she reaches Gray Hawk, he says,

"Men ridin' this way."

She changes quickly, gets into the wagon, and drives it out onto the road, headin' back towards town.

"Hey lady, did you see an Indian woman ridin' a big paint horse?"

"No, I didn't."

"Thanks. She must've turned off a ways back. Let's go, men."

When the men get out of sight, she turns the wagon around and heads toward the Indian village.

She meets Jake and Gray Hawk the next mornin' at the village.

"Rose, ya've gotten two of the Densen brothers. I think ya better lay low for a while. They'll be expectin' ya and try to git ya first. Let's let 'em think about it for a while."

"I need to visit my ranch. I'll be leavin' in the mornin'. I should be back in about a month."

"Okay, Jake. That's a good idea."

Jake rides out in the mornin headed for his ranch, he's been away a long time. A week or so later, he rides through the gates of his ranch. Everythin looks great, and he's pleased. Curly sees Jake ridin in and calls Bob, "Jake's here!"

"Howdy, Jake."

"Hello boys, how you been?"

"Just fine, Jake."

"Where's the kid?"

"Sam is out ridin around checkin on the ranch. Say, Jake, he sure is a fine boy."

"He's gettin good with his gun, he's fast."

"I think it was a good idea to teach him how to use his gun properly, he practices every day."

"It was a good idea if he respects that gun and uses it as a tool, not a game."

"Boys, I want you to feed and water Big Black, then rub and brush him down. He's gettin old and needs a long rest. I think I'll put him out to pasture."

"How's his son doin'?"

"Jake, that is a great horse. After you worked him with that long shank bit when we were in town, he responds perfectly to the regular bit."

"Jake, he's one fast horse, he might be faster than Big Black."

"Right now, he's out on the range with a few new mares. I guess he's bred them all by now."

"Bob, in a week or so I want you to bring him in."

"Alright, Jake, let me know when."

"When I ride out in a few weeks, I'll be ridin Big Black Jr."

"Bob, would you go round up and bring in Black Jr.? Take Sam with you."

"Okay, Jake, if we can run that horse down—he's faster than any of our horses."

They ride for an hour lookin for Big Black Jr.

"Hey Bob, look up on the hill!"

"It's that black horse."

While they're lookin up at Black, he rears up and comes a runnin down the hill towards the two riders. He runs right by them and takes off runnin across the plains. They chase him for about a half hour, then he stops, turns toward the men, jumpin around and tossin his head.

"Sam, that horse is playin with us. Let's stop chasin him and turn and ride towards the ranch. We can't catch him anyway."

When they turn and start to ride away, the horse stands still and watches them. When he sees they're not gonna chase him, he begins to follow them.

"Look, Bob, he's followin us."

When they get close to the ranch, the horse remembers the feed he was given. He races by Bob and Sam, runs right through the gate, and into the corral. He runs around the corral bouncin on his front feet and tossin his head, then goes to the waterin trough and takes a drink. Bob rides up to the gate and closes it.

"See, ya caught him okay."

"Jake, I think he caught us. We chased him around, he was playin a game with us, then he came in on his own."

"When he calms down, he needs a good brushin down."

"I'll take care of it, Jake."

"Thanks, Sam."

The next mornin after breakfast, and after the stock had been taken care of, Jake says to Sam, "Hear you been gettin fast on the draw."

"Jake, I've improved, especially over the last month."

"That's good, boy, let's see how fast you are. Bob, put a couple of cans up on that fence and pick up a stone. Sam, when he drops the stone, draw and shoot."

Bob drops the stone, they draw—Jake's bullet hits the can, then Sam's shot strikes the can.

"Son, you have become fast."

"I don't think I'll ever be as fast as you."

Bob says, "Nobody ever will be as fast as Jake."

"Son, remember what I told you—use your gun to protect yourself and others. Never put your gun out for hire."

Bob says, "Sam, let's you and I try that trick."

"Sure, Bob, go get your gun."

Sam has no idea how fast Bob is—Jake does. He remembers the day Bob helped him in the saloon.

Bob returns with his gun and holster, strappin it on as he walks to Sam and Jake. Jake picks up the stone and says, "Ready, boys?" He waits a few seconds, then drops the stone.

One gunshot is heard, but both cans fly off the fence. They fired at the same time, so it only sounded like one shot.

"I hit the can first!"

"No you didn't, I did."

"I'm tellin you I did."

Jake laughs, shakes his head, and walks away. "You boys will be arguin about that as long as you live." And they did.

"Hey Bob, how come you never wear that gun belt?"

"Don't want to use it. If I don't have it on, I can't. Sam, I've had to kill men before, and I don't like it."

Walkin away, he undoes his belt buckle and puts the gun and holster back in his room in the house.

Two men ride into the Indian village lookin for trouble. They have their guns drawn and start shootin. They're not aimin at anyone, they're just tryin to drive the Indians off their land.

Gray Hawk comes out of his teepee and confronts the men. The men try to run him down with their horses. He grabs the bridle of one of the men and pulls his horse down. The man gets up off the ground, picks his gun up, and shoots Gray Hawk in the shoulder.

Just then, Rose comes out from behind a teepee. She's wearin her gun.

"Look, a white woman with a big gun. What are ya gonna do with that gun, honey?"

"I'm gonna put a hole in both of you."

The man standin on the ground points his gun at her, the one on the horse draws. Two shots ring out through the Indian camp. Both men lie dead on the ground.

She tells the braves to tie the men on their horses and turn them loose. The braves carry Gray Hawk into the old woman's teepee. She takes the bullet out of his shoulder. He lays unconscious for two days.

When he comes to and his eyes open, the first thing he sees is Rose lookin down at him with a smile on her face. He tries to move, but she tells him to lie still.

"Drink."

She gets some water, sits him up, and holds him in her arms while he drinks. Their eyes meet for a few seconds, then she lays him back down and tells him to rest.

She thinks, for the first time, that Gray Hawk, with his large physical build and that shinin long black hair, is a handsome man. When she was holdin him in her arms and lookin close into his eyes, she had a feelin come over her she hadn't felt since her husband died.

She went out and sat on the rock she so often sat on and watched the river rush by. She thought, watchin the river, no matter how much she liked Gray Hawk, he could not take her husband's place—no man ever could.

Jake rides Big Black Jr. around for a week off and on to get used to the horse. When he feels good under him, he decides to head back to the Indian village. He tells the ranch hands, "I'm a-leavin in the mornin. I got some unfinished business to take care of. The next time I come home, I think I'll stay. Think I'd like to spend the rest of my days sittin on the front porch smokin my pipe, sittin in this old rockin chair."

Jake mounts Big Black Jr. and heads out for the Indian village. He rides for about a week before he reaches the village. He rides into the camp, Gray Hawk sees him comin.

"Rose! Jake back!"

The braves give him an Indian cheer.

"Jake, you ridin new horse."

"Yup, this is Big Black's son."

"Do you call him Big Black?"

"Yes, that's his name, Rose."

"Gray Hawk, what happened to your shoulder?"

"Got shot. Rose tell you."

Rose explains what happened to Gray Hawk.

"Rose, this sort of thing is beginnin to happen all over—greedy men wantin Indian land. There'll be big trouble before it ends."

"Rose, are you ready to go back huntin for the Densen brothers?"

"Yes, I'm more than ready."

"How about Gray Hawk—he healed enough to travel?"

"Yes, I think so. Why don't you ask him?"

"Because even if he wasn't, he'd say he is."

"Hear you, Jake—me good. Okay to go."

"Well, let's plan to leave in a couple of days after I rest up these old bones of mine."

"Okay, Jake, it's time to eat. You hungry?"

"Hungry? I could eat the hide off a grizzly bar."

"Well, let's eat then."

"That was a good meal, that deer was tender."

"Who shot that deer?"

"Rose did—with bow and arrow."

"I heard the Densen brothers headed west. There's three towns a few days ride from each other, but they're quite a distance from here."

"I'm gonna ride to the area of these towns and find a place to stay while I ride into each one and see if I can locate the Densens. In a couple of days, head west—I'll meet up with ya on the trail."

After a few days rest, Jake rides out in the mornin. He rides a few days and reaches the mountains in the area of the three towns. He rides the trail up into the mountains and runs across an old abandoned trapper's shack. He thinks this would be a perfect place to stay— there's an excellent view of the trail below.

He sets up camp at the shack, then heads out to meet Rose and Gray Hawk. He meets them on the trail—Gray Hawk is ridin Rose's Pinto stallion, Rose is drivin the wagon with her Indian princess outfit in a small trunk in the back. She's got a rifle by her side as they ride along.

"I found the perfect place to hole up—back up in the mountains. We can git to any of the three towns within a couple of days ride."

They reach the shack as the sun's settin behind the hills. Jake sits outside smokin his pipe, watchin the sunset paint changin colors in the sky. When darkness sets in, he couldn't see his hand in front of his eyes. All grows quiet in the mountains—once in a while, the hoot of an owl and the howl of a coyote can be heard.

The mornin sun shinin through the cracks in the shack wakes them. They have breakfast and sit around drinkin coffee.

"You two stay here—I'll go scout out the towns. When I find a Densen, I'll ride back and get ya. Then we'll all ride out and find a spot for Rose to park the wagon and become Appachy Rose."

Jake rides out to look around town. The first town he rides into is small—a few stores, a Sheriff's Office, and a saloon. He rides Big Black Jr. up to the hitchin rail in front of the saloon and dismounts. He takes his hat off, dusts off the trail dust with it, and walks into the saloon.

"Hey, old man."

"Howdy, boys."

He walks up to the bar and orders a beer. He hears one of the men softly say, "That's Jake, the fast gun. Look—he rides that big black horse tied up out front."

"Wonder what he's doin here."

Jake keeps lookin at his beer with his back to the men and says, "Just passin through, boys."

"Say, Jake, do you still draw against others shootin at beer mugs?"

"Nope, haven't done that in a while."

"He must have slowed down."

"Could be, boys."

Just then, the three Densen brothers walk into the saloon. Jake takes his beer, walks to a table where his back is against the wall, and sits down. He pulls the front of his hat down and leans back as though he's sleepin—listenin to every word that's said.

One of the brothers says, "We're gettin low on cash."

Another says, "Pete, why don't you ride to the ranch and pick up some money?"

Jake thinks, I didn't know they had a ranch in this area—that must be why they don't just rob a bank. They hole up here and don't want trouble.

Pete says, "I'll rest up a couple of days and head for the ranch—it's about a day's ride from here due south."

Jake slowly gets up, walks out of the saloon, gets on his horse, and leaves town. When he's out of town, he kicks up his horse and gallops toward the mountains.

"Rose, change into your Appachy Rose clothes—I'll explain as we ride."

He tells her that in a couple of days, one of the Densen brothers will be on the trail leadin south out of town. She'll have to ride hard to meet him.

She races her horse down the mountain trails, jumpin over logs and roundin sharp corners until she reaches the trail. She rides all night and most of the next day—both she and her horse are tired. She stops at a place where she can see anyone ridin from the north on the trail.

She waits all day and into the night, then falls asleep. The mornin sun wakes her. She watches the trail for a few hours, then sees a rider comin. He looks like the man Jake described—he wears a black hat and rides a gray horse.

When he rides closer, Rose rides out in front of him, stoppin him.

"What do you want with me? Why did you kill my brothers?"

"Kill you now—draw!"

When she says that, the man reaches for his gun. Appachy Rose draws and shoots the man straight in the heart. He leans over on his horse. She ties him on and heads toward town, leadin the horse.

When she gets close to town, she puts a silver dollar in his belt where it'll be found and hits the horse with her reins. The horse takes off runnin into town. He runs right up to the hitchin rail where the Densens tied their horses.

Appachy Rose rides back up the mountain to the shack.

Back at the store, the old boys are listenin' to Sam's story. One man asks Sam what it was like bein' young and workin' on Jake's ranch.

"Ah, that was a great life, everyone was good ta me, especially Bob and Curly. Jake was seldom there, but when he was, it was a great time. Never thought Jake would leave the ranch ta me."

"Hey Sam, I wanted to ask ya, where did the old Indian woman git a black wig?"

Sam laughs. "She made it from the hair of a horse's tail."

"Sam, did she ever git the last two brothers?"

"Well boys, that's a story for the mornin'. I'm headed for the ranch now."

Jake leaves the store and heads for his ranch.

The old boys sit around talkin'.

"That was some story Jake was tellin' us."

"Yup, sure was. Can't wait ta hear the end of it."

One of the old boys is sittin' quietly. The others notice how serious he is.

"Hey Pete, are ya okay?"

"I was just thinkin' about Sara and the day she passed away. Remember we found that old tin box and the letter inside?"

"Ya, it was full of money, and there was a note addressed to us. Let's read it again."

One of the old boys softly reads the letter:

"Well boys, if you're readin' this note, I am no longer with you. I knew you boys would find this box. I hope you will open the store for the townspeople, seein' how I left the property to all of you. I've been savin' this money for years—feel free to use it to stock up the store. I made a deal with the Western Feed Co. to sell their feed. If you decide to contact them and sell their feed, you will have to use some of this money to buy lumber to add a large storage room on the back. Be sure to make a large door in the storage room on the side so you can unload and load the feed into wagons. I thought you could make a road around the store so wagons could drive in, load, and drive around and out without havin' to carry the feed to their wagons. Well boys, I wish I was there to help, but the Good Lord had other plans for me. Be seein' you boys someday here in the clouds."

They all sit down, a couple with tears in their eyes, and pour a shot of whiskey. One of the old boys says, "Here's to you, Sara—we miss you dearly."

The next mornin' the old boys await Sam's arrival. The aroma of coffee brewin' filled the store when Sam arrived.

"Coffee sure smells good—let's have a cup."

"Sure thing, Sam."

They sit awhile drinkin' their coffee. One of the old boys says, "Well Sam, did Apache Rose git the last two Denson brothers?"

"If you remember, she just met and shot one of the brothers on the trail and sent his body into town."

"Ya, Sam, she had ta do a mighty powerful bit of ridin' to catch up to him on the trail. She could ride that horse of hers as good as any cowboy."

"One time there was a horse race in one of the towns. There was a cowboy there that would race against the local fast horses and bet money with them on the race. His horse was fast— it was a thoroughbred race horse. He wasn't as fast as some of the quarter horses at the start, but in a long-distance race, the quarter horses didn't have a chance. Jake rode into town and bet the thoroughbred's owner that he would lose the race. He took Jake's bet—it was for two hundred dollars."

"Ya mean Jake bet two hundred dollars on a horse race?"

"Yup."

"Did Jake ride Big Black in the race?"

"No!"

Apache Rose, dressed like an Indian Princess, was hidin' in the woods behind the startin' line. When the gun sounded and the horses took off, she came racin' out of the woods. It didn't take long for her horse to catch up with the others. They raced for two miles—Rose's horse and the thoroughbred were runnin' neck and neck. Then they headed for town and the finish line.

Apache Rose and her horse crossed the finish line three horse lengths ahead of the other horse. People were cheerin' her on as she crossed the line. She stopped for a few minutes.

"Hey Indian, what's your name?"

"Apache Rose."

She raced out of town before anyone could get a good look at her— she didn't want anyone to tell she was white. Jake collected his winnings of two hundred dollars and rode out of town. As he was ridin', the owner of the thoroughbred yelled, "Hey old man, want to race that big black horse of yours?"

"Nope, you couldn't win—he's faster than that Indian's horse."

"Boys, back to my story."

Now, the two Denson brothers left were in the saloon when a cowboy came in a-yellin', "Your brother's been shot dead, his body just came in tied to his horse." They go out and take their brother off his horse.

"Look—a silver dollar tucked in his belt."

"The poor kid, he never had a chance against that squaw."

"She'll be after us next—we're gonna stay together until we get her."

"How we goin' ta do that?"

"She has to be fast with her gun to outdraw our brothers. When she gets into town, I'll face her in the street, you'll be on the roof of that shop over there. When I tip my hat, shoot her right in the back."

Jake rides into town and goes into the saloon. A cowboy comes a-ridin' into town and runs into the saloon.

"Hey, I just saw that Indian girl ridin' that big pinto horse headin' for town."

"Go git on the roof like I told you—take your rifle."

Jake hears the plan. He sneaks out the back door of the saloon and hides behind a buildin', waitin' for her. He's positioned himself so he can see the man on the roof.

When Rose rides into town, she sees Jake. He says, "There's one on the roof, I'll get him. You'll hear the gunshot—don't turn around, watch the one in front of you." She rides on into town.

The Denson brother walks out of the saloon into the middle of the street, feelin' confident knowin' his brother is on the roof. She gits off her horse and leaves him standin' in the street. She walks toward the man standin' alone.

She says, "Today you die."

"Who are ya? Why do you want to kill me?"

When she gets closer to the man, she sees the scar on his face—she remembers his laughter when he was assaultin' her.

She says, "You killed man, attacked wife, set house on fire. You thought funny when ya flipped silver dollar on naked belly. I return silver dollar."

She throws the silver dollar at his feet.

"What does this all have to do with you?"

"Don't matter—you be dead."

He reaches up and tips his hat. A shot rings out—he wonders why she doesn't fall. Then his brother's body falls from the roof.

He says, "Wait a minute—what's goin' on?"

She says, "I give you chance—draw when want."

"I won't draw, you can't shoot me—it'll be murder."

"Draw—I kill now."

He drops to his knees and begs her not to kill him. Everyone in town has heard the entire conversation and is laughin' at him. She shakes her head and turns to walk to her horse. She hears the cockin' of his gun—she turns, draws, and puts a bullet in his forehead, just like he did to her husband.

Jake has run around and inside the saloon through the back door, then comes out and is standin' in the street with the town members—nobody knows he shot the man off the roof.

She mounts her horse, rears him up, and says, "Apache Rose rides no more." She rides out of town to meet Gray Hawk, takes off her Indian clothes, and wipes the red paint off her face. She takes the saddle off her big paint horse and then the bridle. She hugs the horse and kisses him on the nose.

"You served me well—I rode you hard, maybe too hard, I'm sorry. I don't need you anymore— Apache Rose will never ride again. Go be free—have many sons and daughters."

"Gray Hawk, we will ride the wagon into town. I'll look for somethin' that will be much quieter than ridin' around as Apache Rose."

"I go with you for while."

"Okay, I will get you a horse so you can return to your village."

The people in town cannot believe what just happened. Ridin' in the wagon, Rose and Gray Hawk are stopped by a man who asks, "Hey Injin, do you know who that Indian girl is?"

"Apache Rose."

"Did you see her?"

"Um, ridin' north on big black and white pinto. She Indian woman from Northern tribe."

Jake walks over to the wagon and says, "I'm headed home to my ranch."

"We'll meet up again, Jake—take care of yourself."

"Sam, what ever happened ta Apache Rose?"

"Well, she rode her wagon into a town and started a small business. You know Gray Hawk never left her—he stayed by her side till he died."

"Boys, pour me a cup of that coffee—my story's not done."

"See that gun and holster hangin' on the wall behind the counter—have you ever wondered why it was never for sale?"

"Never gave it a thought, Sam."

"What about it?"

"Go look at it close—it has a rose carved into the holster. See that pearl-handled gun?"

"Yup."

"That gun shot and killed six men—the two that raided the Indian village and the four Denson brothers."

"How did Sara get them?"

"Apache Rose's name was Sara."

"You mean our Sara was Apache Rose?"

"Yup."

"Well I'll be."

"Hey Sam, we buried Sara here on her property and placed a grave marker on her grave. By the way, did you ever see a gray hawk?"

"No, not really—now that I think about it…"

"Come here, Sam—look at Sara's grave marker."

"Well I'll be—a gray hawk sittin' right on her marker."

You could see that gray hawk sittin' there every day at sundown, as though he was protectin' the grave of Apache Rose.

+OLD COWBOY'S LAST RIDE
by Bill Hagenburg

My cowboyen days are thru:

I'm just sitting here getting older it's true.

Laying by my camfire alone:

Sleeping resting my head on a stone.

I was once young and bold:

Now I'm just growing old.

Lord I know my time is near:

The angles heavenly voices I hear.

My eyes will close, I'll take my last ride:

Up into the clouds ridding by your side.

Never more to ride alone you see:

Because I will be with thee.

The End
Written Dec. 15,2019